The Pink Room

There. From a distance. Soft and faint like rain on the roof, a melody floated down from above. Notes that jabbed the air like probing fingers. A sound like fairies dancing in an acid dream.

Fur Elise.

For Cain, it was like stumbling into some terrible scene he might have written himself. His entire body went cold. He felt a pounding in his temples as the adrenaline of fright fueled his pulse. He was aware of a full bladder and had to concentrate to contain it.

He fumbled with the sleeping bag zipper and squirmed out of it as though it were full of spiders. He knelt on the hard floor and strained to listen. Still the music played, the quick melody losing energy but still recognizable. Fur Elise from the snow globe, floating down from the very top of the turret. Beautiful, terrible music from the pink room.

It wound down. I heard it wind down. There was not a single note left in those springs and cogs.

He stood and pulled on a pair of jeans. He reached for the flashlight and switched it on. He aimed it at the staircase, terrified at what he might see there. But again, there were no leering faces or crouching ghouls. Only the darkness of the second floor. And above that, the turret from which the haunting melody continued to play.

I can't go up there. I think I'm physically incapable of climbing those stairs.

10-Digit ISBN 1-59113-853-1
13-Digit ISBN 978-1-59113-853-2

Printed in the United States of America.

Booklocker.com, Inc.
2005

The Pink Room

Mark LaFlamme

To my mother, Janice, who always had faith even in the worst of times. And to my wife, Corey, who has taken up the same cause with the same courage.

Writing a novel is great fun. Doing it right is a lot of work. This book would not exist were it not for the guidance and expertise of Dave Griffiths, the masterful editor who doesn't mind barking at his students once in a while. You're amazing, Dave. Thanks also to Gail Tarr, a friend and visionary. Your excitement over the project renewed my own. To classic cops Matt Cashman and Tom Slivinski for answering frequent and annoying questions about police matters and other manly business. To Dr. Dave Stuchiner of Central Maine Medical Center in Lewiston, Maine, who has advised me in previous works on the many terrible things that can afflict the human body. To Gerry Boyle, the great Maine author, for years of inspiration and support. To my wife and my mother, both hawk-eyed perfectionists who can spot errors a block away. Thanks for following me around and cleaning up my many messes.

Most of the science in the following story is real. Quantum physics does not need a novelist to elaborate on it's weirdness. The science is strange enough on its own.

Prologue

From the Winter 1912 issue of the* Aroostook Almanac, *available in Bangor, Houlton and Presque Isle for 10 cents a copy.

Late spring this year will be marked by cosmic drama as a rare alignment marks the changing of the seasons. In mid-June, Mercury, Venus, Mars, Jupiter and Saturn will be visible at twilight moving steadily together in the western sky. It's a rare grouping of planets that began two years ago and which will culminate on June 21, the summer solstice. The coinciding of the solstice and the planetary gathering will not occur again for nearly a hundred years and is considered a marvel by both astrological and scientific standards. Those with mystical proclivities will recall that ancient civilizations regarded planetary groupings as a show of force from the gods. Those with more scientific leanings will enjoy the chance to observe the cosmic landscape as it has not been seen since the era of Vikings.

In 1912, the stretch of land that would someday be called Mulberry was not yet established. The rugged, mountainous region near the northern tip of Maine was mainly a resting point for loggers. These men were mostly French Canadians, hired to clear swaths of land near the border and to prepare the timber for the long journey south.

These were the lumberjacks of lore — rugged, hard men who worked the woods by day, drank and fought at night. Most spoke English, though it was fragmented and clipped. When they came to the township that would later be known as Mulberry, it usually meant a day to rest tired muscles, to drink at the saloon and to fish in the chain of lakes that surrounded the area.

The afternoon of June 21, 1912 was unlike any other in the small oasis in the Maine woods. Woodsmen were loud with song and bickering inside the saloon that occupied the bottom floor of

Tookey's Inn. Canadian and American currency mingled as the men paid for showers and shaves, bought bottles of booze and played poker with local farmers who bluffed poorly. The wide room smelled of pipe smoke, sweat and whiskey. A disoriented wanderer through this anachronistic township might have believed the year was 1812 rather than a century later.

By 8:30 p.m., the sky had darkened to a deep blue and most of the shadows had vanished. Pale stars twinkled in the moonless sky and the temperature never dipped below 55 degrees. The air was thick with mosquitoes and black flies and night birds seemed particularly agitated.

At Tookey's, a mood of merriment had given way to a collective gloom that manifested itself in mutterings and a few fistfights. Card games turned ugly. Arm wrestling bouts turned into brawls. Nobody paused to wonder why the normally congenial men found themselves averse to the company they kept.

At 9 o'clock, a Frenchman was thrown through a window and then beaten as he lay bleeding in the gravel outside. The barman who tried to intercede was jumped by a pair from the same group and pummeled until he was unconscious.

A cocker spaniel that ran into the bar, barking and snarling, was seized and picked up by the biggest and strongest of the woodsmen, a 45-year-old Canadian named Francois Robitaille, who raised the yelping animal above his head and then brought it down with frightening force upon his upraised knee. A collective gasp and then a brief silence followed the sharp, explosive sound of the animal's spine snapping. The cocker spaniel twitched and quivered and a milky string of blood dripped from its snout. Robitaille, with forearms and biceps bulging beneath a red, woolen shirt, hurled the dog across the bar where the carcass crashed through long rows of liquor bottles before smashing into a mirror on the other side.

The killing of the cocker spaniel was particularly troubling because Francois Robitaille was known as a gentle man. He had a special affinity for critters and once kept a raccoon as a pet after rescuing the animal from a washout.

A year back, when Francois was running a crew up near Van Buren, they had come across a dying fawn in an area where the land turned marshy. The work had become more difficult because no maps had shown these spongy areas — the lumber here was soft and there were disagreements over what to take and what to leave.

Francois, who once ordered his men to keep working after one of them lost half a foot to an axe blade, came to a stop before the struggling doe and ignored his men as they gathered around him. He bent and scooped the animal into his arms, walking away with it solemnly, like a pall bearer. He lowered his six-foot-seven inch frame down onto a fallen tree, cradled the fawn's head in his lap, and stroked its fur as it died.

The men stood in silence, leaning on axes, meal bags slung over their shoulders. Those who were wearing hats removed them. One began to pray under his breath, detected someone looking at him, cleared his throat. A few of the men later swore that tears glistened in the big man's eyes as he watched the fawn die in his arms. Others refuted that idea and at least one scrap resulted from the debate.

In either case, it was particularly troubling to see Francois Robitaille break the back of a 30 pound cocker spaniel the night of June 21, 1912 in Tookey's Inn. And after the deed was done, the big man turned his hot gaze from table to table, daring anyone to question him. Under normal circumstances, that gaze would have been greeted by averted eyes and the heaviest of silences from brutish, but wise men.

Things were far from normal this night. A short but bearish man by the name of Claude Desjardins decided that he would be the one to call Francois on this brutal display. It wasn't that Desjardins particularly liked dogs. He was a bluenose from New Brunswick and it was well known that Desjardins would butcher a puppy and feed it to his mother if it meant a few pennies in his pocket. He was also a bit of a coward who ducked out of danger whenever possible and then made up wild tales of heroics and bravery.

But tonight, as silence filled Tookey's for the first time all day, the 19-year-old jumped from his chair, knocking it over just a few feet away. A glass danced back and forth on the table before tumbling and breaking on the wooden floor. Desjardins hitched up his grungy, green pants, spat upon the floor, licked the entire length of his greasy mustache and leveled a finger at Francois Robitaille.

"You sonoma bitch. Whatchoo do dat for, you big fugging bastard? Cog sugger. Why you kill dat dog?"

At that, Francois grinned. And as fond as the woodsmen were of fisticuffs, they were not eager to seen the tiny Nova Scotian ripped to pieces by the gentle giant gone bad. And that surely would have happened had Rodney Saucier not, at that precise moment, appeared in the doorway pale, trembling, bleeding and half naked.

Saucier was 62 and easily the oldest of the woodsmen who typically came through the town that would someday be Mulberry. He was tall and thin with an almost artistic, gray mustache. Saucier was the funniest of them, the smartest and the best storyteller the men had ever encountered. He was also calm, stoic and as emotionally sturdy as any man could be.

Only tonight, he was a quivering, blubbering and babbling mess.

The business of the cocker spaniel and the likely demise of Desjardins forgotten, the men rushed to Saucier, eager to learn what nastiness had reduced him to this state. They forced a shot of whiskey into him, offered him a hit of the pipe and shook him by the shoulders.

The man only babbled nonsense.

"M-m-my mother," he said, squatting on the floor, hugging his knees with both arms. "For hours. Hours! She been chasing me for hours with that long, brown strap she like to beat me wit'. Oh, she was growling and laughing and...she moved so damn fast through the woods!"

Of course, Saucier's mother had been dead for decades. As far as any of them could remember, she had died when Saucier was ten years old. But there was no consoling the man. The normally slow and deliberate speech was replaced by the staccato stammering of a frightened child. Saucier insisted his mother, "dressed in that old, wool cloak, and her hands all gnarled and strong" had pursued him through the woods at Olive Hill where he'd been trying to spook loose some partridge. She clawed him, bit him, slapped him and pushed him down as he tried to flee.

"I don't know when I came to the road, but I fell onto it, crying and screaming and I wouldn't open my eyes. I ain't sorry to admit it, neither. I could feel her breath on my face and it smelled like rhubarb. I could hear her giggling in my ear and then her lips...then her lips..."

There was an earnest debate over whether someone should slug old man Saucier to put him out for the night. They liquored him up instead and he eventually slept under a bar stool.

Rodney Saucier's encounter with his dead mother was not the strangest thing to happen in northern Maine that night. Francois Robitaille's deadly assault on the dog was not, either. It was hard to quantify the strangeness. Few people tried.

Ovilda Gerhaty, the 17-year-old daughter of a preacher, came to the township from St. Agatha that night and gave herself to three woodsmen, one-by-one. Gerhaty had never entertained the idea of losing her virginity in such a fashion. She had not thought about it much at all; not until the sun went down and the air smelled so sweet and she fancied she heard murmuring behind her wherever she went.

Gerhaty returned home at midnight and faced the wrath of her father. She was sore between her legs and her crotch had been dripping for hours. After the beating, she hobbled to the tub, drew some water and then slit her wrists with her father's razor.

St. Agatha had a population of 300 then which was huge by the standards of the townships around it. Greater numbers didn't mean greater strangeness. Just more of it.

Everett Meade, the wealthiest man north of Houlton, hanged himself in his barn after waking from a nap on the porch. He'd had the most dreadful dream. In it, his dead wife stood over him, dropping beetles onto his face and reminding him what he had done to their 10-year-old daughter all those years ago — the night he got really drunk at the grange hall. Everett woke up, shook his head and rubbed his eyes. He then wandered off to hang himself with the kind of forethought and precision that had made him rich.

Amos Duprey burned his house down because he was sure there was something underneath it he needed to have. He watched with hypnotic calm as flames devoured the farmhouse he had saved all his life to build. When the last of the walls came down in thunderous, blackened heaps, Amos Duprey tried to remember what he had been searching for. It wouldn't come to him. After an hour of considering in the smoke clogged air, he decided it was pointless. He had destroyed his beautiful home and now he could not remember why.

Sonny LeMasse, teenage son of a wealthy lumber man, spent a sinful hour making unrestrained love to his older sister. It was something he had dreamed of many nights for the past two years. And it was wonderful how she gave herself to him.

In the throes of his orgasm, he screamed her name and gazed into her beautiful eyes. Only it wasn't Sandra LeMasse, age 19, who lay beneath him. It was a dead and reeking goat he had apparently strangled in a fit of erotic insanity.

Robin Baxter, the town dentist in Frenchville, came face to face with a man he had killed seven years ago in a medicinal experiment gone awry. The man was a blackened, grotesque horror. And mean. The man pinched Baxter with rotted, puffy fingers. He kneed Baxter in the groin. He called Baxter vile names. Ultimately, he instructed the dentist to drink from a can of lye and Baxter complied, if only to make the rotting man go away.

Catherine Corriveau threw her children's kittens into the wood stove and giggled as she listened to them screech and thrash. Mark Gellineau put ground glass in his nine-year-old son's food. Tony Baril, a school teacher, dug up the remains of his mother, father and little brother and burned their bones right there in the family plot.

It was collective insanity in a straight slash through a small swath of northern Maine. Fourteen people died, through suicides and strange mishaps. Completely sane men and women awoke from dreams that they had visited with long dead loved ones or bitter enemies. Upright men committed atrocities that would shame their family names for generations.

The strangeness lingered, though the intensity of it diminished. For days following the solstice, people reported feeling out of sorts. Things felt off center, that was all. The world looked the same, but felt different. They felt pressed upon, influenced, by forces they could neither see nor hear, smell nor touch.

No one noted that the forces of dementia appeared to overtake people in a straight line across the northern tip of the state. To do so, a person would have had to acknowledge the phenomenon and to reveal his own indiscretions. It was best not to talk about what madness had befallen them for that short time. It was best to forget about it and not to wonder.

Some forces of the world could not be grasped by the intellect of mortal man and it was foolish and dangerous to try.

Part I
Second Empire

One

There could not be a darker place on the planet than northern Maine after midnight. Jonathan Cain walked in the center of the road and made an earnest effort to make out one speck of artificial light. Just one little pin prick in this awesome darkness.

But there was none. There were stars twinkling above and a vague shadow of mountains ahead. There were pine trees on either side, and Cain thought they might stretch into infinity.

Twice, he stretched his arms out in front of him and was fascinated that he could not see his hands. It was enthralling, this depth of darkness.

The air smelled of pine and of something high and sweet, like a flower. Summer night smells. And summer night sounds.

To the left, not far into the woods, the sound of a snapping twig. There was a brief silence and then something scuttling away. To the right, something chirped or sang or hissed. Cain didn't know the sounds of the woods. But he liked them.

He also liked the sound of his shoes on the pavement. Very rhythmic and soothing. A deliberate, confident sound. He was a domesticated presence in all the wildness around him. There might be a hundred wild eyes staring at him this very moment. Moose and deer, coons and coyotes. Cain wasn't afraid. He felt honored to have this place among the beasts.

He became aware of a fuzzy hum in the distance behind him, an invasive sound that intruded on his ruminations. He was surprised by the depth of his disappointment. The sound was too precise and steady to be generated by anything but a man. His solitary distinction among the wildlife was ending.

It was five minutes before the lights of the car shone upon him. The beams hurled Cain's shadow onto the road ahead of him, making him look stretched and alien. Then the sound of the engine was louder and the car was beside him, rolling to a stop just inches from where he strode.

Cain took a few more steps and then stopped. He turned to look at the long, black car. There was the buzz of an automatic window lowering but nothing but blackness beyond it.

Cain stood in the road, hands stuffed in his pockets. He half expected the car to vanish before his eyes and a moose to take its place. A Maine mirage.

Then a deep, clear voice said: "Hello there," and Cain was almost disappointed that this visitor was something so mundane as a man.

He took a step closer to the car, curious and nothing more.

"I say, hello. Would you be Jonathan Cain?"

Cain bent to peer inside the car. He could still see nothing. He straightened again and shrugged.

"Uh huh."

He heard the driver slap the gear lever into park. The engine purred. An interior light was switched on and two men sat staring out at Jonathan Cain. Both wore suit coats over dark T-shirts. Both were muscular, with close cropped hair. The driver leaned over the passenger slightly for a better look.

Cain waited.

The passenger spoke. "Kind of a weird time of night to be walking out here."

Cain looked to his left. The car taillights cast twenty feet worth of a red glow, beyond which nothing could be seen. He looked to his right and reconsidered the hulking shadow of the mountains.

He turned back to the men in the car. “Kind of a weird time of night to be driving around, too. Now that you mention it.”

The driver looked puzzled. The passenger grinned. Far off, something cawed and then was silent.

“You probably wonder how we know who you are or why we care. Probably seems a little spooky.”

“A little, maybe.”

The man nodded. The shadow of his head bounced up and down over the dashboard.

“Don’t mean to be. We’re harmless. Really. We work for a group of people who are interested in asking you a few questions, that’s all. It’d be great if you’d hop in the back there and let us take an hour of your time.”

Cain considered the car again. Looked like a Crown Victoria, either black or dark blue. A government car. Cain wondered distantly why feds didn’t pick up the occasional Pinto or Pacer for discreetly cruising the back roads.

He stared into the car.

“My mother told me never to accept rides from strangers.”

Anger flashed in the driver's eyes but the second man’s smile never wavered. He looked like the older of the two. Cain pegged him at 45 and guessed most of those years were military.

“Mine too,” he said. “Let me clear that right up, then. I’m David Reyes and my driver here is Carlton Loomis. Now, I swear we can get you where we’re going in just a few minutes and then drive you back when you’re ready to go.”

Cain looked over the men a moment longer. Funny how this encounter didn’t trouble him. He had been in northern Maine fifty minutes, maybe less. Already, mystery was afoot.

He expected mystery. Plenty of it. Just not in this form.

“What the hell. My mother was a drunken old bitch who babbled a lot, anyway. Just a short ride?”

David Reyes smiled and held up his hands. “Fifteen minutes, tops.”

“Alright. Take me to your leader.”

Two

Rathbun hated living in the tin can. It was miserably hot in the summer and deadly cold in the winter. No matter how he arranged equipment and furniture, he could not disguise the sad truth that they were living in an arched, corrugated can in the middle of northern Fucking Maine.

As far as Benjamin Rathbun was concerned, this Godforsaken place should be described just so on the maps: northern Fucking Maine.

The people up here were yokels. They spotted him as a Fed the very first day he came to this wretched town. They regarded him with a sort of amused fascination.

When he went into Lions Bait and Feed, or whatever the hell the goddamn corner store was called, chatter would come to a halt. The locals would carry on their business but stop speaking altogether, as though they continued conversations telepathically when a stranger approached.

It was unnerving. When someone smiled and offered him a greeting, it was even creepier. This place was Stepford with a drawl.

They would offer their hands and ask about his day, but Rathbun wasn't fooled. The smiles were props. The banter was designed to confuse him so they could learn about his business.

A few weeks ago, a man who looked like a lumberjack offered him a free kayak lesson out on the lake. Business was slow, the man said. He needed to get people hooked.

A sexy woman in cutoff jeans and a shirt tied at her midriff asked if he'd eaten at the Hearthside Grill yet. A shirtless teenager told him about a hot fishing spot and pointed toward a good stretch of road to watch for moose.

It drove Rathbun crazy. He trusted no one. The people of Mulberry presented themselves as honest folks living and working in what they called the Real Maine. It was potato land up near the Canadian border and to Rathbun, who was from San Diego, it might have been another planet.

Once, driving too fast down Route 11 just after dawn, he had drifted too far to the right and struck a black lab trotting on the dirt shoulder. The dog had a red bandana around its neck. An identification tag hung from a blue, canvas collar. The front bumper of the Crown Vic had punched a hole in the dog's left side. The animal whimpered and drooled blood onto the dirt. Its rear legs kicked as it lay on the side of the road.

The sight of the beast disgusted him. The dog was not mortally wounded and probably could have been saved by even a mediocre vet. But there was no way Rathbun was going to hoist the dirty mutt into his car and drive it into town. No friggin' way. Too many questions. Too much attention.

Besides, he didn't trust the people of Mulberry.

The road stretched for miles ahead of him and nothing moved upon it. Behind him, the road was likewise silent. Around him, nothing but pine trees spreading out forever. Not a structure or a soul in sight. Yet, as he stepped to the dog and pressed his foot onto its throat, Rathbun had sensed eyes upon him. Eyes hidden in the shadows of those goddamn endless pines.

The dog had looked up at him, too. The brown eyes had gone milky, but remained fixed on him, as if promising a free kayak lesson, dinner at the Hearthside or the best fishing spot in the whole county. Anything mister. Please don't stomp the life out of me.

Rathbun had stomped the life out of the mutt, bearing his weight down on the animal's throat until it sputtered and died. Then he put gloves on and rolled the dog over an embankment. He wiped his foot on the side of a tree. Goddamn beast had drooled blood on him.

The rest of the day, Rathbun felt he was being watched. Maybe followed. Definitely watched. He spent that evening inside the tin can with an extra bottle of gin and the .45 particularly close at hand.

Rathbun supposed he had been paranoid. He was probably paranoid beyond reason. The people of Mulberry did not seem outwardly sinister and they were not the most intelligent people he had ever encountered.

Still. He trusted none of them. Theodore Currie may never have been a member of the Mulberry tribe, but he had lived among them and only a year ago. Rathbun hated Theodore Currie. Absolutely despised him.

The man had been a genius, there was no denying that. But he was a genius with a silver spoon up his ass and Rathbun loathed him for it. The man was born into scientific glory and it only got easier for him over time. His dad had been the top government scientist during the anything-to-win days of war in Korea and Vietnam. Jefferson Currie was no scientific giant, but the word was that the old man knew more of the government's dirty little secrets than anyone alive. And Jefferson Currie used that knowledge like an upraised weapon the rest of the life. God only knew how much of his money came from high ranking politicians with dirty pasts. God only knew if he'd used that leverage to advance his only son through the finest colleges.

Goddamn Curries. It brought Rathbun no measure of comfort that both of them were dead. No comfort at all.

He was more than half drunk on this warm night. He sat in a hard chair in front of a computer whose screen had gone blank. He had a martini glass in one hand, but it was filled with straight vodka. Why be epicurean up here in Shitsville, where most of the inbreds drank Schlitz beer?

He lived in what was nothing more than a giant culvert which had been erected in one day just to house a merry band of glorified babysitters. And now that he thought of it, where the hell were Loomis and Reyes? Probably off mingling with the locals. Morons.

The two men had taken to Mulberry like a pig takes to its own shit. This was a vacation, to the big jarheads. They fished, they threw around a frisbee, they ate lobster every other night. Christ, what a couple of tools.

Reyes and Loomis didn't have to worry about scientific formulas fading with time inside that big, inaccessible house. The men were soldiers, not scientists. If a gun were pressed to their temples, neither could name two of the four forces of nature. What did they care that the ultimate secrets of time-space might be written down in a spiral notebook just a few miles away? Reyes and Loomis extracted information, disposed of enemy personnel or just flared their nostrils as a means of intimidation when called upon.

No wonder the idiots liked it here, Rathbun thought. They were surrounded by a population as goddamn dumb as they were.

The ride took ten minutes. Along the way, in an area where the trees gave way to a marsh on the left side of the road, the driver stomped on the brakes for a moose that had ambled into the roadway. All three of the riders lurched forward in their seats. The driver cursed and laid on the horn, but the moose only glanced at the car with cold, black eyes.

"Big bastard," Loomis said as he drove around the animal.

Cain sat back in the seat, hands behind his head. Welcome to Maine, he thought. The way life should be. Federal agents included.

Then they were turning from Route 11 and bouncing along a small, dirt road barely wide enough for the car. At the end of it, gleaming in the headlights, was a Quonset hut made of corrugated steel. To Cain, it looked like something struggling to grow out of the ground. Out here in the woods, it looked like a shiny, metal secret.

"Home, sweet home," Reyes said.

Before they stepped out of the car, a garage door nearly the height of the entire building began to rise. The screech of metal on metal was obscenely loud. Cain thought he heard something crashing through the woods in a fearful flight. Then the metal door rolled to a stop. The silence that followed was somehow more imposing than the clamor.

Three

Cain accepted a seat in a black easy chair that looked like it had never been sat upon. Across from him, on the other side of a metal desk with nothing upon it, sat a tall, thin man with a long nose and a tan button-down shirt with rolled sleeves.

"I understand you've been inside the house. I'm very interested in talking to you about it."

The man's name was Ben Rathbun. He offered no more than that — no rank or position. Cain didn't ask for one.

"Afraid I can't help you there. I haven't even been up the driveway. Just parked at the end of it and started walking. To tell you the truth, I can't even verify there is a house."

Rathbun was rolling a pencil between his fingers. He did not look at Cain.

"Oh, but there is. The Currie house. Home of the late, great Theodore Currie, noted scientist in the field of quantum physics. Compared to Hawking at 25, to Einstein at 30. Blah blah. I suspect you know all this, Mr. Cain."

Cain said nothing. He knew all this, it was true. Currie was the reason he had come to Mulberry. Currie and his mysterious house in the middle of nowhere.

Rathbun sighed. He continued to fidget with the detachment of a man preparing to deliver a speech he'd recited a hundred times.

"Theodore Currie. Educated at Cambridge, Stanford and Cornell. Published his first paper on quantum mechanics at Cornell at the age of 22. Winner of the Nobel Prize at 26. Invited to speak with the president a year later, but turned down an offer of a lucrative job in a government think tank."

Loomis and Reyes, who had been hovering around the desk, wandered off. Cain guessed they were either bored or disappearing on cue. Rathbun didn't seem to notice.

"Currie was considered the man most likely to develop and prove a unified theory, Mr. Cain. This was one man in a field full of geniuses who mostly resigned themselves to the notion that such a theory would not be discovered in their lifetimes.

"When Currie published a paper claiming proof of extra dimensions, the majority of string theorists yawned. Then they examined the data more closely. And re-examined it. And then gasped, applauded and got down on their knees to hail this generation's Einstein."

"You don't sound like one of his fans," Cain said.

Rathbun stopped twirling the pencil and offered a faint smile.

"Is that how it sounds? I'm sorry. I'm just not convinced he was that close to a unified theory. His so-called proof of the extra dimensions was never fully explained. Mr. Currie took a sort of leave of absence, you see..."

"After his daughter died. In a fire at their home in Tarrytown, New York."

Rathbun looked at him, still with that faint smile.

"Right. When Angel Currie passed away in 2002, Theodore disappeared from the scientific community. He bought land on a hilltop here in East Bumfuck, and he hired builders to erect a big Victorian fashioned after his daughter's favorite dollhouse. The prevailing rumor at the time was that he had gone completely nuts and used his mother's wealth to pay for construction. He offered a hundred thousand dollar bonus if the crew could get it done by spring of 2004. And they did."

Cain sat with his arms folded over his chest.

"Do you know why he wanted the home built so fast, Mr. Cain?"

Cain said nothing. Rathbun sighed again and let the pencil drop to the desktop. He leaned back in his chair and laced his fingers behind his head. There was no sign of Loomis and Reyes.

"It was generally suspected," Rathbun went on, "that Theodore Currie believed he had found a way to prove the existence of higher dimensions. He was the one man with perhaps the greatest grasp of the workings of string theory, remember. And with that knowledge, he may have believed he could somehow contact the dead."

Cain unfolded his arms and leaned forward. Slowly. Taking his time. "And if he could contact the dead, maybe he could find his beloved daughter. With the help of ley lines and cosmic alignments."

"Whatever. Of course, he was certifiably insane at this point, by all accounts. It is one thing to mathematically prove there are dimensions beyond the four that we know. It is another thing entirely to propose that our dead exist in one of those extra dimensions."

Cain shrugged. He held his arms out and smiled. *Hey, I just got here. What do you want from me?*

Rathbun sat forward in his chair again, staring at Cain now like a co-conspirator.

"Let me be straight with you. I think Theodore Currie was a goddamn lunatic at the end of his life. He disappeared into that house and never came out again. I'm not interested in any of his desires to communicate with his dead daughter. Not at all. But I am interested in whatever science he may have indulged in. Good old quantum physics. Planck's constant, super symmetry, Kaluza-Klein."

"Of course," Cain said. "So, why didn't you and your people buy the place and go nuts."

He thought Rathbun might have flinched, but couldn't be sure.

"My *people* and I tried that very thing. We tried it all neighborly like and we tried it in court. So far, no luck. The elder Mrs. Currie is a powerful woman and quite influential, too. There are court orders prohibiting us from getting close to the house and from pursuing our ambitions to buy it. There are court orders keeping us from a lot of things, frankly. We'll win sooner or later. In the meantime, important science may be growing mildewy up there or it may burn up in a fire. Nobody can step foot on that property without a quick response from Olivia Currie's considerable team of lawyers, and so we have to ignore what may be the most important science to come along in a century."

"That's got to be galling," Cain said. "For the United States government."

Rathbun smiled, but there was no humor in it. To his credit, he did not deny government involvement. He did not elaborate on it, either.

"You can probably understand that it concerned us a great deal to learn that a writer of popular fiction would be moving into the Currie house. After a year of obstinacy, the stubborn, old bitch has granted permission for a novelist I've never heard of to take full control of the house. No offense."

"None taken. I guess you just have to assume that Miss Currie has more confidence in a man who writes lies for a living than she does in the government."

Rathbun looked as if he'd been slapped. He started to speak but then his mouth snapped shut. His face began to redden and he had picked up the pencil again, squeezing it this time in a fist. Cain watched as the man struggled to contain himself.

"I'm sorry you feel that way," Rathbun said after a considerable pause. "I had hoped you'd be more understanding of our predicament."

"What, as a patriotic member of the team?"

"No. As a human being. A human being interested in knowledge and progress."

Cain got to his feet and stood in front of the chair.

"I *am* interested in those things. Right now, it's not my problem."

"Not your problem," Rathbun said, standing. "But you could help us with ours. All we want is a little information about..."

"No thanks. It's not my house, sir. I'm only a guest."

Cain turned toward the door. Loomis and Reyes stood there side-by-side, arms crossed. Cain wondered if they learned that pose in the military. He looked back at Rathbun.

"Do I get a ride back? Or is this where a beating commences."

Rathbun scowled. It was an angry look, but Cain thought he spied a hint of desperation in there, as well.

"Take him back to where you found him," Rathbun said to the men, before turning his attention back to Cain.

"You know Currie was covered in bite marks when they found him, don't you? I've seen the autopsy reports myself. Bite marks all over. And no one can explain where they came from."

Cain said nothing. He waited. Rathbun waved his hands at him and turned away. Cain started for the door.

"Another thing, Mr. Cain."

He turned slowly to look at Rathbun, whose face was redder than ever.

"I understand your wife recently passed away. I'm sorry to hear that. I only hope that misfortune has nothing to do with your interest in the Currie house. That would just be doubly tragic."

Cain thought of a retort but then dismissed it. He only nodded acknowledgment instead. The memory of Kimberly pricked him — a real, physical sensation that felt like glass in his chest. He'd have to give the parting shot to the bad guys.

Four

I must be crazy. I must be out of my goddamn mind.

Fifteen years ago, Jonathan Cain was unloading trucks at a warehouse on Lake Erie. He worked 12 hour days and sometimes took boxes of cotton to work to stuff inside his gloves. The cotton helped soak up the blood that dripped from his cold, cracked fingers chilled by the winter winds off the lake.

He lived in a crummy walk-up apartment on the bad end of town. He wrote on a loud, electric typewriter while Kimberly slept on the pull out sofa. Lean times. Hard times, but happy times. Somehow happy.

Then one particularly cold night, Cain and his bleeding fingers came home to an apartment full of burning candles. Exactly 66 candles spread across the drafty, three room hole on the third floor. Sixty five of those candles represented a publishing house that had reviewed and rejected “Such Beautiful Children,” his first novel.

The final candle — and the biggest of them all — sat on the battered coffee table casting dancing shadows across Kimberly’s smiling face.

“I’ll give you one guess,” she said, rising and slinking across the living room in the skimpiest gown Cain had ever seen. “Either I’ve taken up witchcraft, or a publisher called today who was very interested in your book.”

Much, much later that night, they awoke wound in a braided rug, naked and with wax hardening in hard to reach places.

In the past 14 years, Cain had published a dozen novels. Ten of them went to the best sellers list and three were made into movies. His wasn’t exactly a household name, but he had a good following and the money was damn near staggering. It still floored him when he thought to check on his various accounts. He was rich and successful by all definitions. His fingers rarely bled anymore.

Cain wrote horror stories. His books were about genetic mutations and hideous things hidden in basements. He wrote about government experiments gone amok and things that lived on bone marrow.

Cain's first best seller was about a graveyard where dozens of people had been buried alive. The atrocity was revealed when a nearby river flooded the cemetery and coffins and corpses bobbed to the surface. The final hours of each victim was recounted and man, Cain had spooked himself with that one.

That was the very point. His books were based on bad dreams. They were born of unholy ideas that crawled into his head at inconvenient moments; ideas that came often unbidden. Cain did not summon the thoughts that would later become novels. Often he did not want them at all.

He wrote his books mostly in a daze, taken over by the hypnosis that comes when imagination is set free to wander.

And the readers wrote adoring letters that tended toward the dramatic. Readers, Cain had learned, often think of the novelist as an omnipotent force, high above the chaos and calamity of the story. The writer as puppeteer, powerful and controlling but entirely untouched by the emotional impact of the tale. The slow construction of the story, they reason, must surely inure the author to the beauty or horror of the completed work.

A ridiculous notion. The slow construction of the horror novel only meant that the writer had that much more time to suffer with it.

On those hellish occasions when he had to speak to a group, Cain tried his best to emphasize that the writer is as much a victim of his imagination as he is the beneficiary of it. That which frightens, angers or stirs the reader was created piece-by-piece in the storyteller's mind, and thus it was felt more powerfully there.

It was fancy talk, nothing more. What Cain knew but tried to sugarcoat was that he was vastly different from the heroes and heroines that graced his novels. Those brave souls confronted horrors with valor, either inherent or born of desperation. Cain, on the other hand, could not — absolutely *would* not — sleep with a foot dangling over the edge of the bed.

He did not wander cemeteries at night for inspiration. Noises in the basement caused his mind to race with conceived possibilities. He would rather stay up all night with the television cranked up than explore the source of a creaking sound in the attic.

Two summers before Kimberly got lost right outside their home, they had driven to Prince Edward Island to spend a week in a tent. It rained almost nonstop for five days. But one night, as they sat playing cribbage on a picnic table under a tarp, the sky cleared almost freakishly. A wind sprang up from the east and the clouds parted, revealing stars that seemed to twinkle with renewed luster.

They gathered what remained of the damp firewood, crinkled every page of every newspaper in the car, and spent an hour getting a fire going. It was a beauty and they squatted around it, feeling the heat after days of dampness.

"Okay, professional storyteller," Kimberly said to him, her voice rippling and far away across the fire. "Earn your keep."

Cain had dozens of stories that never made it to the page and he unleashed a few that night in the Prince Edward Island woods. The disfigured boy who ate his parents and his sister and who now roamed the island woods.

The old abandoned church *just a few miles from here* where an entire congregation gave themselves over to Satan one afternoon a quarter century ago. The killer of school girls who had to be hanged a dozen times because he kept coming back. The ugly truth about the lighthouse witch who sent her children out to punish the island invaders.

And on and on. Classic ghost stories with Cain twists. As the fire burned down and the clouds returned, Kimberly was delightfully spooked. Cain, on the other hand, was completely unnerved, his imagination sprung free and his senses profoundly acute. Every dripping tree limb, every snapping twig made him jump. He imagined far worse things than those horrors he had created for the campfire. By the time they crawled into their sleeping bags, Kimberly yawning and already forgetting the tales, Cain was a mess. He gobbled two Valium and washed them down with warm beer.

Cain was no sissy. He was a schoolyard scrapper as a boy when being the dirt-poor son of a single mom gave him plenty to fight about. He played hockey through his second year of college before dropping out. Cain, the skater, was known for an eloquent combination of aggressive play and finesse with the puck.

He got in maybe a half dozen bar fights during the hard-drinking days of his early 20's. Points given for remaining upright, Cain figured he won more than half of them.

He was tall and rugged, though he tended toward the lean side. He had intense blue eyes and a little extra rise on the groove of his upper lip. Other men regarded the feature as a sneer. The ladies saw it as a boyish pout. Winner on both counts.

Before he was married, Cain was a risk taker. Later, he learned to live more reasonably while diverting recklessness into his fiction.

Cain the writer was known for boldness. In the real world, where weird shadows could be crouching creatures, and things always went bump in the night, Cain the man was a bit of what the kids would call a wuss. He suspected most men were, if they had the intellect for it. They would do battle with any man or beast that threatened their families or insulted their mothers. But creaks in the attics or thumps in the basement, well...Best to leave those to hell alone.

So, as he walked the long, twisting driveway to the Currie house, leaving the Explorer behind him near the road, he could not shake the notion that he had made a gigantic mistake. With each step, with each new sound, he came to believe he would be unable to force himself to step inside that place at all.

His sneakers ground into the gravel, creating sharp echoes that bounced off the trees that pressed in close on either side. The driveway twisted to the right and then to the left, rising up the side of Olive Hill. The dark was seamless. It felt to Cain that he was walking into doom. At any moment, a hideous monstrosity might appear in front of him. Or maybe just a man, with a pale face and red eyes.

His breathing was so loud, it seemed to come from his head. He could hear his heart beating and that too seemed impossibly loud. Cain walked with his hands in front of him, lest a stray branch come for his eyes. There were quick, frightening screams from the woods that ended so abruptly, he wondered if he'd imagined them. There were chirps and chatters and the occasional far away grunts.

The driveway was a quarter mile of carnival of horrors. Yet, when he came to the last of it, and ascended a steep rise where the gravel turned to grass, Cain considered turning around and rushing back into it.

In the darkness, black on black, the Currie house loomed over him. The trees had been cleared around it, creating the illusion that the house had grown out of the hilltop like a horror movie castle. From this angle, the house seemed fantastically huge. It was two stories of mansard windows and jutting eaves. But most dramatic, a feature that beckoned the attention like fingers at the chin, was the massive turret on the north end of the house. It stood like an upraised thumb. The highest point of the turret reached a full story higher than the second floor roof top. It was fashioned in the shape of a bell tower, but Cain knew there was no bell up there. The top of the turret was the epicenter of the Currie house, the purpose of it. All the rest, as grandiose and beautiful as it was, was mere garnish.

The turret was home to the pink room. And the pink room was what it was all about.

No, Cain thought. *Kimberly. Kimberly is what it's all about.*

He moved forward, steps quieter on the long grass. Thinking her name was empowering. Kimberly, Kimberly, Kimberly.

Better. He felt ashamed that for a time, love had given way to fear.

This was crazy, yes. Currie might have been nuts, and Cain might be, too. But if there was just a sliver of a chance...

He strode toward the house, eyes fixed on the turret as if fearing it might swoop down upon him. He walked carefully up the wide stairway to the long porch. The boards beneath him groaned predictably. The key joined the conspiracy by refusing intercourse with the lock. And when he finally thrust it in and sprang the lock, the door swung away on its own with a long, petulant creek that opened on the uncertain promise of darkness within.

Five

The paper was soft, like tissue. Touching it, there was a sense it had been crumpled many times. Crumpled and unfolded again. Crumpled, unfolded. Words scrawled in pencil there were almost lost in a web of wrinkles. Countless seams had deteriorated the rigidity of the paper so that now it was fragile and easily torn.

Olivia Currie took pains to see that it did not get torn. The note was one of few personal things she had left of her only child, beyond the books and papers and stacks of awards. It was the only thing that had been taken from the house in northern Maine.

A week after Theodore was found dead in the woods, Olivia was flown to Mulberry in a private jet. There, she saw for the first time the home that had consumed her boy. The house was magnificent and bizarre. It resembled the dollhouse she had bought for her granddaughter and Olivia knew exactly why that was so.

She wheeled through the house with nervous, silent servants at her side. She was carried to the second floor and then to the top of the turret. When one of her men began packing up Theodore or Angel's things, Olivia had screamed at him. She ordered the house locked down and signs posted across the property. No one was to come here. Nothing was to be carried out of the house. Nothing but the tattered scrap of paper from the desk, which she now examined from the gloom of the enormous French chateau in Marblehead.

The paper was special, though troubling. If she'd had fingers to flatten and smooth the paper, she would have done so cautiously and tenderly. Instead, she had Gary, who removed the paper from the desk, and spent five minutes laying it out for her. She watched him sternly, but inwardly, she was amused. Gary handled that old scrap of notebook paper as though he were handling explosives.

"That's enough. Set it there. Turn the damn lights up so I can read the thing."

He wheeled her closer to the desk, each movement slow and careful. Gary did not want to rip the paper and he did not want to upset the old woman. He moved her this way and then that. He waited for her approval.

"That's good. Thank you, Gary. Now the lights, please? Then you can leave me."

He twisted a dial and bright, yellow light filled the room. Light seemed wrong in this place and Gary frowned. He quickly corrected himself, screwed the neutral expression back to his puffy, oval face, and glanced across the room at his employer.

Her head was hanging over her torso. She looked a colorless flower drooping on its stem. She was reading. The old woman was absorbed and sad.

Suffolk Pink. Not to be confused with Dashberry! White for the trim around the ceiling.

Rocking horse. Brown and white. There is pink crayon on the neck where Angel tried to color it. Right eye is rubbed away Left front paw is broken, about two inches. Refer to photographs.

The bureau has five drawers. The knobs are painted pink, except for the top one which is a purple flower. What kind of flower? The mirror is oval and trimmed in pink. Picture of Uncle Ray's puppy in the lower end.

The snow globe is the size of a softball and winds from the bottom of the base, which is pink with a circle of flowers. Inside, Strawberry Shortcake sits on a strawberry. The globe plays Fur Elise. Angel liked it when it was wound up tight and played fast.

Bedspread is also Strawberry Shortcake. Red, pink and white, with horses and little girls. More red than pink. Aunt Janie ordered it from a catalogue. Ask her where.

White dust ruffle with pink flowers. May have come with the spread.

Stuffed animals: white teddy bear (a foot-and-a-half tall) with pink ribbon around neck. There's a small, silver locket hanging from the ribbon. Red M&M with white arms. Pink, hairy thing that giggles when you tap it. Ask at the toy store.

Night stand is white with square, pink knobs. Three drawers? Angel scribbled on the top of it. The name of that boy she sang with in the kindergarten play. Robbie? Bobby? Ask Principal Kaplin.

The pink clock on the wall over the night stand is flower shaped. Red arms and numbers. There is a green sticker on the face we tried to scrape off with a razor.

The poster over her bed is a white cartoon horse with a pink mane. The horse has big, brown eyes. Almost human eyes. The word Milkshake at the bottom. The horse's name? The poster came with a lunch box and other stuff. Ask at the toy store. The right, top corner is always falling down because we used that yellow putty to hang it.

The chair under the window has a clown on the seat. Sort of like Ronald McDonald only more colorful. Angel put tomorrow's clothes there each night. Red dress. White turtleneck. White socks with hearts on them.

Priscilla curtains are white with pink trim. There may be little, pink flowers on the curtains. Angel kept them tied back with pink ties unless she was scared at night. Refer to photographs.

Fuzzy, pink area rug. Estimate it to be three feet by four. Angel spilled cocoa on it last year. May be a small stain.

Pink bean bag chair near the closet door. Always losing its stuffing so may have been ripped. Angel sometimes sat there with her coloring book. What kind? Strawberry Shortcake? Get crayons.

Poster on the back of the door has two cartoon girls in it. Blueberry Muffin and Strawberry Shortcake. They are in a field with mountains that look like ice cream cones.

The closet door has a full-length mirror on it. Angel sometimes puts a blanket over it at night when she's scared. The blanket is mostly white but has red trim and red flowers on it.

Hang the clothes in the closet, with all the pinks and reds hung together. Shoes on the floor.

The dollhouse. Should be ready for inspection on Friday. Double check: Spaniard red with white trim. Second Empire style with mansard roof. Turret must have railings at the very top and three windows below. The dollhouse sets on a white table, exactly centered.

The dollhouse must be exactly centered.

Suffolk pink for the walls. Not Dashberry. Suffolk pink. The curtains are pink. The rug is pink. It has to be the right size. All of it has to be the right size. Remember! The walls are Suffolk pink. Remember Suffolk! Not Dashberry!

The memo moved her to weeping every time she read it. It was ridiculous, really. It was just the inventory of a young girl's bedroom. Olivia remembered the bedroom and it was beautiful. Teddy had not missed a detail. Teddy did not overlook details in matters about which he was passionate.

Olivia Currie had no arms and only stubs for legs, the result of bacterial meningitis contracted during a trip to Africa the year after her husband died. She lived in a $20,000 wheelchair with every assistive gadget that had been invented. She could propel the chair by breathing into a tube and adjust speed and direction with a series of sips and puffs. With a joystick she prodded with her chin, Olivia could engage a mechanical arm to perform rudimentary tasks or fire up a laptop computer. With various movements of her head, she could tilt the chair this way or that way, play music, turn on lights and televisions or dial a telephone.

Olivia rarely used these gizmos. In personal matters such as this, the technology seemed crass and invasive. It was too bad because emotional storms were particularly complex for a quadruple amputee. Crying was a real bitch when you had no hands to wipe away the tears. It was a bitch because you couldn't put your hands to your head and try to hold back the grief, either. You couldn't cover your mouth to stifle a sob and you couldn't pound your hands in frustration.

Crying was just not practical. Olivia called to Gary. He was at her side a moment later.

"Turn it over. That's all. Just turn it over and leave me."

He did as he was told and did so with great care. He picked the paper up by a corner as if it were a live thing. He reversed it and lay it gently on the desk. He straightened it, looked at her for approval and then glided from the room.

The flip side was less dramatic. Teddy's work had never made much sense to her, though she reveled in his accomplishments. The meaningless mash of letters and numbers stirred little emotion in Olivia and that was fine. That was just dandy. Crying was just not practical for her at all.

North 47 degrees 20 minutes, west 68 degrees 27 minutes.

200 random point run. 39 five-point, 10 six-point and 1 seven-point array.

Zj>Xj+iYj

Non-vanishing harmonic spinor?

Hough transform negligible.

4 2
6n /k

Merc., Ven., Mars, Jup., Sat. 06/06/04 19:27 PM EST
M42 1976 Ori 05 35.4 -05 27 5.0 85 x 60 DfN 1.6

M110 205 And 00 40.4 41 41 10.0 17 x 10 Gal 2200
M11 6705 Sct 18 51.1 -06 16 7.0 14.0 OCl 6

Olivia sat dry-eyed in a mansion that overlooked the ocean in the most coveted section of Marblehead. She was worth $450 million dollars. She had a team of servants that tended to her around the clock. But immense wealth had never meant much to her, and it meant even less since she'd been hacked to a stump.

Teddy had been her only glimmer of happiness in an existence that was otherwise like living in a straightjacket. Teddy and his beautiful daughter who looked so much like Shirley Temple. She looked forward to their visits weeks in advance. She sent Gary out to buy them lavish gifts. She doted as much as a person could with no arms to hug and no legs to leap for joy.

Now she had one speck of purpose left in her truncated life and that was the writer. The writer whose books Gary had read to her and which had moved her in ways she had not expected. Cain wrote about monsters and things that live in closets, it was true. But Olivia Currie knew a metaphor when she saw one, and Cain's stories were full of them. Cain wrote about the pain of betrayal, the agony of loss, the inexplicable misfortunes that befall good people while evil men thrive. The writer tacked wings and fangs on these things and called them creatures. But Olivia saw through that. The writer exorcised his own demons in a way that entertained and terrified his readers. Most of them probably didn't know or care that they had unwittingly partaken in the writer's therapy.

She admired Cain and liked him immediately upon their first meeting. Now, somehow, she needed him. She needed him to provide a bridge to the troubled mind of her dead son. Because when his time at the house in northern Maine was over, Cain would be back to reveal what he had learned. The writer had promised.

Six

Cain spent his first night in the Currie house in a sleeping bag on the living room floor. Only, you couldn't really call it a living room. The first floor of the great house was a picture of unfinished business.

Walls had been constructed to divide the rooms, but no final touches had been added. The fireplace had no mantle. There were no built-in bookshelves or nooks nestled into the dark, pine walls. The place still smelled like plaster and paint, though it was faint beneath the stronger smell of dust and inactivity.

Banisters had not been assembled around the flying staircase winding to the second floor. Light fixtures had not been installed on the high ceilings. Electrical outlets around the room looked ugly and dangerous without plates over them.

Electrical power to the house was scheduled to be switched on today. Linemen would come out to check the connections and then radio in to have the juice switched on. Or they would climb a pole and pull a lever. Whatever. Cain had no idea.

His first night in the house was a dark one, with long, sneaky shadows bouncing across the walls as he wandered the first floor with a lantern.

The wandering was brief. A quick glance inside the kitchen, with no sink tucked into the square cutout at the center of a marble countertop. A peek into the dining room, which was nothing but a perfect square of a room painted white.

There was an immense library with French windows, but the room felt cold and antiseptic. The first floor did not feel like part of a house that had been vacated. It felt like a building that had never been a home.

But then, Cain thought, squirming from the sleeping bag like a giant larvae, Currie's business here had never been about comfort.

There was an office on the second floor somewhere, Cain knew. What gadgets and oddities filled it remained to be seen. There might be a bed up there and maybe a personal item or two. But he did not expect humor calendars or framed photos hanging on the walls. He did not anticipate vases for flowers or shelves for knickknacks. Currie had come here to work. Cain, too.

He awoke with gnawing unease about the encounter with the men in the Quonset hut. It was not a surprise that shadowy government agents held an active interest in the house. Olivia Currie had warned of their curiosity. Still, it was unnerving to learn they had set up shop here in Aroostook County, and that they were bold enough to announce themselves so quickly.

He was slightly hung-over from the six beers that had put him to sleep. Booze was an uncertain thing for Cain. There were times when it fueled his imagination like a spray of gasoline on a campfire. There were times when it dulled his intellect and reduced him to the literary equivalent of monosyllabic speech.

He was grateful that last night's drinking had led to stupor. By the fourth beer, he was no longer taking involuntary glances at the stairway that wound in a half loop to the dark second floor. He was no longer imagining the jolt he would feel at discovering a pale face standing and staring from that darkness. The white face of a young girl, perhaps. Or an old man. Or a grinning specter face of indeterminate age.

Now it was morning and there was light. Lots of light. Sun poured into the house like water filling a sunken ship. Cain stood, dug shorts and a T-shirt from a duffle bag, and walked out onto the porch. There was no coffee to ruminate over, so he stuffed his hands into his pockets and walked down the stairs and onto the grass.

Cain had heard that warmth had a hard time finding Maine in the spring, but it was warm enough for him today. The sun floated in a bright sky and something buzzed like electricity in a faraway tree.

He walked through the grass and felt insects colliding with his bare legs. A dragonfly whizzed around his head. He turned in all directions but could not see beyond the thickness of pine trees anywhere. There was no hint of a town beyond them — no far away hum of a passing truck, no buzzing boats to be heard.

He turned to look at the house. It was a beauty and a monstrosity. It could be home to epicureans or a funeral parlor. The house was a deep, blood red, a color that seemed somehow obscene against the backdrop of gentle green trees and the soft blue of the sky.

The square turret on the northern end was magnificent. It was stately yet sinister. Homey yet haunting. A neat square of wrought iron rails on the very top looked as though it might cage a very small prisoner. The house could have been designed by Michelangelo or Walt Disney.

He walked through the grass until he could see the other side of the turret, with its giant window facing north. Trees had been cleared on that side of the house so a person gazing from that window would have a wonderful view of the sky. He imagined Theodore Currie standing at that window for hours after sundown, staring out upon countless stars and marking constellations he could name by heart. The brilliant Theodore Currie staring into light years of space while waiting for signs of something that might be much, much closer.

Maybe he opened the window and whispered his daughter's name into the night. Maybe he sat on the bed and touched her toys, gripped by fears that his calculations had been wrong. Cain wondered what it would be like to sit in that room. He wondered how it would feel to be surrounded by pink walls and a little girl's bright playthings while the rest of the world was dark.

Seven

Reggie Lyons once spent a night sleeping in a tree while coyotes circled on the ground below him. The animals howled and paced in excited loops but Lyons got in four hours of solid sleep before the sun rose. In the light, he had power over the beasts again and the animals knew it. They scampered back into the deep woods and Reggie climbed down from the giant oak. It took him twenty minutes to find his way out of the woods and he was at the store on time to serve breakfast to the first customer.

Reggie didn't find the story interesting enough to share with friends, so he didn't. He forgot about it himself by the end of the day.

There was the time Lyons spent two days and nights trapped in a mangled pickup while his buddy lay dead behind the steering wheel. That had been a pickle, all right. It was the middle of the night when Rover Reed swerved to miss a moose and flipped the truck over an embankment along Route 11. The truck rolled end over end through a space between a pair of trees, like a misshapen football sailing through the uprights. It bounced off a refrigerator-sized boulder and then slammed down in the hard packed mud next to a stream. No mangled trees to signify a wreck. No dramatic ball of fire. No worried friends back in Mulberry staring at their watches and scratching their heads.

Lyons and his oldest friend had been returning early from a trip to Portland and nobody expected them back for days. To make matters worse, they had crashed in one of the unpopulated townships, where few people stopped unless it was to take a hasty leak by the side of the road.

Lyon's head and shoulders had smashed through the passenger side window in the wreck. The rest of him was pinned beneath a ton of steel. It was the middle of July and the state was in the blast of a four day heat wave. A man could bake out here in the mud, if the goddamn bugs didn't devour him first.

Some might have suggested that Reed was the lucky one, having crushed his skull against the windshield and dying in short order. Lyons never thought so. He thought it was pretty damn unlucky to have your brains dripping down the front of your shirt.

It was an unpleasant couple of days out there, Reggie would allow that much. His face was pressed into foul smelling mud at the side of a stream and he could only get one arm free of the wreckage. But so what? That free arm hosted an intact hand which managed to retrieve a beer that had landed close by and Lyons nursed it for two whole days. That free arm also swatted away hornets and bugs and in one instance, a ferocious-looking fisher.

By the end of the first day, Rover had already begun to stink. It was a pungent, fishy smell and it got worse by the hour.

On the second day, there was a sizzling sound from inside the truck and then a putrid odor filled the afternoon. It was hot. The bugs were heavy and the smell coming from Lyons' best friend was eye-watering bad.

Lyons scooped up black mud with his free hand and caked it under his nostrils. Compared to the aroma of Rover's innards, the scent of the thick, foul mud was a sniff in a flower garden.

Shortly before dusk on the second day, a state trooper rolled to a stop on the roadway thirty feet above. Lyons yelled up and then calmly finished the hot, gritty beer. With that gone, he crumpled the can in his fist and flicked it away.

"Took you so fucking long?" Lyons asked the trooper, who'd climbed down the embankment.

Later, in the ambulance, Lyons looked down at his busted legs and was only slighted appalled to see a good portion of Rover's brains splashed across them.

"I didn't think old Rover had that much," he quipped to a paramedic.

Lyons once shot a man trying to smash into his house in the dead of night. He was once written up in the Bangor newspaper for hauling three teenagers out of an overturned car along I-95 just before the Volkswagen exploded. Two years back, he fought a former NFL linebacker when the giant tourist insulted a waitress over at the Hearthside. Reggie broke two of the man's ribs and sent one of his teeth flying. The former pro had even apologized to the waitress before driving himself to a hospital up in Fort Kent.

Reggie Lyons was a tough man and a well loved one, to boot. He was 53, a widower and childless. He was the town constable and the owner of the Lyon's Share Market on Route 11. It was a stupid name for a store, but some of the tourists liked it and screw the locals. Let them cross into Canada and pay ten bucks for a pack of smokes.

The constable position paid $5,000 a year and Reggie considered it gravy. He was paid to look out for 300 full-time citizens and to keep the additional 200 summer residents from burning their nuts off with fireworks. He broke up the occasional fight, lectured drunken teens and played referee to brawling couples.

There were three fatal car crashes and seven boating wrecks in Mulberry over the last twelve years. State Police handled the former, the wardens investigated the latter.

There were dozens of unattended deaths, but all but one was easily explained. Locals died of heart attacks, household accidents and drowning, mostly. More than a few drank their way to graves and a handful got hooked on city drugs.

The only unfinished business, as far as Reggie Lyons was concerned, was the Currie mess a year ago. The State Police had ultimately handled that one, too. The Staties and some quiet, federal guys who asked a lot of questions but answered none that were put to them. Screw ‘em, Lyons decided. He knew plenty. He had been the first person on the scene after Currie had been found bled to death in the woods. The man had been bitten. Chewed, was more like it, but by no animal Reggie could identify. That was a freakish one, all right, but everything about Currie had been freakish.

As constable and lifelong resident, Reggie Lyons was also the unofficial Minder of Business. When someone new moved to Mulberry, Lyons knew most of what there was to know about him by the time they took their first shit here. He did this through police contacts to the south, through Mounties and border patrol officers to the north, and through a vast network of people who loved him or owed him favors.

This week, new business was old business. Someone had moved to the Currie house and the town was buzzing. The news would have been juicy under any circumstances. It was particularly zesty since the new tenant was a fairly popular author.

“You ever heard of him, Reg?”

“Sure I heard of him. My sister down in Houlton read a couple of his books. Says he ain’t bad.”

“What kinda books?”

“Spook stuff. Stella calls it gothic horror.”

“Whatever that is.”

Fred Descoteaux was stuffing his face with a double cheeseburger with bacon and a side of fries with beef gravy. Fred was 260 pounds and probably two years from his first heart attack.

“The Currie house. That’s where that scientist lived a couple years ago, right?”

It was Bobby Erenfried, who moved up from Orono six months ago. Erenfried was striving desperately for acceptance in Mulberry. He was a good man, with his own plow and a fishing boat. He’d gain acceptance right after he stopped trying to get it.

"That's right," Reggie said, leaning against the counter and gazing out at the gas pumps. Pauline Dufresne was having trouble figuring out how to use her credit card again.

"That Currie fella is the one whose daughter died, right?"

"Right."

"How old was she? How'd she die?"

Reggie and Descoteaux rolled their eyes in unison.

"Six years old. Burned to death in a house fire down in New York."

"No shit." He took a bite of his sandwich, mulling that. "Anyone else die?"

Descoteaux sighed. It was a sound of tired disgust, but he was warming to the subject. The big man liked to be the one with information and it seldom happened.

"Nobody else home. Kid's mom died giving birth to her. Her dad was off in Connecticut or something getting a big award. Babysitter was hooked on smack and was out trying to score. That's heroin, you know."

"I know what smack is. Jesus Christ, Fred."

Pauline Dufresne gave up trying to pay for her gas at the pump. She came in and angrily slapped a ten dollar bill on the counter and left without a word.

"Nice lady," Descoteaux said.

"Yeah. I'd fuck her."

The three men laughed and then looked around guiltily. Descoteaux finished eating and pointed to the coffee pot behind the counter. Reggie slid a cup to him and began flipping through the newspaper. Erenfried was still working on his tuna melt.

"So, the kid die at the hospital or right away?"

"Right away. Burned up pretty bad. Heard they found her on the floor of her bedroom, trying to claw her way into the closet. Probably thought it was the doorway out, I dunno."

"No shit."

"Yeah. And the fire started cus the junkie babysitter left a cigarette burning in the bathroom. Goddamn dipshit. She should have been hanged."

Erenfried looked up at Reggie who nodded over his paper.

"That's terrible," Erenfried said. "And the dad went pretty crazy, or what?"

"That's what they say. Wouldn't you? Bad enough he loses his wife. Then he hires a drug addict for a babysitter and his little girl goes up in smoke. Jesus Christ, man. I'd go fucking bananas."

"God."

Penny Forrester came in shaking her 17-year-old ass around the store before buying a bottle of water. She snapped her gum and flirted with the men. She complained that she was bored and then stretched, puffing out her grapefruit-sized breasts. Then she left the store, giving an extra shake or two on the way out.

"Donny Forrester's kid," Erenfried said, like he was answering a question on a game show.

"Yeah. You could get your arms broke just for looking at her."

Erenfried looked up at Reggie, who nodded again.

It was 4 o'clock. There would be a rush of business soon as working men came in for coffee and smokes, the free and clear came into gas up boats and ATVs.

Erenfried, who worked at the Hearthside bussing tables, pushed his empty plate away from him.

"So, what's the deal on the writer? He a big drunk, or what?"

Reggie fielded this one himself. It was okay to give Erenfried charge of old business. New matters belonged in the hands of the constable.

"No, not a drunk that I know of. Seems okay. No record or anything since he was a kid. He's richer than God, too, by our standards. Has a full-time house down in Cape May and another one in North Carolina."

"Huh. What brings him here, then? Thinks he's Hemingway come to hunt big game? Wife made him move because she heard there's no crime in Maine? Or what?"

Reggie began wiping down the counter. Fragments of tuna and beef dotted the Formica like soldiers on a battlefield.

"Wife's dead. Got a brain tumor about a year ago. Died in about a month."

Descoteaux winced. His own wife survived breast cancer four years ago.

Erenfried stood, stretched, groaned and pulled out his wallet. He punched his companion on the shoulder. He felt confident he was up to speed. Hell, he might even know a thing or two more than his neighbors.

"What is it about the Currie house? Great place to mourn or hold séances, or what?"

There was no answer right away. The other two men didn't believe there was anything inordinately spooky about the house on Olive Hill. It was an odd place built by an unbalanced man, that was all.

Still, the house had taken on a certain Halloween ambiance for the rest of the town. It sat up there invisible, for the most part. But there were a few areas — a tote road off Route 116 and the snowmobile camp at the top of Mount Orange, for instance — from which a corner of the house could be seen. Looking at it that way, with that massive turret poking above the pines, it looked like a segment of a really bleak secret creeping into view.

"You know Erenfried?" Reggie said, whipping the dish cloth over a shoulder. "You say 'or what' too much."

Eight

In one of his early novels, Cain wrote about a character named Devon who had to open a coffin exhumed from the basement of a church. Inside the coffin might be enough jewels to allow the character to flee the country a wealthy man. Or it might be the tortured corpse of his younger sister. The scene marked the climax of a story about a cat-and-mouse game between a loveable criminal and a twisted, old millionaire.

The story was a transparent rip-off of the "Lady or the Tiger" parable. But the book sold near 500,000 copies and the ending was a blast to write. The fate of the protagonist came down to the lifting of that coffin lid. A high squeak of hinges, a falling of shadows and bliss or agony was at hand.

Jonathan Cain felt like the man lifting that lid as he ascended the flying staircase to the upper floors of the Currie house.

It was night outside, though a thin band of darkening blue still held on at the lower edge of the western sky. Night creatures were chirping and buzzing and cawing with such vigor it was almost deafening. The stars were dazzling. The air was warm.

For the first time in a year, electrical power pulsed through the Currie House. Hours earlier, Cain had produced a dozen lamps from a box in his car. He assembled them throughout the lower rooms of the house and switched them on as he went along. Artificial light invaded long-dark corners. If he was climbing to the upper floors, Cain wanted the warm comfort of light at his back.

The light switch at the foot of the staircase had done nothing for the darkness above, so Cain produced a flashlight with fresh batteries.

He started up. He walked evenly and without drama, like a man merely going upstairs to take a leak. He tried whistling. But his mouth was dry and he knew it was a farce, so he stopped. Cain was terrified.

Not of shrieking ghosts that might lurch from foul smelling closets, or of demons that might descend on him.

Cain was afraid of his purpose here tonight. It chilled him to think of Currie up there night after night trying to summon the dead. It unnerved him even more to contemplate his own motivations.

The stairs were polished wood. Each step sounded to Cain like he was walking on a piano. The staircase wound to the right and the ascent was strangely disorienting. Cain normally thought it was bad luck to count one's steps, but he counted anyway. And eighteen steps later, he was stepping into the darkness of the second floor.

He took a breath, switched on the clunky, yellow flashlight and moved toward the first door on the right. *The hinges will scream when I open it. There will be strange shapes in there, but it's only abandoned boxes and maybe some drop cloths.*

The door opened smoothly. There were no chairs or bureaus to cast strange shadows. The room, long and rectangular, was empty. The white tube of light from the flashlight slashed through darkness like a laser but there was nothing to see.

Cain backed out of the room and pulled the door closed. His feet scraped on the planked floor and sharp echoes shot down the hall. He jumped and resisted the urge to wheel around, aiming the flashlight like a gun. He turned slowly instead and faced a second door across the hall. Ornate wood so dark it looked black. Cain stepped toward it, twisted the knob and shoved it open.

There was a gust of air like stale breath. Something lunged from the other side of the door. Long arms reached for him and flapped in the dusty dark. Cain felt something smooth and cool brush his face and he flailed at it with the flashlight. He screamed and stumbled back, waiting for a horrible face to appear over those massive, reaching arms. The flashlight slipped in his fingers and he almost dropped it. The beam danced crazily across the walls and ceiling. There was a deep, abrasive sound followed by a thud that shook the floor. He took another step back and collided with something behind him. He screamed again, wheeled and banged his face against the door he had opened moments earlier. Dizzy from fright, he spun back around, expecting to see hideous hands sweeping in to shred his skin, claw his eyes, squeeze his throat. He turned the flashlight beam toward the right, where he thought the staircase should be. A tall figure appeared in the light and Cain jumped once more, this time catching a scream before it departed his throat. It was a ladder, abandoned next to a wall where the hallway cut down on more rooms.

Alarmed that he could not find the staircase, Cain wheeled to his left again and faced the doorway that housed the long-armed horror.

There was nothing but a square of darkness from the open door. Dust floated like snow in the flashlight beam. On the floor, a long, thin object poked just an inch or two from the doorway. Cain turned the beam towards it, ready to spring at the slightest movement.

The leg belonged to a tripod that seated a massive telescope now laying on the floor like a fallen creature. Peering into the room, Cain saw that the scope had been covered with a thick, dark cloth which now was pooled around it on the floor. He poked it with his foot. Thick, scratchy cloth and nothing more. He moved the flashlight to examine the rest of the room. More shapes and shadows, but nothing that lunged or flapped. Everything was covered with dark cloth, so that it appeared as a room full of sleeping gnomes.

His heart was pounding. Sweat streamed down the sides of his face and from the hairline at the back of his head. He turned to examine the door behind him and ascertained it still open. No ghouls, ladders or optical equipment sprang from it. Cain laughed a nervous laugh. He rubbed his face where he had struck the door across the hall. There was still the rest of the second floor to explore and then the turret room. The real work lay ahead of him. But first, a drink. Maybe two drinks. And then he would return with all the lamps he had left and maybe a trunk full of light bulbs.

Thirty minutes later, he was back on the second floor. He had three more rooms conquered and no more contusions to show for it.

There was a mattress, three folded blankets and an empty box in what was surely supposed to be the master bedroom at the far end of the hall. There was another metal ladder in the center of what would have made a great reading room. There was a box full of empty soda bottles in a corner of that room and a coil of rope on top of it.

Beyond that, no great discoveries were to be made. The bathroom up here was elegant and huge. A giant, sunken tub in a far corner with a sky window overhead. A large, square shower across from a long vanity with twin sinks. There was an acrid smell in there that Cain could not place. Like he had in the other rooms, he screwed light bulbs in wherever they would go. He set lamps where they were needed.

Back in the room of the long-armed horror, Cain plugged in two lamps and switched them on. He got the telescope righted and examined the lenses. Nothing appeared to be cracked. It was a black Meade with an 8-inch aperture and a chrome steel tripod. The son-of-a-bitch probably weighed a hundred pounds. He set it in a corner.

On the back wall, a long row of windows had been covered with more of the dark green cloth. Beneath the windows, more heaps lay covered. Cain began ripping cloth away and revealing the marvels beneath.

There was a long, cherry wood desk with an attached bookcase. Atop it was a Dell computer with cords coiled around it like a nest of snakes. There were a dozen stacks of paper on the desktop and stray scraps running loose among them. To Cain, it looked like someone had tried to straighten the desktop before giving up abruptly.

There were maybe three dozen books on the shelves. Half were standing, the rest leaning or laying flat. Cain ran a finger over some of them and scanned the titles. He knew a thing or two about quantum physics and cosmology, but these books might have been written in

Hebrew. Weak gauge bosons, flop transitions, Kaluza-Klein and tachyons. Heavy stuff. But then, he had not expected a Louis L'Amour, Grisham or King on Currie's reading list.

There were a half dozen or more wads of paper squeezed into tight balls on the floor. Cain thought dimly about the men he had met last night. He wondered why they hadn't sent someone to break in to the Currie place and steal scraps of paper just like these. The computer, the stray scraps of paper...these were the kinds of things that made government men pee their pants.

There was a drafting table shoved against a wall, with rulers, gauges and pens strewn on the floor around it. A larger ball of paper lay on the floor in front of the table, dusty and dull, like a dust bunny seen through a microscope.

In a corner near the covered windows, incongruous among the technical tools of a scientific genius, a teddy bear lay face down in a heap, half covered by a hanging cloth. One white arm was outstretched, as if straining for a helping hand. Cain knelt and picked it up, holding the bear at arm's length to examine it. And as unexpected and uncontrollable as a sneeze, he was swept by a blast of sadness that was so quick and powerful, it was like a breeze from an icebox.

The bear was white with a wide, goofy smile stitched below round, black eyes. There was a pink ribbon around its neck and the small remnant of a gold chain that may have once held a locket. The bear was white and yet most of it seemed to have been soiled a cancerous yellow. Cain, a former pack a day man, was reminded of the ugly nicotine stains that once yellowed the curtains in his writing room.

Gingerly, cautiously, he sniffed the bear. It did not reek of cigarette smoke. He rubbed his hands through the faux fur and found that it was coarse in places. *Wet*, he thought. He imagined Theodore Currie clutching the bear tight night after night, as he struggled for sleep with memories of his burned, dead daughter clogging every thought. Cain imagined tears soaking the once soft fur, the fingertips of a madman sinking into the foam.

The image was unutterably sad and he set the bear on the desk. It tipped drunkenly to the right, but Cain caught and straightened it. With that wrong righted, he started out of the room. The toe of his right sneaker collided with the larger of the wadded balls of paper. It was an unplanned field goal. The paper ball went airborne in a perfect arc, and sailed through the uprights of the doorway. It landed in the hallway with a harmless bounce.

Cain walked to it, plucked it off the floor and stepped back into the room. Slowly, like a very old man opening a Christmas present, he pulled the paper open, wincing at the brittle sound of old creases coming apart. The paper was almost poster sized by the time he had it smoothed out. Only a few words scrawled there. Letters with dramatic, fly away curves, like the legs of a dying spider.

"It is eternity in between."

Nine

Theodore Currie was buried in a cemetery that was too neat to be beautiful twelve miles from his home in Tarrytown. His wife's grave was to the left of his, Angel's was to the right. A stranger visiting this plot would assume the three had died together in some tragic way. Until they read the dates on the stones and discerned that Theodore Currie had grieved plenty before he was taken.

The stone above his grave was even and square and short on adornments, much like the life he had led. There was no eloquent epitaph below his name. The stone did not proclaim that here lies Theodore Currie, noted physicist and advancer of current theories. His was another bland stone in marching rows of many. The trees around them were also in rigid rows and they were manicured and neat. There was nothing fanciful or singular about any of them.

There were fresh geraniums on either side of the headstone, and the flowers were getting whipped and battered by a rainstorm that had sprung up earlier in the night. An observer with a flair for the dramatic might have suggested that the wind and rain accurately reflected the emotional turmoil of Currie's life. The observer would have been guilty of understatement.

On the last night of his life, Currie understood the true nature of the universe more than any person walking the earth. There was nothing supernatural about this knowledge. At the time Einstein unleashed his general theory of relativity, it was said that only a handful of people truly understood it. Most scientists readily accepted that claim.

Currie, like thousands of others, knew that to accept the notion that all particles in the universe are made up of tiny, vibrating strings, one had to also allow that no less than eleven dimensions exist. The eleventh dimension was particularly appealing. In a ground breaking paper on the subject, Currie had suggested that this one dimension was as close to all of us as the shirts we wear. It was as close as the sweat that slicks our bodies or the perfume we spray on our skin. Yet we could never see this fantastic realm, Currie explained in his decidedly non-theatrical writing style, because the eleventh dimension was no more than a trillionth of a millimeter in diameter. It was invisible to any technology available to man, yet it was infinitely long. Gravity, the weakest force, slipped in and out of it all the time. The eleventh dimension was also the final destination for certain forms of energy cast from our world into seeming oblivion.

Currie, calm and bookish, quietly dismissed other theories trying to take off in the scientific community. He had no use for the idea that the universe floated in a membrane full of other universes. For Currie, all of the cosmos consisted of tiny strings and extra dimensions for them to reside in.

Even for the geniuses of the world, the concept was hard to wrap the mind around. All that we see or do exists in a world of up and down, left and right, back and forth. The three spatial dimensions that rule the universe.

But over time, as general relativity and quantum mechanics continued to defy each other, more and more scientists came to believe that string theory was the only way to unify the workings of the very large with that of the subatomic. It was the last chance to explain the astounding weakness of gravity in relation to the remaining forces of nature.

Faced with lack of evidence to share with the non-scientific public, theorists began using basic analogies to explain the invisible dimensions of string theory. And the eleventh dimension was particularly inviting. Imagine, they implored a bored and skeptical audience, an ant crawling across a stretched garden hose. Watching from a distance, they said, that hose appears as a mere line, only one dimension for the insignificant bug to move in.

Yet on the surface of the hose, the ant is aware of another dimension, invisible to the observer, in which it can travel — the curvature of the tube on which it walks.

Eureka, said the scientists. To the bewildered observer, it is as though an extra dimension was revealed curled up on every point of the garden hose. And this is the way it is with the universe. We are surrounded by other dimensions indescribably close to us — as close and prevalent as the air around us — and yet we can never see them.

Suddenly, quantum theory was cool. A Columbia physicist wrote a 400 page book about string theory and sold a million copies. Perfectly normal men and women were reading it on the beach. They were proudly displaying it on coffee tables. It wasn't quite the presentation of scientist as rock star, but it was getting there.

With unprecedented interest in their work, top theorists began to boast: proof of strings and extra dimension will come with the help of super colliders in coming decades. But even those who boasted the loudest did not truly comprehend the theories they were expounding. They were clutching shaky science and clinging to hope that their measly contributions would be validated while they remained alive to glory in it.

Not Theodore Currie. Mathematics, for the acclaimed scientist, was intuitive and visual. It was instinctive. Faced with an intricate knot, his brain would work out a solution well before his fingers touched the twine. When he listened to classical music, he would close his eyes and see the octaves, harmonies, waves and tempo in mathematical form.

Currie somehow was able to compute the elusive math of string theory that confounded others, and often without ever putting pencil to paper. More importantly, he was able to visualize and understand the looping, swirling math of the science that exhausted even the most astute. Currie got it.

It was widely accepted that in 1915, the majority of human beings possessed minds incapable of truly grasping Einstein's theory on the workings of time, space and gravity. Einstein grasped it completely. That did not mean he could make another person understand.

Likewise, Currie could not have explained what he naturally intuited and knew to be the truth about a universe full of extra dimensions and coils of invisible strings. He could not explain but he could experiment.

Over many nights in northern Maine, Currie tapped into the unseen dimension he had come to believe was occupied by the energy of the dead. But his ambition was not to crack the oldest mystery in the history of cognizant thought. He cared nothing about science on those final nights, other than that which was needed to bring back the daughter he so adored.

Theodore Currie was not a sane man in the final months of his life. The loss of Angel had left him in a never-ending state of delirium, his head a cacophony of debilitating memories and quantum formulas that played in his head like chords on a haunted piano.

Before moving to Mulberry, Currie spent days wandering in a daze, unable to consolidate the image of his delicate, brown-eyed daughter with the uncompromising properties of death. He thought he heard her crying for him at all hours. He imagined he heard her voice from his bedroom doorway at night, soft and lisping because Angel had lost a front tooth just a week before she burned.

Some nights, he slept in a ball on the couch, remembering how he would lay there exhausted after a 12 hour day at the university, Angel sitting on his legs and reading fairy tales to him. Such a bright girl, but so shy and meek it was almost crippling.

Angel would have never been a tomboy. She was more comfortable with frilly dresses than with jeans or cutoff shorts. A dead bird on the front lawn would inspire her to tears that would last most of an afternoon. A raised voice or an unkind word from a neighborhood child would set her chin to quivering.

Angel resembled the mother she never knew, with hair so long and coiled into such fantastic springs, she looked like a doll propped in the window of an antique store. Angel was an ethereal creature and one coveted by her otherwise intense and passionless father.

So, on the days and nights when Theodore Currie imagined his precious, delicate daughter choking in a room full of smoke and crawling across her bedroom floor, it wasn't just guilt or grief that gripped him by the throat. It was the kind of pain that pumped through the body like acid and ate a person up like cancer.

That his little girl was irretrievably lost was not an idea Currie could fit inside the mind that could otherwise make sense out of anything. It couldn't be. It wouldn't be.

Denial is a fancy that visits all of those who grieve for an angry, fleeting period. A stage of grief, a temporary madness. But few, if any of those who have raged against the finality of death have had anything close to the power to defy it. Currie was different. There was nothing at all fanciful about his designs to reclaim his daughter from the clutches of doom. Currie knew the science. Currie was perhaps the only man alive who really knew it. The knowledge was at once a comfort and a curse.

Clinically, Theodore Currie lost his mind the moment he learned of his daughter's death. He was at Yale, tolerating the accolades from a roomful of adoring peers, when two Connecticut State Police troopers walked solemnly to his table. They beckoned him out, spoke to him softly and drove him to New York where another pair of troopers took over and drove him to the burned relic of his home. By then, Currie was gone. True sanity never returned. He was brilliant, yes. He was as methodical and intuitive as he'd ever been. But the ability and desire for rational thinking was something he'd left back at Yale with a roomful of peers he would never see again.

Currie lost that but he never fell all the way down the rabbit hole into the oblivion of the visibly insane. There was classic mourning, but resolve and determination cut it short. Currie was back at work. And the pace of his studies intensified over a period of weeks as he made preparations to bring his daughter back.

He began with ley lines.

Currie was intimately familiar with the bands of energy that cross the planet in ways nobody really understood. Ley lines were not an integral part of his study of quantum mechanics or his passion for cosmology. Yet, in some intuitive way, he had always felt there was a relationship — some beautiful interaction among gravity, the unseen dimensions and the magnetic forces of the earth. And so he studied them, for no other reason than that he found the concept intriguing and might someday find them useful.

Currie had examined the maps. He had visited Stonehenge, Nazca in Peru, the Great Pyramid at Giza, Ayers Rock in Australia, Sedona in Arizona and Mutiny Bay; each a place of awe and each believed by some to sit on the elusive lines of energy that cross the planet in a grid.

Ley lines were a theory. There were those who believed birds and fish used the magnetic forces to travel thousands of miles across the globe with eerie precision. There were those who suspected ley lines were behind the mysteries of the Bermuda Triangle.

Nobody had offered up anything close to proof of their existence. Yet, with a few simple calculations and the consultation of easily accessible reference books, Currie had found what he was looking for and not too far off at all.

The closest ley line was a 50 mile slash that crossed northern Maine, and Currie could not have wished for a better location. There had not been a population explosion in that region of the country and securing an optimal spot would not be a problem. Currie needed an area that was reasonably private. He needed to be close to the center of the ley line and he needed to build up high.

With coordinates and a global positioning unit in hand, Currie visited Mulberry and found himself on Olive Hill, a good distance from the town below him. It was perfect. It was ideal. He bought the land from a man who owned virtually all of Mulberry and who didn't give a whit about Olive Hill.

Currie contacted builders at once, refused to haggle over costs and presented his incentives for quick work. Then, with hammers pounding and saws buzzing in Mulberry, he returned to New York for the last time to indulge in the oldest and sweetest of his passions. He turned his attention to the sky and methodically charted out the time table for the coming alignment.

Currie was not sane at all. But his capability to compute complex math was not diminished by his emotional instability. He was determined, he was confident, and he was endowed with the finances to carry out his ambitions.

By spring of 2004, the Second Empire home was finished, and it looked like a gigantic version of the dollhouse Angel had so cherished. It was strange and sad to look at, but Currie did not linger long in reflection. The house stood in the precise spot indicated by his calculations, with magnetic energy in the earth below and the power of the cosmos above. That was what mattered.

Currie hustled the baffled workmen away before they could complete their finish work. He had what he needed. He didn't need valances and cornices and fancy bookshelves. He needed little of the house, beyond the small room in the turret he would make cozy for his daughter.

It was night when he began unloading the Ryder truck of all the things he needed to tempt her back. The rocking horse she bounced back and forth on for entire afternoons. A snow globe which played a tune that made her think of fairy tales. A bed, a bureau, a clock, a nightstand. All the things needed to entice his beautiful, brown-eyed Angel home from the invisible dimension that kept her.

The entire body of knowledge Currie had accumulated in a life of study culminated in a simple pink room in the turret of a house that had been precisely constructed. In the end, the scientist traded scales and beakers for cans of paint and a child's play things.

Ten

Cain didn't need the lamps he carried into Angel Currie's room. The lights in here worked just fine. The ceiling lamp lit up with a flick of the switch. The horse head lamp on the nightstand clicked on with the twist of a knob.

It was very pink indeed. Surrounded by four pink walls, and pink trinkets splashed elsewhere throughout the room, Cain felt as though he'd fallen into a bottle of Pepto Bismol.

He sat on the foot of the small bed marveling at the incongruity of the room. The pink room did not belong in the Currie house. It was too bright and soft. It was too warm and vaguely soothing. The room felt as though many happy years had been spent here, though Cain knew it was not so.

The trip up to the pink room had been a horror. The staircase to the top of the turret was narrow and twisting. Cain had been expecting a more modern ascent, but instead felt like he was climbing inside a fairy tale castle. There was a single light fixture on the wall half way up the stairs. The light did not work, even with a fresh bulb. Cain was resigned to climbing in darkness.

Halfway up, there was a thunderous sound from a floor below him. His heart at first seemed to stop and then began to jackhammer. He tried to spin around and only twisted into the wall beside him. His hands and feet went numb and he nearly dropped the box filled with lamps and bulbs. He froze and waited for another deafening thud. It would be closer this time. It would be at the foot of this claustrophobic staircase as the terror from the second floor lumbered toward the intruder...

There was no follow up noise. There was no echo. Just one, nasty thump and then a dreadful silence.

The telescope. The goddamn thing fell over again and this time, the lens probably shattered into a thousand pieces.

Cain was not convinced, but forced his feet to move again. He would ignore the sound for now and continue to the pink room.

And now he was here. Inside the room that had called him out on this strange adventure. A place he had first heard about from his publisher and then from Olivia Currie herself. The pink room. The place where the loved and lost might be seduced back from the shadow.

He stood and began to take inventory. He reached up behind the bed and rubbed his hands over a wall clock in the shape of a flower. Dust coated his fingertips and he absently wiped them on his jeans.

He touched the nightstand next to the bed, the square, pink knobs cold and slick. He did not open the drawers. The idea felt both disturbing and perverse.

The name "Bobby" was scribbled in crayon on the white surface of the stand. It looked as though the letters had been written by a child. Cain knew it had not.

A white, cartoon horse with a pink mane was displayed in a poster on the wall over the bed. Part of the horse's face was hidden behind a corner of the poster, which had pulled free from the wall and curled down.

The curtains over the window beyond the bed were white. Behind them, a square patch of black that Cain knew would be the northern sky. There would be a terrific view of the stars from up here, unobstructed by treetops which the turret towered over.

He stepped around the edge of the bed and almost tripped over a pink bean bag. He caught himself and then spied his reflection in the full length mirror on the back of the closet door. In it, Cain looked pale and afraid. He examined his face a moment and then noticed that the closet door was slightly ajar.

He felt suddenly cold. It was the same sensation experienced when he wrote a particularly spooky scene in one of his novels. When that happened, he normally savored it, enveloping himself in the crawling chill to work it into a zesty piece of narrative.

He did not savor the feeling tonight. Stepping past the beanbag, he reached out for the closet door. His hand moved comically slow, inching toward the door knob. He was aware of this underwater speed yet he could not correct it. The house was so silent, it buzzed. The crevice of darkness beyond the closet door was sinister, the ultimate representation of a man's fear of things that lie just out of view.

Jesus. Just open the goddamn door.

He grabbed the knob and pulled the door open. The hinges creaked, high and loud, and he jumped. Beyond the door, a whirl of motion, like floating fairies. Something stark white flapped toward him. Cain stopped breathing but stood his ground, watching as a dozen dresses, blouses and shirts adjusted to the draft of air that had invaded the closet. There was a tinkle of clothes hangers clanging against each other. To Cain, it sounded like whispering.

Breathing again, he reached out and ran his hands over a row of red dresses and skirts. He twirled red corduroy between his fingers, examining the texture. He studied a row of shoes, most of them black, lined neatly on the floor beneath the hanging clothes. A little girl's closet with little girl things. No stunning revelations. No gruesome clues into the last days of Theodore Currie.

Cain was grateful for the latter.

He stepped back, decided nothing was going to lunge from the darkest depths of the closet, and shut the door. He pressed it until he heard the latch snap closed. He turned to continue the inspection of the rest of the room.

The dollhouse sat perfectly centered on a table next to the doorway. It was a disorienting thing to look at because, Cain knew, it was a perfect replica of the house in which he stood. And the recreation was eerie. The main doorway looked as though it might open with a tug. The mansard roof was topped by what appeared to be real bits of shingle, and the rails around the turret were black metal.

He bent and examined the turret. Such a good imitation. He imagined seeing a little Jonathan Cain staring out from the window at the top.

The thought made him shudder. His imagination was grinding away again and that would not serve him well tonight. Imagine, he thought, seeing that little Jonathan Cain standing in the window, an alternate me in a wee, little place. What a wonder. And imagine, then, seeing a shadowy, disfigured shape creeping up behind him...

He turned away from the dollhouse and shook the thought. He walked to a bureau and examined a snow globe sitting on top of it. Again, his hand seemed to move freakishly slow as he reached out to it. He watched his fingers grasp the glass orb and pick it up. He reached beneath to twist the winding key.

Why am I doing that?

When tiny snowflakes began to shower the globe world and the music began to play, Cain jumped and almost dropped it to the floor.

It was Beethoven's Fur Elise, a tune that was both beautiful and deranged. Cain imagined it was a melody a lunatic might hum under his breath while mowing down a schoolyard full of children with an assault rifle.

The smiling, elfin girl inside the globe sat among the snowflakes and the music played at a slow clip. Cain stood mesmerized, watching and waiting as the tinny music wound down. The flurries were ending. The agonized music struggled for life, coming one feeble note at a time. There was a final ping and the music died, as though a very tiny man had collapsed on a very tiny piano. The pink room was humming with silence again. Cain gently set the globe down and moved away from the bureau.

Except for the small ripple he had left on the foot of the bed, it was neatly made. There was no sign Currie had slept here in his final days, weeping into the pillows and murmuring his daughter's name. There was no sign anything unusual had happened here at all. It was a little girl's room and nothing more. A little girl who had been reduced to ashes in an urn and buried in the ground nearly a thousand miles south of here.

Cain switched off the bedside lamp. With his foot, he shoved the box full of lamps into the hall. His hand on the wall switch, he took one last look around the pink room. He imagined how it would look in a week or so with its décor completely changed. There would be a bigger bed with a quilted spread. There would be bamboo blinds and deep blue curtains. There would be paintings and books and a battered old trunk at the foot of the bed. There would be a papasan in a corner and a bottle of massage oil in a nightstand. There would be a tattered notebook full of musings and aborted poetry.

This will be our room, with everything she cherished. I won't forget a single thing.

He shut the light and pulled the door closed, bracing for the descent down the weird, winding staircase.

Cain would have been enormously relieved to find the expensive telescope overturned and surrounded by shattered lenses on the second floor, but that easy explanation was not to be. The scope was upright and unmoved from where he had left it. Whatever had caused the explosive sound, it was not the Meade.

He took a cursory look around the room and saw nothing out of place. The white teddy bear smiled goofily at him from the desk, its pink ribbon slightly crooked. If the bear knew what had caused the noise, he wasn't saying.

There was really no reason to climb down the stairs and into the basement. It was a new house and there was not likely anything accumulated down there. And anyway, the Currie house was all about what was up here, above ground and in the light. It was built high on a hill to be closer to the sky, with its massive turret facing north. Theodore Currie had been watching the sky. He would have had no use for the subterranean portion of the house. It was a mere necessity of architecture.

Nursing a beer, taking small sips and trying to make it last longer, Cain knew he had to go down. There may be nothing in the cellar but a furnace and hot water heater, it was true. But the examination of the house would not be complete until he had descended to see what lie beneath it.

He poured the last of the beer down his throat and savored the sting of alcohol on the back of his tongue. He left the bottle next to the sleeping bag and got to his feet. He walked across the living room and to the kitchen. He found himself humming and forced himself to stop. More whistling past the graveyard. It was unsettling how easily that habit took over.

The cellar door was between the kitchen and dining room, just a square of wood with a brass knob. Next to it was another door, this one with glass panels, that led outside. What a choice to make — to the right, cool air and a million miles to run. On the left, a descent into claustrophobia and uncertainty.

Cain opened the cellar door, aware of a hundred terrible movie scenes that advanced in such a fashion. An ocean of darkness greeted him on the other side. A dry, fetid aroma floated up. It was a basement. No doubt about that.

Cain once wrote a story about an antique collector who sneaked into the basement of an abandoned house in search of treasures. Among the items he found in the dark, dusty place was an odd pair of eyeglasses constructed of what looked like animal teeth. Putting those glasses on was the last thing the hapless antique man did as a sane man. The spectacles afforded him a glimpse into hell and all the wretchedness that resided there. There were mothers eating babies.

There were deformed children inching like slugs across the floor. There were damned men vomiting spiders and elderly women being ravaged by dogs. There were shrieking women on fire and young girls with their eyes plucked out. There were...

Cain shook his head and forced himself to stop. That story had been poorly written and it garnered him maybe a hundred dollars from an obscure magazine. What the hell was it doing haunting him now?

He reached into the darkness and fumbled for a light switch. He had decided hours ago that he would not go down there if he had to carry a flashlight. Nossir. Not a chance. It was bad enough that basements were absolute representations of the human psyche and things that get hidden away. It was bad enough that spiders tend to hang from webs and unseen things scurry underfoot. He did not need bouncing shadows and a narrow tube of light through which to observe. Better to wait until tomorrow, when at least small helpings of sunlight floated through basement windows.

The point was moot. He found a light switch and somewhere beneath him, bulbs began to glow. The basement instantly became yellow instead of black. A set of unpainted stairs slanted straight down to a concrete floor. Conditions were prime for Cain to make his way down to explore the area beneath the Currie House.

Shit.

He walked down the stairs leaving the door open behind him. The fetid smell was stronger halfway down. It was much cooler down here. Once his feet were on the concrete floor, he quickly turned in a complete circle to ensure that nothing carnivorous was about to lunge at the invader from above.

The basement was truly unremarkable. Examining it from a fixed point, it seemed nowhere near as large as the house above him, in terms of square feet. There was a massive chimney in the center, with a tall water heater next to it, covered in insulation. On the other side of the chimney, a stout, square Burnham furnace that was still and quiet. Wires and pipes slashed in all directions across the ceiling, neatly fastened. There were no dangling cords or pipes gnarled and bent with time. Staring up, Cain decided that the support beams overhead were higher than in most cellars. Stretching a hand up over his head, his fingers were still a foot away from the planks.

He stepped away from the stairs. He did not like the feeling of leaving the doorway behind him, but it was vital that he look over the entire space down here. Just once, and he would be through with it. No washer and dryer hook-up, no ping pong table.

His shoes scraped against the floor and sharp echoes bounced off concrete walls. He forced himself to walk more gracefully. He touched the furnace, which was cool. He tapped the brick chimney with his knuckles and no Edgar Allan Poe cat screamed from within.

So far, so good.

On the far end of the basement, an oil tank crouched in a corner like a giant, headless pig. It was massive and black and would utter a terrific gong if a person were to rap on its side. Cain did not rap. The chimney was between himself and the stairs right now and it unnerved him. The trip to the sublevel was thus far uneventful and he aimed to keep it that way.

He examined a box of circuit breakers. There was a pile of lumber scraps leaning against a wall and he poked through them, ascertaining there was nothing of importance hidden behind them. He began to hum, jumped at the echo and swore once before falling silent again. The trick was to get this done before his imagination got cranking again like a generator roaring to life. Cain did not want his mind turning to morbid fancy down here. He did not want to stare at the small, rectangular windows above him and imagine a small, pale face staring down at him.

Jesus!

He forced himself *not* to look at the windows and picked up the pace. He had just about completed the circumnavigation of the cellar and there was nothing of note down here. Now, unless the lights suddenly went out and the door slammed above him, this had been a very successful tour.

Goddamn it!

He was approaching the stairs from the opposite side now and he allowed himself the luxury of rushing. Why the hell not? It had been a tense evening and this was the culmination of it. The sooner he was done, the sooner he could go back to the beer cooler and maybe breathe normally for a while. Yeah. A few twelve ounce sedatives would be just the thing.

He was about to step on the first stair when his eye caught a splash of white beneath the staircase. At first, his eyes did not want to acknowledge it. This was not a curiosity hunt. The less Cain found down here, the better. But whatever was under there, it somewhat gleamed from the shadows.

Shit.

He stopped, just inches from the staircase. He stooped slightly to peer beneath it. Yes, there was something down there. Let it be a stack of oily rags left behind by careless workmen. He would burn them in the front yard and call it a fire hazard eliminated.

It wasn't a stack of oily rags, but a heap of bones. They were spread out under the stairs like relics of a great feast. Cain bent for a closer look, disturbed and fascinated. The light was poor under the stairs, but he could see enough. There were tiny ribcages that had once been birds. There were short, thin bones that no doubt belonged to coons or squirrels. To confirm this theory, he spotted a bushy, gray tail poking from beneath a small, staring skull. Next to that was the remains of a larger animal he could not identify. The skull showed a snout that was too short and stubbed to belong a dog. The torso was long and it appeared all but one of the legs was missing. There were still scraps of fur clinging to some of the bones. Cain thought he could hear flies buzzing down deep within the carnage. He decided at once the sound would mark the end of his archeological ruminations for the night.

They were only the remains of dead animals. Probably creatures that crawled in through a broken window or a crevice somewhere and then could not get out again. Other animals had been perhaps lured by the stench of easy prey. And one by one they died. Ugly but easy. The carcasses should be cleaned out of the basement, surely. But not tonight. Tonight, the heap could stay right down here with the furnace and the oil tank. Tonight, Cain was going to surrender to the beer cooler and not think much about much at all.

It was silly, really. What few amenities there were in the Currie house were on the second floor. There was a mattress up there and a spacious bathroom with a sunken tub. There was a large writing desk and what looked like a decent computer. Yet, he slept on the floor in the living room below and bathed in a tiny bathroom off the kitchen. He spent two hours a night sitting on a hard, wooden chair, writing in a notebook propped on a windowsill. His hand cramped from writing longhand and his back screamed from hunching over. The window looked out on nothing but trees.

It really was silly, but it was what it was. Cain lived on the first floor of the big house. The upper floors were for the work at hand.

Eleven

Bucky Letroy was a literary agent, but he liked to think he could drink as heartily as any of the great, alcoholic writers of any generation. He was the last to leave Bobo's Bar for the third straight night and he was still feeling peppy. All the pussy journalists at the bar had tapped out by midnight and the rest of them got called away by wives or gay lovers. It was pathetic.

New York was bordering on hot tonight and the city buzzed. Letroy wove along the avenue with thoughts skipping like a rock on a pond. He was also somewhat lost. Had he parked the Mercedes in the garage tonight or on the street?

A bear of a man with an untucked shirt and crooked tie, he pushed his way through throngs of sparkling men and women who looked as though they'd stepped from the pages of a fashion magazine. Breakable figurines was what those people were. They came from wealth, soaked in privilege and really never learned the hard lessons that made men and women of true character.

He considered writing down that lofty idea, but even as it was conceived, the thought turned to lint in his head.

Letroy was essentially a failed novelist, but to his credit, he knew it. He was a fierce master of marketing representing a half dozen established authors. He lived vicariously through geniuses and took his 15 percent. By most standards he was rich and by most standards, happy.

Now, with nine or ten drinks warm in his beach ball belly, he found the Benz illegally parked on a corner and he fumbled with his keys. A horn blared. A siren wailed. A girl shrieked with delight from the park. Letroy dumped his body into the front seat, ran a hand through his beard and pulled the door closed. He sat in silence a moment, his mind a vacuum. Was it business he'd been thinking about? Or pleasure?

Earlier, he'd tried to pick up a Rubenesque blond in a tight, black dress sitting alone at the end of the bar. His lines were crisp, his body language precise and his intentions glaring. But Letroy didn't need any of that. The girl was a pro and could have been his for $250 and a hotel room.

Gloomy over the aborted conquest, he'd retreated back to his table for more scotch and turned his attention back to business. He was worried about Cain.

Two nights ago, Letroy had gotten a call at his office. The voice on the other end of the line belonged to a woman who was blubbering into the phone. It was Grace Popst, wife of the two-time best-selling author, Gerry Popst.

The couple had split a year ago, not long after Gerry received a $150,000 advance for his third crime novel. The writer's life, once calm and uneventful, became chaotic almost immediately. He still wrote well, but there was talk about hard drinking, skirt chasing and maybe a little rock now and then. There was an arrest for indecent conduct involving a hooker, a set of handcuffs and a Fooz ball table. Once a high school teacher and struggling writer, Gerry Popst had become a literary punk rock star.

Letroy had flown out to see the man in his new beachfront bachelor pad in Santa Monica. Popst had been hammered at noon and full of high-priced good cheer. He had also been in hot denial about his turbulent lifestyle and downright nasty in defense of it. Letroy had finally given up and reminded the writer about his deadline. Popst mailed out his manuscript a month ahead of time and it was his best work yet, a taut piece about a San Francisco gumshoe who ends up chasing a suspect to ancient Egypt. Letroy stopped bothering the writer about his meandering and cashed a commission check.

Then Grace Popst called with news that Gerry had downed two dozen Valium with a bottle of wine, tied a plastic bag around his head and died in a hot tub at his swank, rich man's apartment. Another drunken writer swirling into oblivion. Another asshole novelist who struggled for success and then couldn't handle it when it came. Letroy was overcome by sorrow for his lost friend, but also by some degree of guilt. The writing had been hot and so he'd shut his eyes to the rest of the man's failings. It was his second author to opt out by way of the pill bottle.

Now there was Cain. There was no indication the man was falling apart or considering a cozy night with a handful of happy pills. None whatsoever. But Letroy had been thinking more and more about Theodore Currie and what he had gone to northern Maine to achieve. The grieving genius. A brilliant man descending into lunacy over the loss of a loved one. There was a great story to be told there for sure; one with tragedy, madness, genius and mystery. It was a story Cain could tell with his fast, violent style that was sometimes like a boxer beating a story into a reader's head.

But the circumstances were too immediate. Powerful grief was something Currie and Cain shared and it was funny how Letroy had not thought of that before.

He recalled how Cain never went anywhere or made any big decision without his wife. He recalled the playful looks, the furtive kisses, the secret jokes that no one else would ever get. It was a fairytale marriage and a fairytale success story and the glory of it was that the writer was wise enough to know that.

And then Kimberly got a rotten egg inside her head and she was dead before her husband had even absorbed that news. Like that. The glory and success was over. The blessed couple was walloped with a blind-sided curse so swiftly it was blinding. And then Kimberly was gone and Cain bore the suffering alone.

Letroy, who was 49 and never married, tried to imagine the power of that kind of grief and could not.

Cain was strong and by all appearances, he was coping. Still, the agent worried. He had a funny feeling; a nagging uncertainty about

Cain's residence at the Currie house that was like something lodged under an eyelid. It troubled him and it made him brood over his liquor. Was Cain entertaining the thought of killing himself? Was he considering something even more insane?

Letroy decided he was too goddamn soft about the people he represented and he grumbled over it. Now, sitting in his car and trying to talk himself out of driving, he snatched up the car phone and squinted at the numbers. His meaty fingers probed the key pads until he found the number for his top selling client. He dialed, pressed the tiny phone to his ear, and waited to see if the call would go through.

It did. Miracle of miracles. Letroy imagined northern Maine as just slightly more civilized than the Congo, but the line was ringing. Once, twice, three times. Then Cain picked up. The agent roared into the phone.

"Jesus Christ, I can't believe it. What, are you standing out on the roof to get reception?"

"Bucky? What the hell. How you doing?"

"Great, Jon. Great. Been drinking pissy J and B and hitting on whores. The fucking usual."

Cain laughed on the other end. It was two in the morning, but the writer was known to keep weird hours. Not that it mattered. Letroy would have called him anyway.

"Look, I've been thinking about you up there in Frankenstein's castle. Maybe we were a little too ambitious about that deadline, waddaya think?"

There was a pause. "Not sure what you mean, Buck."

"What I mean is, the Currie story could be a good departure book for you. But let's face it, Jon. You're a fiction writer and this ain't fiction. You've got all that freaky science to wade through and a lot of puzzle to piece together."

"We knew that going in, Bucky. I got all summer up here and that's plenty of time."

Letroy grunted. “I’m thinking maybe you shouldn’t spend the whole summer up there. Maybe cut it short.”

Another pause. A longer one. Cain said: “Why would I want to do that?”

Letroy ran a hand through his hair. He switched the phone to his other ear.

“I just think it might be a bad time for you to spend so much time up there by yourself. It hasn’t been a year since Kim passed away, man. I mean, I feel like I pushed you into it, you know? Christ, you’ve got a ton of shit in your old trunk the publisher would cream over. The Currie story can wait. You can get a taste of the place and maybe head back next year. It’s not like anybody else is...”

“No,” Cain said. “It’s gotta be this summer, Bucky. I’m right where I need to be.”

The agent tried to measure the meaning of that response. But shit, he was still buzzing and a little cloudy on everything. He sounded like the one with emotional issues right now.

“I just don’t want you to get... I don’t want you to get caught up in the history of the place. It’s fucking depressing when you think about it. I should have thought of that before I got a hard-on about the story and sent you up to cow country.”

Cain chuckled. Through the static on the phone lines, it sounded sinister.

“You didn’t send me up here. This is something I wanted to do from the start.”

“For the right reasons, I hope...”

Another pause. More static.

“What do you mean by that?”

Letroy stared down the avenue, where beautiful bodies spilled out of gleaming bars and danced away sparkling with youth and vibrancy. This neighborhood was so damn glossy it was sickening.

“I’m just worried about you, Jon. You jumped on this assignment a little too fast. I heard you met with one of Currie's old buddies before you left. Some professor. I heard you grilled him for a week.”

Cain laughed again. “You’re drunk, Buck. Of course I met with the guy. I want at least a half-assed understanding of what Currie was doing up here. Jesus.”

Buzzing and cracking over the phone line like indecipherable messages from space. Letroy tried to blink away intoxication and clear his thoughts. Would he remember this conversation in the morning? Would he feel like an ass about his theatrics? Who the hell knew.

“Okay. Okay, man. Let’s talk about it again though, huh? Maybe I could come up there and spend a few days, hunt some buffalo or whatever the hell people do in Maine.”

Cain mumbled something but it was lost in the increasing fury of static. He assured his agent he was working and nothing more. Letroy sat behind the wheel of the Mercedes and decided he was fine to drive. It was just a few blocks and there was a nice drinky treat waiting at home. The agent was done worrying about his star author. He was thinking about refilling the tank again.

“I’ll talk to you later. Just do me a favor while you’re up there, will you?”

“What’s that?”

“Don’t try to raise the dead.”

“G’night, Bucky.”

“Yeah, g’night.”

Twelve

Of all the agonies Cain suffered following the death of his wife, the dreams were perhaps the worst.

They were not dramatic, theatrical dreams at all. There were no reunions in sunny fields where they danced and laughed at death. There were no reflective dreams that took him back to the first date, the first time they made love, or the altar. No fairytales or grand illusions.

The cruelest element of Cain's nightly dreams was the mundane nature of them. In sleep, he mowed the lawn while Kimberly sat in a lawn chair and handed him bottles of water. He sneaked up behind her while she washed dishes in their sunny kitchen and wrapped his arms around her slender waist. He lay beside her with a book in his lap, near hysterics because she had started to snore with her mouth wide open.

In dreaming, Cain floated back to all the prosaic pleasures that made the marriage blissful. Once he dreamed that they were doing a Stonehenge jigsaw puzzle together on the sunporch. They completed it only to discover one key piece was missing and then argued bitterly over who had lost it.

He dreamed they were shopping for kayaks. He dreamed they were buying paint for the back room they would transform into a workout room or a library. He dreamed they ate Chinese food in the bathtub.

Ultimately, it wasn't the dreams that tormented him, but waking from them — waking in that cottony gray place where dreams and reality hold equal footing. Not remembering that Kimberly died without recognizing him, or that she could neither speak nor see in the final days. Not remembering the sickness at all.

There were drinking binges that went on for days and ultimately left him dehydrated and too weak to get out of bed. But suicidal boozing never stopped the dreams. It only made the spells of sleeping and waking more frequent.

Many mornings, he awoke believing his arm was draped over her shoulder or hip. His eyes would open and he expected to see dark hair pooled on the white pillow. He would anticipate the fragrance of her and the brown eyes watching him.

For all the talent he possessed with the written word, Cain would never have the ability to describe with any sort of adequacy the plunging despair at waking up and remembering. In one comfortable moment, she is there next to him waiting for him to rise. A blink of the eyes, an ascent above the waterline of sleep and she is gone — forever gone and eternally out of reach. Those first moments of recollection were far beyond any form of physical pain that could ever be administered. It crippled him. It left him frantic to return to the lie of the dream. Many days, it left him convulsing with grief, as he wept into the pillow and pounded the mattress with a fist.

It was not like that when his eyes fluttered open in the dark two hours after the unsettling phone conversation with Bucky Letroy. Tonight, Cain awoke at once and immediately knew where he was. There was no deception in waking, but there was confusion. There had been a disruption to the pressing silence of the house and he had yet to identify it.

His heart thumped. The sleeping bag squeezed him like the throat of a snake. The floor was hard under his back. Cain stared at the ceiling, but did not see it through the darkness. He rolled his head to the right and the giant, red numbers on the alarm clock reported it was 3:37 a.m.

A sound had awakened him, he was sure of it. It was a sense rather than physical knowledge. Something sly had invaded the night and now Cain lay in a panic that had no real basis.

He sat up and tried to adjust his eyes to the dark. He pulled his arms free of the sleeping bag and sat perfectly motionless. The hum of the quiet house roared in his ears and yet there was something beyond it; outside of it. Cain cocked his ears like a forest animal to listen.

There. From a distance. Soft and faint like rain on the roof, a melody floated down from above. Notes that jabbed the air like probing fingers. A sound like fairies dancing in an acid dream.

Fur Elise.

For Cain, it was like stumbling into some terrible scene he might have written himself. His entire body went cold. He felt a pounding in his temples as the adrenaline of fright fueled his pulse. He was aware of a full bladder and had to concentrate to contain it.

He fumbled with the sleeping bag zipper and squirmed out of it as though it were full of spiders. He knelt on the hard floor and strained to listen. Still the music played, the quick melody losing energy but still recognizable. Fur Elise from the snow globe, floating down from the very top of the turret. Beautiful, terrible music from the pink room.

It wound down. I heard it wind down. There was not a single note left in those springs and cogs.

He stood and pulled on a pair of jeans. He reached for the flashlight and switched it on. He aimed it at the staircase, terrified at what he might see there. But again, there were no leering faces or crouching ghouls. Only the darkness of the second floor. And above that, the turret from which the haunting melody continued to play.

I can't go up there. I think I'm physically incapable of climbing those stairs.

Even as the thought was born, Cain was stepping toward the staircase. He had to go up. He could not be chased from this place by a busted toy or twisted springs. And that's all it was, surely. An old, temperamental snow globe you probably have to slap with your palm to silence. A fluke of tiny machinery.

He started up the stairs, holding the flashlight ahead of him like a gun. His legs felt weak. He paused halfway up and cocked his head. Fur Elise, winding down and down, but still playing. Cain imagined the tiny strawberry girl with her tiny, pink bonnet smiling as the music died.

On the second floor, he shone a light down the hall. Dust floated like pollen across the beam. A few shadows scurried from one side of the hall to the other. Cain turned toward the turret stairs and then paused at the foot of them.

Okay, I really can't go up. The staircase is so narrow, it's like walking into a tomb.

But again, his right foot rose to the first step. The music was louder now, but sluggish. It was like a band playing in a bog, each note a dying gasp. Cain's heart battered his chest and now his bladder was throbbing. He held the flashlight in front of him as he climbed the winding stairs. Shaking hands caused the beam to bounce.

He was out of breath when he reached the landing. He jerked the flashlight from one side to another, convinced that something was up here waiting for him. His hand was shaking badly as he cast the light upon the bedroom door. The silver knob gleamed like a star under the ray. A final note clicked inside the snow globe and then there was silence. The coils had unwound completely.

He took a long breath. He glanced behind him at the dark stairwell. He turned his attention to the door again and reached for the knob. It was cool under his hand but it turned easily. The click of the fasten was loud as it came free. Cain pulled the door open and a draft of air moved over his face and tousled his hair. He stood back and held the flashlight in front of him like a swordsman. Light wormed into the room and fell upon the rocking horse in the corner. The horse was smiling wickedly, almost mockingly. Cain moved the light away from it and reached his free hand into the room, sliding his palm against the wall, searching for the switch.

A strong, cold hand will clamp down on my wrist and pull me into the room. The door will slam shut behind me and there will be a low, throaty chuckle...

His fingers found the light switch, lost it, found it again. He slapped at it until warm light filled the room. His heart was pounding. He felt a few warm drops of piss at his crotch. He heard his lungs sucking and exhaling air as if it were coming from someone else.

The pink room was unchanged. The bed was neatly made. Small, furry animals were splayed across the pillows. The clock on the wall still displayed frozen time and a corner of the poster drooped over smiling cartoon horses.

Cain glanced over his shoulder once more and then stepped into the room. He moved past the replica dollhouse and forced himself not to look at the windows.

The snow globe sat precisely centered on the bureau. The girl on the strawberry sat smiling eternally at the world beyond the glass. A few synthetic snowflakes floated around her head. There should have been no music left beneath her. The snowstorm had ended hours ago.

But maybe globe world gets shaken just enough due to the same malfunction that causes the thing to play in the middle of the goddamn night.

Weak but possible. Cain was no genius when it came to moving parts. Still, the sight of the little girl in the snow caused him great unease and he wondered what to do about it. Stuff it in a drawer? Leave it alone? Take it downstairs where he could smash the shit out of it if that wretched music began again?

Cain smirked at his own jitters and decided he would take the tiny girl and her huge strawberry downstairs with him for company. He began reaching for it but then froze. His eyes slanted toward the closet door. It was slightly ajar, just as it had been earlier in the evening.

I leaned into it. I pressed until it clicked shut.

But again, what did he know about door latches and the oddities that plague houses built in haste? Nothing, that's what. All houses have their peculiarities. Live with them awhile, a person ceases to notice.

Still, he decided it wouldn't hurt to toss the bean bag in front of the door this time to keep it from opening. A little compromise between himself and the house.

Cain stepped toward the closet door to push it closed again. He paused and looked at his reflection in the mirror. The reflection staring back looked like a man with hornets up his ass. He looked like a man who has lost a battle with his wits.

So open the damn door one more time. Demonstrate how brave you are and let's be done with it.

He gripped the knob and pulled it open, braced for the tattletale whispers of the coat hangers.

The little girl was standing on the other side of the door, staring out. The face was bloodless and gray, the face of sickness. The upper lip was curled in a lupine snarl. The eyes were slit in rage. Hideous, springs of hair fell over the forehead in matted, dingy loops. The teeth were yellow and rotting. One front tooth was missing and a dark, terrible tongue poked at the socket. The little girl hissed from what sounded like a throat full of sand, a dry, gritty sound not much louder than a whisper.

"You touched my things!"

Cain was frozen, hand still on the doorknob. His mouth fell open and he pissed himself. The flashlight fell from his hand, thumped to the floor and rolled away. He was aware of none of these things.

"Bastard! You touched my things!"

The little girl was gray, dirty horror. Her hands twisted together under her chin. Distantly, as if watching through a telescope, Cain became aware that the girl wore red corduroy overalls, with a white turtleneck underneath. He recognized it as one of the outfits he had touched during the earlier inspection of the closet. The thought formed in his head and then blew away like tumbleweed. The entire world seemed to be dwindling to a little pinprick of light. His lips moved, but the voice that came forth sounded very far away.

"Angel..."

Now the girl bared her teeth. She stretched a small, gray hand toward him and Cain was aware of a fetid smell, like old books that have been kept in a damp basement. His hand slid from the doorknob and he took a step back. He felt like he was falling. The little girl with slimy, dripping hair stood in the dark maw of the closet as if she were floating. Her teeth gnashed together and her nose was curled like a carnivore's.

"Asshole! Stay out of my room."

Cain took another step back and felt his bare foot press up against something spongy. He held his arms in front of his face in a warding off posture and now he waved them for balance. The girl snarled and her features twisted like a jack-o-lantern face on a rotting pumpkin.

"This is *my* room!"

Angel Currie lunged, like a ghastly figure in a funhouse. Cain felt her small body slam against his belly and he screamed, instinctively bringing one arm around to fend her off. The crook of his elbow wrapped around the back of her neck and she felt greasy. He stumbled, almost toppling with her under his arm. He felt her writhe in his embrace and there was a sharp, stinging sensation in his left bicep as her teeth sank down into his flesh. He screamed again and tried to pull away, feeling her teeth biting and gnashing his skin.

She bit me. She bit me and now she's chewing me up.

He struggled to regain his footing and used his free arm to shove the girl away. Teeth ripped free from his arm and she stumbled back toward the closet. She stood there a moment, growling, blood on her lips and bared teeth. Angel glowered, eyes ablaze with rage. She stepped back into the closet, pulling the door with her. It swooped inward and slammed shut. The mirror trembled. There was a clamor of coat hangers and then silence.

The thud of the slamming door echoed through the house. Cain stood with one foot in the beanbag, breathing hard, sweating but cold.

It was momentary insanity rather than courage that compelled him to spring to the closet. Having been thrust over the edge of reason, Cain was not equipped with the fight or flight impulse that should have sent him screaming from this room and from this house.

Panting, grimacing, he pulled the door open. Dresses danced. Shirts waved like flags. Then everything was still.

He slammed the door closed. He didn't wait to hear the snick of the latch. He didn't go scrounging for the flashlight. He ran from the room and barely felt the stairs beneath his feet as he fled.

Thirteen

D*o you believe it? Do you really believe?*

The sun was creeping up in the east. Birds were chattering tentatively outside and dim, gray light tried to seep through the windows. Cain welcomed it. He sat against a living room wall, facing the staircase, with bright lights in all corners of the room.

Soon it would be full light. The terrors of the night world would lose some of their teeth. There would be creeping doubts. There would be a struggle for explanation. But Cain was advancing on that process already — had been for the past two hours.

Do you really believe what you saw? Was it an hysterical delusion brought on by grief, fear and a whole lot of stress? Or did a six-year-old dead girl just lunge from a closet and munch on your arm?

Cain had no problem believing. He didn't fight very hard at all against the irrationality of it. Simple common sense defied it.

He had never experienced anything close to a hallucination and he did not believe stress and fear could create one. There was a jagged, ugly wound on his left arm. He had dumped peroxide on and then covered it with a bandage made from an old T-shirt. The wound looked like a bite. Fresh memories of the horror from the pink room were too stark to be the objects of delusion.

The insanity of it was, Cain was uniquely obliged to believe it all and embrace it. That some manifestation of Angel Currie walked the highest room of the house was ultimately to his delight. If all of it were true — the ley line slicing through Mulberry, the extra dimensions, the sucking of gravity, the enticements — then Theodore Currie really had been the modern incarnation of Frankenstein's genius creator.

It was hard for Cain to know now how much he really had hoped or how much he really believed. But if he had come face-to-face with

Angel Currie, no matter how grotesque she was, it meant the science was valid. It meant Kimberly was not infinitely out of reach at all.

I believe. Oh, yes I do. I will face that hellish little girl a million times if I have to. She is no longer wanted here.

Cain got to his feet and began to prepare for the day.

Fourteen

Rathbun hated the south. Anything between Maryland and Florida was full of bugs and rednecks and he hated them both equally. And the NASCAR, too. And confederate flags and that slow, over-friendly chatter you just can't get away from. The redneck clerks in corner stores took forever to count his change and wanted to ask him about his day. The fat, black woman at the rental car counter drawled excruciatingly and flashed her crooked, ugly teeth as she ranted about the weather. Even the goddamn panhandlers were as cheery as they were insistent.

The south was a swamp that should be sold to Mexico and Rathbun hated it. The only measure of joy he got out of this meaningless trip was that it got him away from the awful hicks back in Maine.

Langley was 800 acres of clustered buildings and Rathbun knew it intimately. For a brief time in the early 90's, he'd occupied a spacious office on the eastern end of the main building. He loved the offices here. He loved the hierarchy and the way pissants knew they were essentially ballast. They sucked up to the scientists at the top of the food chain and they outright groveled at the feet of the officers.

Rathbun would be overjoyed to be inside one of the cozy, air-conditioned offices right now, but no. Franklin Brazel had no interest in putting his visitor at ease. He preferred to have these discussions inside his Lexus, which he drove to the middle of a tarmac, where the blinding sun beat down on them. This was Brazel's way of ensuring that Rathbun understood they were not here to relax or to prattle on like old friends. This was business and the more concise, the better.

"What have you got, Rathbun? No preamble, just give me the facts."

"I've got nothing, sir. I told you as much on the phone. I've got nothing to give you because you won't let me and my men do our jobs up there."

Brazel was twisted in the driver's seat so that he was staring directly at his passenger. One hand hung over the steering wheel. The other clutched a pen which hovered over a clipboard in his lap. In fifteen years, Rathbun had never seen the man without a clipboard. He had also never seen him write anything.

"You *are* doing your jobs. You're keeping an eye on the house from a relative distance. Are you telling me you haven't been able to handle that much?"

Rathbun stared through the windshield. A few men huddled around a jet on the far side of the runway. From this distance, they appeared the size of toy soldiers.

"Keeping an eye on it, yes sir. Without ever seeing it."

"There are court orders, Rathbun. You monitor things by keeping your ears open."

"With all due respect, sir, there's not much to listen to in Mulberry, Maine. There's not much interest in the Currie house, either. Reyes and Loomis could have been in and out of there without so much as—"

Brazel cut him off with a wave of the hand. The pen still hovered over the clipboard, challenging his guest to say something insightful enough to merit a scribble.

"You think like a thug. We're not common burglars, Rathbun. We want to know what Currie left behind in there, but mostly we want to observe."

"Observe? Sir, a novelist is living there now, as you know. A novelist. What can this man possibly do to interest us, beyond destroying or revealing anything he might find?"

Brazel looked disgusted. He was 60 years old and still sported a buzz cut. He was dressed casually in jeans and a T-shirt and he looked like a former marine, which he was. He was also the head of a select group of scientists that operated out of several agencies and universities. Brazel was frequently called to the White House and, on occasion, he showed up unannounced.

He leveled a paternal gaze at Rathbun.

"You know why you washed out as a scientist? Do you want to know why you never went anywhere, in spite of your early success?"

Rathbun resisted an urge to roll his eyes. "No, sir. Please tell me."

"You lack imagination. Completely lack it. You can handle the numbers well enough, but they mean nothing to you."

"I'm not sure I know what you mean, sir."

Brazel laughed. "Well, there you have it. You're too linear, Rathbun. Science isn't all math and formulas. It isn't all hypothesis and experimentation, either. Somewhere along the line, you've got to dream. You've got to burn with wonder before you really strive for the answers. You never had that kind of passion. You don't see beyond the textbooks and test tubes."

"I'm not sure I completely agree, sir."

Brazel stared at him, lips pressed together. He pressed the tip of the pen against the paper on the clipboard and then withdrew it.

"What would we have found if we busted our way into the Currie house, do you think? Some magical formula written down on some gleaming parchment? The answers to all the cosmic mysteries in one glorious string of numbers? The source of dark matter, dark energy and the final unification of quantum theory and relativity all wrapped in one beautiful paper?"

"It's been my opinion from the start, sir," Rathbun replied at once, "that Currie was completely gone at the end of his life. I believe we would have found nothing more than the diary of a madman and maybe a closet full of empty liquor bottles."

"So, you don't believe he was up there trying to bring back his dead daughter?"

"Sure, I believe that. It's the kind of thing that madmen do."

"That's right, Rathbun. If you don't understand it, it must be a fantasy."

Rathbun sighed but continued to gaze at the runway. He hated this part of a briefing with Brazel above all. The man fancied himself everybody's mentor. Van Helsing to a world full of Harkers.

"All I'm saying, sir, is that I don't believe Currie was basing his ambitions on anything rooted in real science at that point."

"No? There is some evidence that he found a geological quirk in that little patch of land up there though, isn't there?"

"If you mean he found a ley line, that hasn't been proven."

Brazel hissed. "Hasn't been proven! You've read the results of the measurements, haven't you? The magnetic energy up there is off the charts. Can you explain that in any way rooted in the science that has been proven?"

"Sir, I just don't think..."

But Brazel was waving his clipboard at him now. "Another indication of your inability to think big. You can't possibly expect knowledge when your mind is shut up tighter than your asshole. That's a fact."

Rathbun chose to say nothing.

"Look, we're interested in knowing what Jonathan Cain, the novelist, does or sees inside that house. Right now, we're more interested in that than anything else."

"But that's insane. Our top priority right now should be..."

"You don't get a say in what our priorities are."

Rathbun paused, cleared his throat, backtracked. "It seems to me, sir, that we should still regard anything Currie left behind as vital."

"And we do. We absolutely do. But for God's sake, try to expand your mind a little bit. This writer recently lost a wife he loved very much. He spent a week with Bobby Dore over at Cornell taking a crash course in Currie's work. He met with Currie's mother. This is a man who has made a million dollars with his imagination, for chrissakes. Don't you think he wonders? Don't you think he misses his wife like hell and wonders if Theodore Currie might have been onto something?"

"I thought," Rathbun muttered, "he was probably planning to write a book about Currie and make another million dollars."

Brazel threw the pen down onto the clipboard. It bounced over Rathbun's knees and disappeared under the seat.

"You're hopeless. Absolutely fucking hopeless. There's a chance this writer might be unwittingly serving as a test subject and you want to break into the house and run away with a fist full of paper. You're a moron, Rathbun."

"I'm only trying to think clearly, sir."

Brazel snarled. "Don't think anymore. Let us do the thinking. You just get your ass back to Maine and keep your eyes and ears open. If Cain goes out to eat, you go out to eat. If he takes a swim, you find a fishing spot nearby. We want to know who he calls and who calls him. We want to know who visits. That's especially important."

Rathbun sighed. He nodded. He was hot and irritated. He was eager to be gone. He was not eager to be back in Maine.

"If I may say so sir, I can't wait until this is over. The solstice is coming, and the alignment, too. If the planets really can exert the right amount of gravity to influence these strings, there's less than a month to prove it."

Brazel shook his head and smiled a rueful smile, like a man who has run out of patience with a slow-witted student.

"Your assignment in Maine is not over with the solstice, Rathbun. You're a fool to think so."

"But the alignment..."

"The alignment is only a part of this. There is far more for us to learn beyond the science. You know only as much as you need to know and you'll do well to remember that."

"Sir, with all due respect..."

"Respect nothing. You will sit tight up there until you're told differently. That's that, Rathbun. And that's pretty much all we need to discuss today. I want you back in Maine."

The news was devastating. Rathbun sat glumly in his seat as they drove back to the office building beyond the tarmac. He was not asked inside. He was not invited to hang around. He was pointed north and sent away, to his exile.

Fifteen

The propeller blade caught the boy on the right side of the face and it ripped through flesh and bone. The water went dark with blood and chunks of the boy's head floated among the gore.

It was pandemonium on shore. The boy's mother, a freakishly thin woman, tried to run into the cool water as if expecting she could skip right along its surface. Her husband, who was enormously fat, tried to pull her away and race past her at the same time. The result was that he crashed into her and both of them went down in a tangle of blubber and bone. Each came up moments later coughing and puking water.

It was another boy, a 12-year-old named Louie McCarthy, who got the bleeding child out of the water. The wounded boy was Dennis Hill, of New Haven, Connecticut, and his face was a Halloween horror. A portion of it, from the right cheek to a point above the eyebrow, was entirely gone. With it into the lake went one eye, a portion of nose and a bit of brain.

McCarthy jumped from the boat, flailed briefly in the icy water and got an arm up under his friend's armpits. Covered in blood, he breast-stroked toward the small beach 100 feet away, towing his dying friend alongside.

Ten minutes after the accident, a group of people surrounded Dennis Hill on the sand. He was wrapped in a blanket, a beach towel was pressed against the side of his head, and he was loaded into a car. His mother and father, coughs turning into screams, were loaded into a separate car that followed.

Cain was about to introduce himself to the burly man behind the counter when the sounds of squealing tires startled everyone inside the store. A green station wagon skidded past the gas pumps, fishtailed dramatically and swiped a pickup truck parked near the road. The driver tried to correct himself by stepping on the gas and the car shot toward the front of the store. There was another screech from the tires as the driver braked again and the nose of the car came to rest against an ice cooler. A cloud of dust rose up and enveloped the car so that it looked like a mirage. A second car, a convertible, screamed to a stop behind it and bodies spilled from both.

"Call an ambulance. Jesus Christ, call for help, Reggie. We got a bad one here."

The man doing the screaming was wearing cut off jeans and nothing else. A long, brown ponytail bounced against his back as he ran toward the store. Others were leaning into the back seat of the station wagon. Paralysis broke inside the Lyon's Share.

Cain ran outside with two other men who had been eating at the counter inside. Behind him, he heard the burly man swearing into the phone as he waited for an emergency dispatcher to answer.

Outside, there were men and women screaming and a boy covered in blood milling silently around the station wagon. A fat man and a thin woman were pushing their way toward the car trying to get into the back seat.

"Does anyone here know CPR? Fred? Bobby? Jesus, this kid is going fast. Sir? Sir! Do you have any medical training?"

Cain, halfway between the store and the station wagon, realized the man with the pony tail was talking to him. He nodded and pushed past him, trying to wade through the knot of people that crowded the car.

"Excuse me. Please. Let me through."

The skinny woman wheeled around and faced him. To Cain, her face looked like a shrunken apple on a Popsicle stick. Dark, wet hair clung to her face and her eyes were wild.

"Can you help him? Can you, mister? Help my boy! Please do something!"

Cain grabbed her shoulders and gently pushed her aside. He poked at the back of the fat man and nudged him out of the way.

"Sir, please let me by. Let me see what I can do."

The fat man and the others looked at Cain and drew away, as if he had jabbed them with a poker. The car door was open and he leaned in toward the back seat. The boy was wound in a pink blanket like a Day-Glo mummy. A bright blue beach towel was soaked with blood around his head. Cain lifted an edge of it and took a look at the boy's chewed up face. The upper portion of it was mangled. Cain saw the hollowed eye socket filled with blood and chunks of bone.

He began gingerly peeling the towel away from the kid's face and shouted back without looking over his shoulder.

"Get me something fresh and clean to cover the wounds with. Moisten it and get it up here. And I'll need gauze. Pads, if you've got them."

The boy didn't make a sound. An arrowhead necklace was jabbing into his throat and Cain pulled it away, breaking the chain. He absently dropped it into a shirt pocket and continued to examine the boy. Cain could see frothy blood foaming at the boy's lips, but there was no visible rise and fall of the chest beneath the blanket. He placed his fingers against the boy's neck, which was cool. The pulse was detectable but sluggish.

"He's in shock. What's the word on the ambulance?"

"Eight minutes. I told them to gun it from Fort Kent."

Cain glanced behind him quickly. The burly storekeeper was peering into the car, one hand on the edge of the door. Behind him, the fat man was trying to keep the skinny woman from lunging into the car.

Cain nodded to the storekeeper and turned back to the boy.

"I'm worried he might have suffered a cervical spine injury on top of everything else," he said. "And he's lost a ton of blood. We absolutely don't move him until the paramedics get here."

The burly man behind him sounded unfazed. "Sounds right to me."

Moments later, the storekeeper tapped Cain on the back and handed him a fistful of gauze. In his other hand he held medical tape. Cain took both and began to tape pads of gauze over the boy's eyes.

The skinny woman began to scream and thrash.

"Why the hell are you doing that? Why are you covering both his eyes? He's dead, isn't he! For God's sake, what are you doing to his eyes?"

Cain was aware of the commotion behind him, but he continued working. The boy was still breathing. Blood was pooling into a small puddle on the car floor. The pink blanket was soaked with it.

"I need to cover both eyes to prevent sympathetic movement. I don't know the extent of the damage. And I still need a clean compress in here. The sooner the better."

"Never mind," the store keeper said, looking over the top of the car. "Ambulance is here."

Dennis Hill's parents rode in the back of the ambulance with the boy. Two others followed in the convertible and the parking lot was quiet again. The man with the ponytail watched the ambulance scream off toward Fort Kent.

"That was a goddamn horror show, dude. Kid's fucked up. Glad you were here, man."

Again, he was talking to Cain, who was wiping his bloody hands on a towel another man had handed him.

"Not much I could do for him."

The storekeeper clapped him on the back. "You were great. You a doctor?"

Cain wiped his forehead with the back of his hand. "No. Not even close. I had some emergency medical training years ago. Just research, though. Not a profession."

Four men were staring at him, including the two diners who stood in the parking lot with matching wife beater T-shirts. One of them, a tall man with a large, hooked nose was squinting against the sun and studying Cain with what looked like suspicion.

"You're that writer. One that moved into the Currie place."

Cain nodded. He wiped the last of the blood from his hands and set the towel on the roof of the station wagon.

"That's me. I was hoping to introduce myself with less drama, but ah, well. Jonathan Cain."

He extended a hand toward the storekeeper, who took it quickly.

"Reggie Lyons. Nice to meetcha."

The man with the ponytail was Randy Dugal. The man with the hooked nose was Bobby Erenfried and the other, Fred Descoteaux. Handshakes all around. For Cain, it was an odd moment. Nothing hastens a bond between a stranger and the locals like massive head trauma, he supposed. So much for being friendly while remaining relatively unnoticed.

The two men in wife beaters went back into the store. The man with the ponytail recounted the story of the boating accident and then walked back toward the beach. Lyons snickered as he watched him go.

"My guess is he wants to beat feet before the Staties get here. Randy's a good guy but he's just about always stoned."

"The Staties," Cain said. "Shit, they'll wanna talk to me."

Lyons nodded. "You got a reason to duck 'em?"

Cain laughed. "No. Nothing like that. I was just hoping to pick up a six pack and get home while the sun's still high. Might make it a twelve pack after that action."

Lyons nodded again and they walked inside the store.

Sixteen

It was 7 o'clock before he was back at the Currie house. The grilling he took from the men at the store was far more vigorous than the questions posed by the state trooper. The locals were not enthralled by fame, but they were curious. Cain answered what he could and was given a few tidbits about Currie in exchange. Customers who came and went asked Lyons about the boating accident and paid little attention to Cain. For that, he was grateful.

He cracked open a beer and began opening windows throughout the first floor. A breeze moved through the house like a restless visitor and the air smelled good. He unloaded a barbecue from the Explorer and set it in front of the house. There were steaks in the fridge and some potatoes he'd cook in tinfoil.

The smell of freshly ignited charcoal stabbed him with memories that were both happy and painful. The smoke drifting up against the green background of trees evoked movie reel images of the many summer days he and Kimberly had mangled steaks as they got caught up in other pursuits and forgot about their chow. He closed his eyes and breathed the smells. He listened to the wind blowing over the tops of pines and he was back at Prince Edward Island, Canobie Lake, Yellowstone. Kimberly would be wearing white shorts and a black tank top and trying clumsily to spin a frisbee on her finger. She would have a half-empty bottle of Corona next to her because she hated beer and could never finish one. They would bicker about whether the potatoes were brown enough and later sit with arms around each other as they watched the sun descend into the treetops. They would stay outside to watch the stars before crawling into the tent to make love and then talk for hours. Birds, crickets and frogs would serenade them. Jonathan and Kimberly Cain were goddamn happy and wise enough to know how rare and wonderful that was. They had a lifetime of barbecues and beaches, tents and hotel rooms to live. Grand vacations and small ones. Together always and always savoring. Always, always, always, until they were old and brittle and ready to sleep after a long and cherished life.

Cain kicked the bag of briquettes and sent small, black squares flying into the long grass.

"Fuck!"

He hurled the beer bottle after the briquettes, a golden spray marking its flight into the wilderness.

"Goddamn it!"

He pounded a fist into a palm. He did it again and said "fuck!" once more. He pressed hot hands to his eyes and paced the yard blindly. Tears stung his eyes and the movie reel images played on.

"Son of a bitch!"

He kicked at the grass and huffed at the woods around him. The woods were meant to be a place he'd spent beautiful nights with his wife, telling her ghost stories he made up on the spot. Now he was here a desperate widower clinging insanely to the bizarre science of a dead man. Just to see her. Just to feel her in his world again.

Cain stopped pacing and looked around him. He had walked halfway around the house in this enraged jaunt back in time. The house brooded over him like a church promising salvation. He let his head fall back and gazed up at the turret, the altar of his hope.

A small face stared from a corner of the top window. A little, gray face with dirty, ugly springs of hair falling over the eyes. The little girl was gazing down at Cain and smiling. She opened her mouth as if to speak but Cain fancied she was laughing. A chill ran through him like an electrical shock. There was a flicker of movement and then the curtain fell into place. The little girl was gone and the window was bare.

Seventeen

Two days each week, Reggie Lyons turned his store over to Paul Gooldrup, a 19-year-old college dropout whom everyone knew would eventually go to work for his father. His father was George "Red Eye" Gooldrup, a man who had made a million dollars buying machinery from farmers at the end of their working years and then selling it to upstarts for a profit. George was now the major seller of farm equipment north of Portland and he expected to one day hand the business over to his oldest son.

But Paul Gooldrup possessed nineteen years worth of stubbornness and defiance. For now, he insisted he would make his millions his own way. And not by exploiting aging farmers or working in the shit-smelling fields of Mulberry, either.

This summer, the young Gooldrup was starting on his fortune by working for Lyons several days a week. He was a trustworthy kid, polite to the customers and too ugly to get involved with sexy, young tourist girls looking to piss off rich parents.

With the kid in charge, Lyons could use his free time to kayak, fish, work around the house or head to Clown's bar to hit on pretty widows.

Today, he planned to combine his activities. He would kayak for two hours and later head to Clown's. It was a classy joint, and many of the women who went there had retired to Mulberry with their husbands, who took to retirement by dropping dead. The jackpot for the likes of the town constable.

His plans were dashed as he was turning from Route 11 to the tote road that would bring him to his secret section of Long Lake. The kayak was on top of the car, there was a bottle of aftershave in the glove compartment, and Lyons was ready for a dazzling day off.

A woman driving a massive, black Lincoln in the opposite direction slowed and began to wave her arms at him. Lyons pulled to the side of the road only reluctantly. The woman was Martha Braintree, a prissy, rich old woman who would talk holes right through a person's head.

But Martha didn't stop him to talk about her hot shit grandson down at Yale or the heroics of her bait sized Corgi. Today, she needed help from the constable and she prissed across the road toward him to get it. Lyons stayed in his Jeep.

"Reggie! Thank gawd. Oh, you're a marvelous sight."

"What's the problem, Martha?"

"Oh, it's a hell of a jam. My niece and nephew are up from Lewiston and they're out on Salisbury Hill with their fancy new truck. One of those SOV's, or whatever they call them. They paid about a million dollars for it and I think it's the ugliest thing I've ever seen. Seems like nobody drives a car anymore, I swear to gawd."

"So, what's the problem, Martha?"

Martha looked momentarily baffled. "Oh! Yes. Seems they took their little rig down that trail the HTV riders use and now they're stuck. Stuck good, they told me over the cellular. I'm not crazy about the cellular, but they sure do the trick at a time like this, don't they, Reggie?"

"So, your niece and nephew are buried in mud up on Salisbury. Is that it?"

Martha reached out to place a bony, cool hand on Lyon's arm.

"No, no. That's not it. Ruth, she gets awful asthma attacks. Gets scared and can't breathe. Been that way since she was a girl turning cartwheels. I guess she's scared plenty now, cawse she's up there hacking and wheezing and not a soul around."

Lyons nodded. Not exactly an emergency he could ignore. He'd have to get a medic up there and a truck with a winch. It really pissed him off. There wasn't a single local person who would drive even a rugged truck down the ATV trail and yet the yuppie tourists tried it all the time.

"Alright. Alright, Martha, no problem. I'll call and get some boys up there and we'll get 'em out of the muck. Now if you just drive back to..."

"Oh, no. No, Reggie, I'd feel better if I went up there with you. Honest to gawd, I would. I get a little shook up myself from time-to-time and I drive like one of those Nescafe racers. Honest to gawd."

Lyons sighed. "Nescafe racers, gotcha. Get in, Martha. Get in."

It took two hours to get the dopey couple out of the mud and Ruth of the asthma attack put on a theatrical display. It was an ugly, aggravating scene and now Lyons' mood was shot. He'd skip the kayaking and go right for the hot widows. Hell, if things went right, he'd get a better workout than rowing could provide and scenery much finer than that along Long Lake. Reggie Lyons was a boob man.

Driving north along Route 11, he passed Olive Hill and slowed. It was a desolate stretch out here, one a person passed by without seeing. But Lyons eyed the narrow slash cut into the trees and thought about the writer living up in that freakish house.

He slowed some more and wheeled the Jeep toward the narrow dirt lane. It was essentially a driveway but it went on and up a long ways. The Jeep bounced and tore through gravel as he made the climb. Sunlight got caught in trees up here and the air felt cooler. There would be deer and moose charging down this snaking driveway at night, searching for a bigger opening to escape the bugs. Lyons wondered if the writer was aware of that fact and thought to warn him.

He drove up over one last rise and came into an opening where the sun poured in over the trees. The house was massive. Lyons had been up here a couple times to check for broken windows or other signs of damage or vandalism. And each time he was freshly impressed with the size of it.

He pulled up next to the Explorer, killed the engine, climbed out. He gazed up at the turret and it reminded him of a fairytale tower. It was a beauty of a house, it was true. Why someone would want it up here was a mystery.

Cain stepped out onto the porch, sweaty in jeans and a white T-shirt, and appeared startled by the visitor. His face was dirty, as though he'd been working on something more physically demanding than writing.

"Mr. Cain. Sorry to come unannounced."

The writer smiled and wiped a hand on his jeans before offering it to Lyons.

"Not at all. Been moving stuff around and getting dizzy. I could use a break. You want a beer?"

"Yeah."

"You got it."

Cain started in and then stopped. He turned around.

"You wanna see the house? I mean, have you been inside?"

Lyons grinned. "No, sir. This is as close as I've been."

Cain walked him through the first floor, pointing out areas that were left unfinished when the builders were hustled away. Lyons admired the wrap-around porch and the marble fireplace. He eyed the sleeping bag on the floor but didn't say anything. Each of them carried a bottle of Budweiser as they stopped to marvel at one feature or another.

"Crazy that he got it to this point and never finished it," Lyons said.

Cain sipped his beer. "Exactly what I thought. Guess he had other things on his mind."

They moved toward the stairs and Lyons stared up. Cain followed his gaze.

"Great staircase. Unfortunately, it leads to just about nothing. Guy had a few things on the second floor, but it's basically empty. There's a tiny bedroom up in the turret but it's not much."

"Unbelievable. All this space and nothing in it."

"Crazy."

"Yeah."

They walked back to the porch where Lyons declined a second beer. The sun was still high and powerful in a near flawless sky. Nearby, a cicada buzzed. The air smelled sweet.

"Anyway," Lyons said, stepping down from the porch. "I came by to tell you the kid didn't make it. The one from the boating accident. Died soon after they got him to the hospital."

"Shit."

"Yeah. His parents are a mess. Came up from Connecticut for a few weeks. Rented a cabin out on the lake and planned to stay through the Fourth of July. The boy has a twin sister who I hear is just about out of her mind."

"Jesus Christ."

"Yeah. Real religious family, too. That maybe helps a little. I guess."

"I hope so."

Lyons thought about it. "Didn't help me when my wife died."

"Me neither."

Lyons nodded solemnly. Then he shook off the mood.

"Well, screw it. We're still here. I apologize for dropping in with gloomy news."

"No problem. Drop in any time. I'll keep beers on hand."

"You're on."

Cain watched the Jeep bounce out of the yard, with a cloud of dust following it like a dingy ghost.

Drop in any time. But, please...Not while I'm working.

Cain had no idea where the thought came from. He turned and went back inside the house.

Eighteen

At first he thought it was thunder. The loud crash, the rolling echo, the fading away of a sudden clamor. Thunder to mark the beginning of a quick but intense storm.

But there was no storm. There was no thunder. The explosion had come from inside the house. Cain didn't know how long his eyes had been open or when he had become aware that something had happened above him.

It was dark except for the soft glow of a lamp left burning in a corner of the room. He lay on his back inside the sleeping bag, a wooden baseball bat hard beneath his arm. Cain touched the bat before sitting up. He turned his gaze once again toward the stairway. Darkness. Nothing more.

He became very still and cocked his head, listening, almost completely certain he would hear the inspired tune of Fur Elise from far above.

Silence.

And yet the echo of that thunderous sound seemed to roll through him still. It excited his heart to pounding. It made his fingers and toes feel very cold.

You have to go. You have to look around.

He got to his feet. It was three days since the drama of the boating accident and it had been reasonably calm since. Today, he had spent the afternoon roaming in the woods and collecting his thoughts. A good day. A day for introspection and planning.

There was a scraping sound above him; a gritty, furtive sound that reminded Cain, for no good reason, of grave robbery. There was something sly, calculated and unholy in it. This, at last, was too much. Cain did not believe he had the fortitude to face whatever lurked on the second floor.

A pest. It is only a pest. You need to face it again before you know how to proceed. This is the path to Kimberly.

Again, the scraping sound, short and stealthy. A slight thump and then silence, as though whatever was up there was listening for signs of detection.

Jesus Christ.

He pulled on his jeans. His bare chest felt chilled, but he did not search for a shirt. He grabbed the baseball bat instead and a replacement flashlight he had bought at the Lyon's Share. He was a two fisted adventurer tonight.

He started for the stairs, still not completely convinced he could do this.

A pest. Only a pest, like a cockroach or a mouse in the wall.

He climbed the stairway in the dark, flashlight off, clutched tight in a sweaty hand. He moved slowly and carefully, as quietly as he could. That he wanted to sneak up on whatever skulked on the second floor was insanity, but here he was.

Eighteen steps and he was on the second floor. It was very dark. Cain imagined there could be something crouching very still in the darkness nearby. When darkness surrounds you, no position is safe. It was not imagination this time, but a real possibility. He did not reside in this house alone.

He aimed the flashlight down the hallway to his left and prepared for unspeakable terror. He pressed the button and white light blazed.

Nothing.

Cain spun to ensure nothing was behind him. His heart raced. He was aware that he was breathing shallowly, softly. He inched toward the doorway on the left. It was closed, as he'd left it. Cain transferred the bat to his armpit, pressed a shoulder to the door and eased his hand around the doorknob. Then swiftly, he twisted the knob and his body forced the door open. He moved the flashlight around like a cop with a gun. The telescope cast a long, gaunt shadow. A heap of books leaned harmlessly on the desk. The teddy bear grinned with eternal glee. Cain drew a long breath and turned to check behind him. An empty hall.

Christ, this is draining. It's a goddamn miracle I haven't suffered a stroke yet just in anticipation of doom.

He was sure this room was the source of the latest calamity, but there was nothing amiss. He was both relieved and disappointed by this fact, but he was not climbing the turret to the pink room tonight. Nossir. Not tonight. His daily adrenaline requirement for one week had been grossly exceeded.

Quietly, anxiety ebbing just a bit, he pulled the door closed and waited until it snicked. Satisfied, he started toward the stairs and then stopped. The bathroom. The reading room. The master bedroom with the mattresses. These rooms were mostly empty, but still...a beam could have fallen from the ceiling. A pipe could have burst. There was no limit to the perfectly innocuous, non-terrifying possibilities.

He checked the room across from the study. Empty. He moved down the hall, clutching the baseball bat tight again, its hurting end up near his shoulder. The flashlight was in front of him as he moved toward what he had thought would make an ideal reading room. He expected to find nothing in here. He was more concerned about the bedroom and the bathroom. Ghosts and ghouls thrived in places where a person conducted his most personal business. Horror writers and movie producers everywhere knew this. Cain was almost cavalier as he shouldered open the door to the reading room.

The man was on his knees in the center of the room. He was rangy and gaunt and what was left of his hair flew around his head. The clothes were tattered. Tan corduroys looked as though they had been torn up for rags. One sleeve of the gray cardigan sweater was torn at the shoulder.

Cain stood paralyzed in the doorway, watching the man struggle on the floor with a six foot, wooden ladder that had fallen in the center of the room. He grabbed at the rungs and tried to pull it toward him, but his arms and hands had been sapped of their strength. Cain could hear the man gasping and sobbing. He watched in silence, the beam of the flashlight encircling the dismal scene like a spotlight.

Then the man turned his face up toward the doorway. The eyes were sunken and dark; unspeakably tired eyes. The bones beneath the eyes were prominent and the cheeks were hollowed. The flesh was gray as granite; ashen, like a corpse.

Theodore Currie. Educated at Cambridge, Stanford and Cornell. Published his first paper on quantum mechanics at Cornell...

When Currie spoke, the voice rolled, jagged and gravelly, as though through a throat full of pebbles.

"She keeps knocking it over. She won't let me do it. She just keeps knocking it over and laughing at me."

Cain's skin tingled as though he'd poked a finger in an electrical socket. He eyed the length of rope coiled near the ladder like an asp. He glanced at the ceiling and saw a thick, wood beam that traversed the length of the room. The dark wood was abraded in an area directly above the unsettling scene on the floor. At once, Cain understood.

"Help me," Currie said, still staring wide-eyed and struggling to get to his feet. "Please. Help me get the ladder up. I know I can do it. I only need a minute."

Cain backed out of the room. Currie, sensing this, lurched to his feet and began to amble toward him. His arms hung limp at his sides. His face bore the expression of lunacy and desperation. Cain spied a black pen poking from a torn pocket on the front of Currie's shirt. That small detail was too mundane, too vivid.

Cain used the handle of the bat to pull the door shut. It swept slowly toward the doorframe and through the opening that remained, he could see Currie stumbling toward it.

"Please! I need to get out! I need to get away!"

The door thudded closed and Cain stepped back from it. There was a rapid-fire drumming as Currie began to pound on the door.

"Pleeeeeeeeease! It has gone wrong! Horribly wrong! It is eternity in between! Help me! It is eternity in between!

Cain stood mute in the hall, listening to the garbled wails of an insane dead man. He clutched the bat and the flashlight, watching the door, expecting to see it fly open and the screeching horror to come gliding out at him.

But the screams were fading, as if the source of them was falling down a hole in the earth. The sound grew fainter and fainter and then was gone. Cain was certain he could open that door and only a ladder and harmless coil of rope would greet him on the other side. But he didn't put that assumption to the test. He moved as fast as he dared down the long hall. He nearly skidded past the stairway, but caught himself and started down.

Behind him, high above the insanity of the reading room, a new noise arose. It was the delighted sound of a child; laughter so joyous it was almost singing.

Part II
The Indestructibles

One

Gary Buchanan genuinely loved the old woman, but his service to her was essentially service to the Lord. Though he tended to her around the clock, Gary's devotion was to Christ. The Currie house was his monastery. This servitude was his humble gift to God. This was Gary Buchanan's way of demonstrating he was worthy of the kingdom. For few things required so much care and commitment as an old woman with no arms or legs. To know the Lord was Gary's ultimate ambition. To walk with Christ was a lifelong dream.

Still, at times he felt shunned. There were times when he felt God was absent and it troubled him. Since he was a boy, Gary had prayed daily for a sign that the Lord was watching over him. Until he happened on the chance to work for Olivia Currie, misery was the only response.

As a child, he had been small and weak, a mincing boy often singled out for abuse on the school playground. His beautiful, tender mother died from complications of pneumonia when Gary was nine years old, and he was left with a drunken, brutish father who had little use for his tiny, timid son.

William Buchanan — Buster, to his friends — was physically abusive and an emotional inquisitor. He was a construction foreman and the quintessence of the steak-eating, arm-wrestling, beer-swilling, gun-toting man of men. He had no tolerance for this effeminate, swishing son whose presence filled Buster Buchanan with disgust.

By the time Gary was a teen, his dad had become convinced the boy was a homosexual. He taunted Gary in front of his drinking buddies. He beat him with a plastic baseball bat when Gary refused to play with neighborhood children. Dear old dad once locked his son in a closet with a flashlight and a skin magazine and told Gary not to come out until he had a hard-on.

Gary prayed inside the closet. For himself, for his father and for the bedeviled souls who graced the pages of the magazine.

When Gary was 14 and already planning to run away and become a monk, his father came home drunk one hot August night and set upon the boy. He battered Gary with his fists and challenged him to fight back. Dad wrestled him to the floor and poured whiskey down his throat, causing Gary to cough painfully through a scalded throat and eventually to vomit. Dad delivered one final blow and left his son bleeding and unconscious in a puddle of his own puke.

In the photo album of Gary's mind, the night of whiskey and vomit was not the worst. Not even close. The worst nights came when good old Buster tried to cure his son of "queerness."

Gary was not gay. Gary had no interest in carnal matters whatsoever. He had stirrings sometimes, and twice he awoke with hot, sticky semen drying on his belly. Those experiences were not pleasant. The wet dreams were not in any way enlightening or relieving. They sickened Gary. They made him worry for his soul.

On Gary's 15th birthday, his father brought home a boozy harlot from the downtown bar. It was not the first time he had come home reeling, with a slattern under an arm. It happened all the time. This one though...This one was a birthday gift from father to son. This one was here to teach.

She wore a tight, flowered dress that revealed the roll of fat like a spare tire around her belly. Her face was tired and worn and she'd tried to paste it together with lipstick and rouge. The result was a face that may have once been pretty but which now looked like that of a melting clown. She was hideous. She was obscene. And she was approaching Gary with liquored breath and a shimmy that dropped the flowered dress to the floor.

Behind her, Gary's dad was grinning drunkenly in anticipated victory.

"We're gonna make a man out of you yet, Gary, my boy. Old Kathleen here has a magic touch. She'll screw the queerness right out of you."

"Watch who you're calling old, sugar."

And with that, she descended on him. She pushed small, frail Gary down on the couch and thrust her hips into his. She reached for his belt and pulled his pants open before Gary could get a hand down there to stop her. When he tried, a swift blow battered his cheek. Foreman Buster was supervising the work.

For a half hour, the melting clown lady ground away on Gary on the dingy living room couch. She pressed her vein-lined breasts into his face, clutching his hands and moving them there. She spoke to him in breathy tones and occasionally winked at Buster, who stood next to the couch leering.

"That's my big boy. Ooooh, yes. You're so big for a little boy, yes you are. Give it to me good now, kid. Yes, like that! Ooooh, yes. You like it inside me don't you, kid? Ooooh, baby! Squeeze my tits. Squeeze them, suck them, bite them..."

The experience was horrifying. After thirty minutes, Gary felt semen squirt out of him and the relief he felt was tempered by the loathing of what had happened. The clown lady sighed dramatically and cooed at Gary as though she were talking to a dog. Foreman Buster roared laughter and punched his kid on the shoulder.

"That's it, my boy. Shot your load into a woman, just like a real man. Remember it, boy. Remember that feeling always. You remember it and get those faggot thoughts out of your head. You're a man now, son."

Later, Gary wept in the shower and prayed for forgiveness. He washed his penis vigorously and wished he could cut it off. He prayed some more in bed and asked for a sign that God would not leave him. None was forthcoming.

Thirty years later, his dad long in his grave and probably telling dirty jokes to the good old boys in Hell, Gary was surprised at how fresh the memory was. He didn't think of those dark times often. But he'd been falling asleep with a magazine in his hand outside Olivia Currie's door. Dreams sometimes sneaked up on him like psychic prowlers. He prayed often for God to take them from him.

He stretched in the high-back chair. He took a look up and down the long, dim hall with its plush, ruby carpet. He rubbed his eyes. He mumbled a short prayer. He glanced at his watch.

"Oh, heavenly father!"

It was late; after midnight. Typically, Gary checked on Olivia at 11 p.m., if she didn't call him before them. Typically, the old woman was sleeping in the vast reading room, and he would wheel her to the second floor. There, Gary would lift her and carry her to the magnificent bed. She would rouse from sleep, he would place two pills in her mouth and then give her a straw to suck on. It was a nightly ritual that stretched back a decade.

Gary got to his feet at once and opened the tall, wooden door. He stared into the gloom of the room and saw her there behind the desk. Quietly, he moved across the room and got behind her. She might never notice the deviation from their routine.

He started to wheel her from the room. He stopped. Something was wrong. The old woman was propped as she was every night, with her chin resting on her chest. But there was no light wheezing of her breath. The old woman was silent.

Troubled, Gary moved to the front of the chair, knelt and looked at her. He had never been squeamish about the appearance of her. He didn't understand those who could not handle the sight. Olivia Currie was a woman who had been through more sorrows than most mortals and yet she persevered with strength and dignity.

Gary held the back of his hand to her lips. There was no soft breath against his skin. Alarm growing, he pressed his fingers to her neck. There was no faint beat of life underneath the flesh.

Slowly, sadly, Gary got to his feet. He crossed himself involuntarily and hung his head. He began to pray.

"Our Father, who art in heaven, hallowed be thy name..."

He prayed long and flawlessly. He prayed for her soul and for his. The Lord, his savior, seemed very far away tonight.

Two

Cain met more people at the IGA on Tuesday, June 14 than he had the entire week he had been in Mulberry.

It was his first trip to the grocery store and long overdue. He had a cart filled with steaks, chicken, ribs, pasta, vegetables and various things he had needed since he got here.

The first person to approach him was a short, shapely lady in cutoff jeans and a tight, red top. Dark hair was pulled into pigtails that for Cain recalled boyhood fantasies about a certain farm girl stranded on a comical island.

"Looks like you might be planning a barbecue," the woman said.

Cain first looked at her dumbly. Then he spotted the packages of meat balanced on the rest of his groceries. He grinned and nodded.

"Yeah," he said. "I'm basically a carnivore."

The woman smiled. She glanced up and down the aisle and then leaned in toward him like a conspirator.

"Look, nobody who's from here buys their meat at the IGA. You go up the road a mile, turn onto Dexter, and there's a butcher shop about a third of a mile down. Better selection. Better prices. And you won't die of food poisoning."

Cain looked to his right. He looked to his left. He lifted a steak out of his cart and scowled at it.

"Thanks. You may have saved my life."

The woman wheeled her cart away smiling and Cain watched her go.

A man and his young son stopped him in the cereal aisle and asked if he was Jonathan Cain, the writer. Cain admitted he was and scratched his signature on the back of a comic book the boy was carrying.

An older woman spotted him and asked if he was the nice young man who tried to help the poor kid from the boating accident. A middle-aged couple overheard the conversation and came over to introduce themselves.

He met a man who professed to be the best angler in all of Aroostook County and who would be glad to take Cain out to a secret spot on Long Lake for a very small fee. He was approached by the night manager of the Hearthside Grill who thought it would be good for business and a “wicked good time” to have the writer come in to sign autographs at the bar. Cain tentatively agreed.

In the parking lot, another couple introduced themselves but made no mention of fishing or writing. They were new in town, too, and wondered how he was getting along. A semi-retarded man in overalls caught up with him near the Explorer and handed him a certificate for a discount ATV rental.

“If you ain’t been out riding yet mister, you ain’t really seen much of Mulberry.”

Cain thanked him and loaded his groceries into the Explorer. He climbed in behind the wheel and paused a moment to take in the slow and easy pace of the people coming and going around him.

He liked the town. He had no intention of mingling much, because there was work to be done. But if fate had not been an absolute bastard, he imagined coming here for entire summers with Kimberly. Mulberry was beautiful and strong. Kimberly was beautiful and strong. It was a match made among a circle of lakes just south of the Canadian border.

Mulberry may get to meet Kimberly yet, he thought. *Give me time.*

Before he could follow the thought any further, there were three men at the driver’s side window and Cain recognized each of them.

“Mr. Rathbun,” he said brightly. “I didn’t figure you came to the grocery store. I thought you’d have your goods flown in by cargo plane.”

Rathbun was smiling cheerfully. To Cain, he looked like a dog about to bite. Behind him, Reyes and Loomis stood impassively, each wearing a tank top and each appearing bored beyond all measure.

"Got a joke for you, Mr. Cain," Rathbun said. "What do you call a woman with no arms and no legs and who died two nights ago?"

Cain looked at him. He said nothing.

"Give up? I'll tell you. You call her Olivia Currie. Or, to be precise, the late Olivia Currie. Get it? Do you like it?"

Cain started the Explorer.

"You got something you want to tell me, Rathbun? Because your breath stinks."

Rathbun went on smiling. "Your friend died Sunday night. They say it was a stroke, although that hasn't been finalized. You'd think they'd be quick about it. After all, how long can it take to autopsy something that's been whittled down to the size of a knickknack?"

Cain wanted to step out of the truck and punch the man in the mouth. The two goons behind him would break his arms, but it would be worth it. And he might get a few shots at them before they put him down.

Instead he said: "You're a real prick, you know it? Your job is so pathetic, you wanna whack off when an old lady dies."

Rathbun held his arms up over his head. "Hey, hey. Don't blame the messenger."

Cain started to roll the window. Rathbun took a step closer.

"Before you go wheeling back to your little chateau, you might want to think about the situation. Currie is gone. Out of the picture. This very minute, a team of government lawyers is working around the clock to determine whether we'll be in that house tomorrow or if we'll have to wait until the end of the week."

Cain smiled. It was a vicious smile and it felt good. He popped a finger out the window and waved it at Rathbun.

"Ah, but I think you're overlooking something here. Olivia Currie signed a document granting me permission to stay in her house for...oh, the rest of the summer, at least. And you might stop jerking off long enough to recall that Currie had a pretty good fleet of lawyers herself. And you know what, you little pissant? I have a pretty fine attorney of my own. Get it? Do you like it?"

Rathbun struggled to keep the smile, but it fell away like a leaf in the fall. He was left with a snarl of rage and it was ugly. His mouth opened and then closed. Opened and closed. Rathbun was a man who was unsure of his words.

"You underestimate us, Cain. Truly. You ought to be packing up your bags and heading back to Massachusetts for the funeral. Imagine the teeny, tiny coffin..."

Cain's smile only broadened.

"Gee golly gosh, Mr. Federal Flunky. You've got me all aflutter." He winked at the men. "I'll tell you what, though. I'll think about that real hard tonight. I'll think about it while I'm burning every scrap of paper I find in that big house. Might burn the computer, too, right there in the front yard. I'm gonna have me a barbecue, Mr. Rathbun. Guess what? You're not invited."

He finished closing the window, blew a kiss to the trio outside and drove out of the parking lot.

Cain pulled to the side of the road a mile from the turn to Olive Hill. He checked the rearview and determined he was not being followed. He snatched up the cell phone, saw that the batteries needed charging, dialed anyway.

Bucky Letroy sounded hung-over and grumpy when he answered. Cain launched right into and pummeled his agent with questions.

"Whoa, whoa! Slow the hell down. You're hurting my ears."

"Is my contract with Olivia Currie still binding, Bucky? I need to know that before I shoot my mouth off anymore."

"Jesus Christ, of course it is. It's the obligation of her estate to honor the contract. I mean, I'll contact Bones about it by the end of the week..."

"Contact him today. Please, man."

Bones was Bobby Barnabas, the lawyer who represented the agency.

"Okay," Letroy said. "Alright. I don't know why you're so wound up. Those government dicks are blowing smoke. The Currie estate will be in litigation for a long fucking time."

"Good. Great. Thanks, Bucky."

Letroy paused to take a drink of something. Cain guessed it wasn't apple juice.

"Hey, Jonathan. Everything all right up there? I meant to call you the other night..."

"You did call me the other night."

"Well then, you see that I'm concerned."

Cain laughed. "Yeah, everything's good. I'd be getting more work done if I didn't have these government spooks sneaking around."

"So, you're writing?"

"Of course I'm writing. What the hell do you think I'm doing?"

"I dunno. I dunno. I just get weird feelings sometimes."

"You and your weird feelings. Sell some books and stay out of the psychic game, will you? Everything's fine up here. Summer's gonna fly by and then we'll be heading south again."

Another pause. A slurp. A smacking of the lips.

"We? Who's we, Jonathan?"

Shit.

"Figure of speech. Man, I'm starting to talk like the locals already."

Shit.

Three

In keeping with her wishes, which were spelled out in precise detail in her will, Olivia Grace Currie was buried next to her husband at Old Burial Hill, on the north side of Marblehead. The cemetery was more than 300 years old and had the distinction of being among the oldest in the country. It was also among the most picturesque. Sad, solemn willows hung down over weather-worn gravestones that dated back as far as the Salem witch trials. The graveyard sprawled across the town's highest point and looked down on the cluster of colonial era homes below. A visitor here could stare over those homes and over the tops of trees to the gleaming water of Massachusetts Bay.

There was no dispute over where the old woman would be laid to rest. It was one of few points in her last will and testament that would not be hotly disputed. Descendants of the late Evan Currie would be incensed to learn that Olivia had listed more than three dozen people as beneficiaries. Many of the people named in the will were not Curries at all. Olivia had left mind-whopping sums and other considerations to men and women who had served her throughout her latter years.

Most infuriating to the family of Evan Currie was the bequeathing of the coveted Marblehead mansion to a group of no less than eight common servants who had been with her more than a decade. The idea of those simple people owning and occupying the grand estate was just unthinkable.

There was no talk of these matters at the graveside service where mourners prayed over the customized coffin holding for eternity the remains of Olivia Currie. There were prayers and sniffles. There were hugs and solemn nods.

It was sunny but cool, with a breeze coming off the bay and wreaking havoc with the ties and veils and various accessories worn by the wealthy and grief stricken. The aroma of the ocean and freshcut grass was overpowered by those of perfume and flowers. And among the enormous array of bouquets that surrounded the waiting grave was a very impressive arrangement sent by the writer Jonathan Cain. The carnations were red and white and they mingled with baby's breath. On the card that had been removed at the funeral home, the writer had substituted simplicity for any attempt at literary flair: "A brief friendship, a world of kindness. You will be missed."

Cain did not attend the funeral. It would have taken an entire day to get to Marblehead and back and an entire day was not something he could afford. He believed Olivia Currie would have understood. In the sky above the Second Empire house on Olive Hill, things were happening fast.

Four

In the early afternoon, Cain drove south on Route 161, toward Presque Isle, and thought about pyramids. It was a funny thing to be daydreaming about on this particular stretch of road, which seemed to be a never-ending cycle of deep woods, long potato fields, and clusters of towns consisting each of a market, a barbershop, a garage and at least a half dozen lawn sales.

Maine was far from the deserts of Egypt, as much visually as geographically. But in his mind, Cain stood on hard packed sand and gazed with zealous awe at the overpowering vision of the great pyramids.

The pyramids were a marvel, a mystery. The arrogance of modern man compelled them to spew lofty rationalizations about their origins and purposes, but Cain didn't buy any of it. He believed that close to nothing about them was really understood.

Years ago, while researching a novel about a curse of biblical proportions, he had studied the monuments of Egypt and the various theories about them. The research was fascinating, but the novel was never written; 55,000 words in, Cain had discovered a huge, ugly hole in his storyline and gave up rather than attempt the massive repair job it would have required to mend the wounded tale. But he had gone back to Egypt again just to experience the mystical exhilaration of the pyramids one more time. And the second time, he experienced it with Kimberly, who was moved to silence at her first sight of them.

Yesterday, Cain knew more than most about the politics, science and spiritualism of ancient Egypt. Today he knew twice as much, thanks to an afternoon spent rummaging through Theodore Currie's desk in the cluttered study on the second floor. For Cain, light was dawning.

In a spiral notebook found deep at the back of a drawer, Cain found a glimpse into the frenzied but ordered mind of the crazed scientist near the end of his life.

It was clear by the scrawlings that Currie had not limited himself to any one realm of science. This notebook was a sort of compilation of the many powers the grieving father embraced to accomplish his work. To Cain, it looked like a cookbook — with precise measurements, specific ingredients and temperatures spelled out to the tenth of a degree. There was no room for error in this particular concoction.

There was much written in the notebook about ley lines. There was more than enough information about higher dimensions, and various drawings to describe the complex shapes of coiled strings. At the bottom of one page, in the lower margin, Currie had written "God is a string" in thick letters. He had underlined it so ferociously, the page was scratched through.

Cain flipped past pages of formulas he would never understand, felt inadequate trying to make sense of things like bosons and neutrinos, finally found comfort in crudely drawn sky maps.

There were several pages devoted to the positions of five planets and the solstice moon during the years 2004, 2005 and 2006. Currie's drawings were crude, yet oddly compelling. He had sketched the charts with a black, felt tip pen and even took time to draw small details, like the rings around Saturn. It would have been almost artistic if not for rows of numbers indicating angular distances, ascensions, declinations, ephemerides and a lot of astronomical jargon Cain did not fully grasp.

In the still of Currie's study, he had kept a nervous eye on the door while pouring through the notebook. He pulled blankets from the windows and opened them wide to let air in.

After an hour, he was comfortable, rapt and taking fewer glances toward the door. Cain was particularly absorbed in reading Currie's hen scratchings on a pair of enigmatic stars called Kochab and Mizar. It was here that his attention drifted to the pyramids and the endless questions about their being.

Historians generally agreed that the Egyptians were drawn to the pair of stars which they came to call the "Indestructibles." Always visible, circling the north pole like guardians, Kochab and Mizar became symbols of eternity and the afterlife, concepts about which the Egyptians were ardent.

Reading through Currie's charts and scattered writings, Cain reflected on what he knew of the oracular twin stars.

For a short time around 2,500 B.C., Kochab and Mizar each was about ten degrees from the celestial pole which lay directly between them. When one star was positioned exactly above the other in the sky, ancient astronomers could find a line that pointed due north.

Cain liked to think about Egyptian priests and astronomers from that glorious age, standing in the night desert, pointing to the north and waiting for those two stars to line up precisely. They waited and planned, foreseeing the construction of a monument that would send their dead kings into an eternal afterlife among the stars.

Currie, like others, believed the Egyptians used "the Indestructibles" to align the Great Pyramid to true north. He also believed they understood the concept of ley lines and that the pyramid was built on one out of necessity.

It took two decades or longer before the enormous project was complete. Debates still rage over how a population that lived 2,500 years before Christ could grasp and utilize concepts and technology that should not have been available to them. The Great Pyramid was aligned with such astounding accuracy, it still baffled modern engineers.

Cain was at Currie's desk for more than two hours. He was coming to understand where the tormented scientist differed from most in the debate over why the Egyptians had built the pyramid in the first place. Currie had believed, like most others, that it was the obsession with the world beyond natural life that inspired them. But he did not believe that the ancient Egyptians wanted to send their dead pharaohs to the afterlife of the stars. He believed they wanted to bring their dead kings back.

Frankly, it gave Cain chills. But there was one more twist in Currie's thinking that was at once more insane and more logical than the rest.

The dead pharaohs were buried in ornate tombs, with their most treasured possessions — jewelry, weapons and in some cases, their preferred wife or concubine, who was put to death to join the king on the descent into the grave.

The modern thinking was this: the treasures were placed near the entombed king so that he could take them with him on the journey to the afterlife. But Currie thought otherwise. In six pages of writing that read like a diary, Currie suggested a more provocative idea: those beloved belongings were interred with the deceased, not to send him away well equipped, but as a means of tempting him back to the world.

Chills indeed.

Almost at his destination now, Cain thought about the Great Pyramid aligned toward true north, just like the turret room. He thought about Angel Currie's cherished items arranged precisely throughout the pink room and about the purpose of his trip to Presque Isle.

Not to send them off to a happy eternity among the stars, but to tempt, entice and seduce them. To trick them back with shiny things to a world where selfish mortals grieve.

Five

The bed, the papasan, the nightstand. Check. The vanity table, the jewelry stand, the trunk. Check. A quilt that was not folded quite right. Deep blue drapes that would need ironing. The bamboo blinds, paintings by Van Gogh and Homer, a giant, painted fan from Thailand. Check, check and check.

Cain was hunched over inside a small trailer in a large, hot warehouse. He made checkmarks on a notepad as he moved from item to item. A bored, portly delivery man dressed completely in brown watched him with his arms crossed. The clerk smelled like sweat and marijuana. Cain ignored him and went through his list again.

"There a problem, buddy?"

"Not yet."

"Cus once you hitch the trailer up and roll outta here, I can get back on the road. Got two stops in Bangor and one in Waterville. It's a haul."

Cain said nothing. He opened the trunk and scanned the items inside. He looked at his notepad and nodded. All here. He closed the trunk.

"Looks good."

"Probably looked good the first two times you went through it."

Cain jumped from the trailer and glared at him. When Cain glared, the rise of his upper lip was almost canine. It was unsettling. The delivery man dropped his eyes.

Ten minutes later, the trailer was hooked to the back of the Explorer and Cain was rolling out. In the parking lot, he paused. He patted his breast pocket and felt a solid chunk there. He wormed his fingers into the pocket and snatched the necklace free. He held it up and the platinum chain sparkled in the sun. The small, red apple dangling from the end looked good enough to eat. Not a scratch, not a flaw. Cain imagined the apple laying against the hollow of Kimberly's neck and had to wipe tears from his eyes with the back of a hand.

An hour before sundown on September 21, 1988, Jonathan Cain, a college dropout with an uncertain professional future, led a striking young woman into an apple orchard on the western edge of Manheim, Pennsylvania. The orchard sprawled across a hundred acres and they were the only people there. The air was cool and the sun was a golden globe perched on the horizon. Everything around them glowed orange under its light. Tree tops were ablaze. The apples that dangled from branches seemed to be on fire.

Cain was in love with the girl. For the first three months, he tried to convince himself he only wanted her part time. He needed space. He need solitude. He needed his heart untethered and his mind sharp.

For the three months following that, he tried to devise a way to convince the young lady, whose hair smelled of strawberries, that they should marry. Cain was as sure of this as he was of his ambition to write his way out of the cold warehouses on Lake Erie. He was smitten. More than smitten. He was consumed by her.

Once, while they were drinking at a wharf bar outside Philadelphia, Cain had too many tequila shots and fell into a gloom. Kimberly had not yet seen the melancholy side of Jonathan Cain and it was a hell of a way to introduce her to it. He descended into grumpy silence. He stared at the water and glowered. He refused to be lured out of his sullenness by Kimberly's flirtations or horrible jokes.

Then he'd started to babble about the various abuses suffered at the hands of a stepfather when he was nine. The beatings, the emotional torture. Stories spouted out of him like vomit while his startled girlfriend listened from across the table.

Without preamble, Cain spewed forth with excruciating memory details of the time the oafish fuck held him under water until he'd passed out. In a drunken growl, waving his arms for emphasis, he described having his hands submerged in near boiling water after failing to shut the door all the way on a cold night.

He told her about the big prick locking him in the trunk of a car. About being beaten with a belt, a bottle, a bicycle chain. He raged on about listening to the vile bastard raping his mother in the next room and about being screamed at when he tried to talk to her about it the next day.

As other bar patrons grew uneasy at nearby tables, Cain fumed on. The evil step dad drowned my cat. The cruel fuck broke my hockey stick into four pieces and burned it in the woodstove. The cocksucker beat me senseless at the hockey rink while my friends looked on in embarrassment and shock.

In the end, he had worn his rage out. It was as though Cain had taken his memories out for a jog and then ran them until they collapsed. He looked up at Kimberly across the table, drunk but clearheaded enough to realize he had probably frightened her irrevocably.

"How long did this last, Jonathan? How long did that bastard live with you?"

Cain had tried to grin. "Two years. Prick got shot while buying a quart of milk at a convenience store. Caught in the crossfire. I wasn't just relieved, Kim. I was fucking delighted."

Yes, Kimberly had seen the melancholy that night. And the anger and resentments and a host of half-buried emotions psychoanalysts cream over. She had taken his hand and rubbed it with a finger. She picked it up and kissed it while Cain sat agog.

"I'll drive with you all night long if you want to go to his grave and piss on it, Jonathan. I'll be your lookout if you want to knock over his headstone and rip up all the flowers. Whatever you need to feel better, baby, I'll be right at your side."

Cain had gaped. He was too floored by the kindness and conviction of her words to react in any real way. He had expected a cliché-riddled speech about forgiveness, and about how things that don't kill us only make us stronger.

He'd mumbled something incoherent, exhausted, the rage gone out of him. He savored the feeling of her cool hand clutching his hot one. He savored her presence and the unexpected devotion.

"I don't hate him," she'd said. "He sounds like a miserable son-of-a-bitch, but I don't hate him. He helped shape you into what you are, Jonathan. And I think I'm falling in love with what you are."

A night later, Cain wrote, in longhand, a love letter and an apology for his behavior. It was mostly love letter. In it, he cited Plato's Symposium, and described each of them as two halves of the same apple.

"...each desiring his other half, came together, and throwing their arms about one another, entwined in mutual embraces, longing to grow into one, they began to die from hunger and self-neglect, because they did not like to do anything apart..."

The letter made Kimberly cry. Two months later, they were alone in the apple orchard in Manheim and almost dancing from tree to tree. Cain led her this way and then that. He carried a basket and picked only the choicest apples, leading her further into the groves.

"Here!" he said, pointing with one hand, holding her hand with the other. "I like the looks of that tree, right there."

Laughing, wondering how a person could get a sense about one apple tree when hundreds abound, Kimberly followed him. They came to a tree that stood slightly taller than the rest. By now shadows were angling sharply to the east and this tree seemed to catch the last of the dying sun's glow.

Cain stopped before it. He pulled Kimberly to his side.

"You kook. What's so special about this..."

Then she saw it. Carved in two-inch letters on the face of the tree, was the finest of his written work: "Marry me, Kimberly."

She wept again. She hugged him, jumped into his arms, and cried hot tears on his neck. She laughed, she wept some more. They made love under that very tree and then bit into apples while coiled there naked. Like Adam and Eve.

"You know," Cain said chewing. "You haven't answered me yet."

They found the apple necklace the following day in an antique store. They were leaving town. The store was a brief stop to savor the last of the trip. The necklace was perfect. It was spooky how they stumbled on it. Cain paid $300 for the necklace, roughly half of what had accumulated in his savings account. Outside the store, he placed it around her neck. It remained there, among Kimberly's most prized possessions, until the day they laid her to rest. The apple was their avatar and their crest.

It would have been natural to bury her with the necklace. At the last moment, Cain had removed it from her, through a blur of tears, as she lay in her coffin. He never understood why he did it. Not until he read Currie's ideas about the ancient Egyptians, and what those jewels and trinkets really signified.

Six

Lyons didn't like the looks of the long sedan riding slowly out past Olive Hill. He passed it on his way back from Frenchville just before dark and dismissed it as a tourist looking for moose.

Tourists loved the moose. Even those from southern parts of the state would spend half their vacations prowling the side roads in search of the spindly-legged monsters. Lyons didn't get it. Up here, moose were nuisances. They would flee the buggy woods and dart onto the road, causing destruction and sometimes death.

There was a spot out on Comet Road, a back way to St. Agatha, where cars would line up on both sides of the road during sundown. It was the most prevalent spot for moose sightings and people jockeyed for the good spots. Lyons didn't get it. He supposed if he traveled to the Sahara, he'd be on the lookout for camel, but still. These were moose and there was nothing exotic about them at all.

There was something sneaky about the dark sedan and Lyons didn't like it. Lyons wasn't certain, but he thought it might belong to those government spooks who claimed to be in town on a geological survey they could not discuss. Lying bastards.

A half mile down the road after spotting the car, he wheeled the Jeep around. Sure enough, the sedan was crawling past the narrow driveway that wound its way to the Currie house.

Lyons thought of Jonathan Cain up there, alone in the big house. The writer seemed like a good guy, mourning his wife and maybe trying to get back to work. Cain could settle in up here, if he wanted to. The town would accept him. There was not much of that 'us and them' crap up here. This was the other Maine, too far north to be closely associated with its more urban twin.

Lyons slowed and flashed the headlights. The car coming toward him sped up as if to fly past him. He flashed his lights more frantically and laid on the horn. The sedan pulled to a stop. Lyons drove up close to it and gave the universal sign for the other driver to roll down his window. After a moment, the driver did so. A young, muscular man stared out at him. Lyons could see another man sitting stoically in the passenger seat.

"Hi there. I'm Reggie Lyons, constable up here. Everything alright?"

The driver flashed a smile full of perfect white teeth. "Sure thing, constable. My buddy and I were just looking for moose. Heard sundown was a good time."

Lyons snickered. "You've been talking to the wrong people, then. Early morning, late at night is when they're gonna be out. And this isn't the spot for 'em. You wanna be on the other side of the lake."

The driver turned to his partner. "See? I told you it was too early."

The men thanked him, promised to try again on the other side of the lake, and drove off. Lyons wheeled the Jeep around and followed them at a distance for a ways. He took down the plate number.

He wasn't buying it. Two men in a pickup truck, each with a beer between his legs, maybe. Two men in a dark sedan who looked like they spent three hours a day in a gym, probably not.

"Unless they're gay," he murmured to himself. "Unless they're out looking for a quiet place to smoke pole."

He laughed and banged the steering wheel. If he'd interrupted a homosexual liaison, he truly felt bad. But Christ, that was a funny thought. Two queers, out in the deep woods of Maine and they still can't find a quiet spot. Good God.

Lyons turned toward town and headed for home. He didn't believe the two men were gay or moose hunting, but they were probably harmless. Still, there was something about that car. He stuffed the scrap of paper with the plate number in his pocket. He'd have it run through State Police dispatch. And he'd make more trips out past Olive Hill just to keep an eye on things.

Seven

From the 2005* Aroostook Almanac, *available across Maine and in parts of Canada for $1.25 a copy.

On June 21, the northern hemisphere will tilt precisely so that the north pole is leaning 23.5 degrees toward the sun, resulting in the longest day of the year and inspiring celebrations across the globe.

Once called "the midsummer day" the summer solstice is steeped in tradition and ritual. Our European ancestors observed the day with extravagant celebrations and festivals of fires. Flaming wheels were rolled down hills. Men, women and children ran across the land with torches and ignited bonfires to ward off evil spirits. Some jumped through the flames to be purified and protected while others prayed that the year's crops would rise as high as the flames.

In Salisbury, England, tens of thousands of people gather at Stonehenge each year to embrace the occasion at what is believed to be an ancient center of power.

Constructed between 3,100 and 1,550 B.C., Stonehenge is a mesmerizing array of megaliths arranged in alignment to the sun on the summer solstice of that time.

In Maine and in most parts of the United States, the solstice is greeted in less whimsical fashion. It is the start of summer and a day when sunlight lingers long. This year, it officially arrives at 2:46 a.m. EST.

Many people still believe that mystical powers are heightened around the summer solstice as the sun enters the Tropic of Cancer. Most just enjoy the long day while remembering wistfully that the solstice also marks the shortest night of the year.

This year, the night of the solstice will be illuminated by a full moon riding strangely low in the sky. The position of the mysterious satellite is controlled rigorously by the interaction of gravity among the moon, the earth and the sun. This year, the great, white orb may be tinged yellow or red as it glows through a lower part of the earth's atmosphere. More cosmic drama to mark the beginning of a grand season.

There was nothing more than a young girl's clothes and shoes inside the closet when Cain opened it the afternoon of June 16. Skirts and blouses hanging neatly on hooks. Tiny shoes with metal buckles lined perfectly on the floor. It was a space utilized by a little girl who once took pride in her things. Colors were coordinated. Clothes were spaced evenly to keep them from tangling and wrinkling.

The red corduroys were no longer hanging inside the closet but this didn't trouble him much. Everything would be gone soon. This was a clearance event.

He tried to be as neat as possible as he pulled the clothes from the closet and packed them into a box. But really. He could barely pack his own suitcase without crumpling everything into misshapen heaps.

He packed the shoes in a second box and slid both into the hallway. The closet was an innocuous square of space with a metal rod running across the length of it.

He produced more boxes and began to work on the bureau. He didn't linger over the items as he packed them away, not even the snow globe. Cain was working with a clinical expedience. The object was to empty the room as quickly and efficiently as possible. He cleared the top of the bureau and then pulled the drawers out one by one. He wrestled it all to the hallway and wondered how he'd get everything down the narrow, winding stairs. He wondered how Currie had done it coming up.

Didn't matter. It would be done.

As he labored, Cain thought about Angel Currie and the unsettling visage she presented. He recalled the sight of her father, sad and desperate in the reading room, and tried to piece together the dreadful sequence of events.

Angel had come back, but she had come back wrong. Cain tried to think of a better word for it, but it was the best he could do. Something had gone wrong. And Theodore Currie, still attracted to this house and the daughter trapped within it, had returned as well. But why? And how?

Cain didn't know. He had to concentrate on the wrongness. It couldn't happen with Kimberly. It wouldn't happen. He was convinced of it, but did not know why.

The solstice was coming. The planets would be together again in the sky and the moon would be full and low the night of the solstice. It was a cosmic fluke that had both benefited and cursed Theodore Currie. But that was last year. Through more reading downstairs, Cain discovered that the cosmic coincidences Currie had anticipated were to be more complete this year.

So why hadn't Currie waited? Why not struggle through another year of grief and wait for a time when circumstances are optimal?

But Cain knew about soul-crushing despair and the pain of missing someone so irremediably gone. Patience was the luxury of sane men. Tell the crack addict to wait a while for his fix. Ask a drowning man to wait a little longer for a breath of air. Cain suspected Currie was emotionally incapable of waiting. There were hints among the half-crazed meanderings in his notebook he may have been considering reaching out for his long-dead wife at another time. The ultimate family reunion through the twisting of strings and the precise tugging of gravity.

A box filled with clothes from the bureau went into the hall. The bureau itself went out with only minimal negotiating. The snow globe was gone, wrapped in a small, white shirt and stuffed into the bottom of a box. There. Better. Cain turned to the nightstand and began to pull out drawers.

The human concept of death was funny. From childhood, man was taught to accept its eventuality. Adults spent good portions of their lives preparing for it and the funeral industry prospered. Young people purchased burial plots while they were still vital and adorned the graves of lost loved ones as lavishly as they could afford.

By the age of ten, most people grasped that death was non-negotiable. Biology dictated that the body would one day succumb to disease, age or trauma and then the physical vessel would decay. Dust to dust.

Yet, people prayed to departed loved ones every minute of every day. They wept at gravesides and invoked God's name in their grief. They prayed that God was merciful and that they would one day see their lost husband or brother, son or daughter again in the afterlife. So unbearable was the idea of absolute mortality, they conditioned themselves to believe in primeval concepts of which no proof was forthcoming. As though belief alone might save them.

"And he who lives and believes in me shall never die."

But men made terrible believers. Their faith was too pliable, too apt to be swayed by new knowledge or fresh ideas. And so they spent as much time trying to stave off their own demise as they did preparing for its certainty. They became obsessive about diets and exercise. Vitamins and herbal medicines were gobbled with abandon. The frantic attempt to dance away from the reaching fingers of the Reaper until medical breakthroughs could buy them more time.

And to some extent, it was happening. Scientists crowed on and on about amazing advances in disease management, mitochondrial alterations, new secrets of longevity. Live longer, live better.

But those advances were slow. To exist with the knowledge of impending doom, a person had to keep what faith and spiritualism he could muster.

In Currie's notes, it was clear that he admired the ancient people for their absolute resolve in matters of death. He considered it knowledge instead of flimsy, assailable belief.

It was Currie's opinion that ancient man had intuitively grasped the workings of the universe more clearly than modern man. There was no explanation for why it might be so. Currie simply believed the ancients knew how to summon back their dead and so they had done so.

What bothered Cain was this: if man once possessed that knowledge, where had it gone? Did that part of the intellect simply get cycled out of evolution as mankind selfishly turned its attention to better means of acquiring comfort and wealth? Like some evolutionary sacrifice that left the science of resurrection behind?

Maybe. Or maybe something had gone wrong.

In his notebook, Currie had clipped a page from the Bible and taped it to a page. It was a section of Deuteronomy that specifically warns the Israelites against divination from the dead.

Then, at the bottom of the page, the scientist listed a few examples from the scriptures where the advice was not heeded. The Witch of Endor, for example, called Samuel from beyond so that he might speak to King Saul. In a more familiar scene, Jesus raised up Lazarus after four days in the tomb. In his notes, Currie had circled the name Lazarus several times.

There was no indication that Currie was religious or that he was troubled by the moral or biblical implications of what he was attempting. The notebook appeared to be nothing more than the observations of a man who spent many hours and days waiting for scientific miracles.

My father's house has many rooms, Cain thought suddenly and inexplicably. He knew little of the Bible, but the phrase had jumped into his head as loudly as a thought could. And with it, an image of those wondrous dimensions that man had never been allowed to see.

My father's house has many rooms...

Troubled for reasons he could not pinpoint, he lugged the nightstand into the hall. He returned to the room and tugged the pink curtains down, letting in more light. It was gray and cool outside. Leaves on the trees were restless in a stiffening breeze. The pale undersides of those leaves had spun so that they were facing the sky. Cain thought that might mean something in weather forecasting lore. He had no idea what.

He chucked the beanbag into the hall so he would no longer trip over it. He hauled the rocking horse out, mind bent on imagining the hollow beast suddenly twisting in his arms, braying and biting. He made to toss the stuffed animals out onto the heap, became unsettled by the idea, walked them there instead.

He peeled the poster from the wall and the one from the back of the door. He rolled both of them inside a pink area rug and took the fuzzy tube to the hall. He took down the pink, flower shaped clock, grabbed the pillows from the bed and added them to the growing pile in the hallway. He peeled the blankets from the bed and left them on the floor to be folded and packed in boxes.

He was tired. The room was starting to look less like a little girl's room and more like a space full of clutter. He walked to the dollhouse, perfectly centered on the white table, and examined it. It really was a marvel. There was no sign Angel had ever tried to pry open doors or windows to set little figurines in there. Of course, Cain recalled, this was not the original. The original had burned up in the same flames that killed the child while her father was in another city collecting pats on the back.

Still, he doubted Currie would have overlooked any flaws or alterations made by his daughter. Its design was not to improve on the original work, after all. It was to recreate it and tempt the girl back.

He reached down to touch the iron railing around the turret. Just like the one outside this room. So impressive. He poked it and the tip of one of the rails pricked him so sharply, his finger bled. Cain withdrew his hand and stuck the wounded finger in his mouth. He glanced at the door.

Theodore and Angel Currie stood side by side, holding hands in the doorway. They filled the door frame, staring into the room.

"You can't do this," Angel said. "This is my room."

"You can't do this," her father repeated. "It is wrong."

Cain stood frozen next to the dollhouse. His finger was still in his mouth. He looked at father and daughter standing forlornly in the doorway. Angel's face still bore an expression of petulant disgust. Her father appeared sad and haggard. But there was nothing menacing about them. Not really.

He pulled his finger from his mouth. "Please," he said, and found that his voice was both assertive and strong. "Go away."

Theodore Currie, arms hanging limply at his side, looked imploringly at Cain.

"You mustn't do this. It won't work. You don't understand how vast space and time is in between. I didn't understand. The strings are impossibly twisted. It is eternity in between."

"You can't have my room," Angel Currie said.

Cain was unnerved but not quite afraid. He longed for a way around them, but there was none.

"I need this room now," he said. "You have to go back. You're not wanted here anymore."

Theodore's face seemed to crumble. "We can't go back! We can never go back. We are caught in between. Don't you see that? We are not completely here. It is eternity in between."

Angel snarled. The gums around the empty gap between teeth looked rotted and grotesque. Her eyes narrowed to slits.

"This is my room. I won't let you have it."

Cain stepped forward. He gazed at them and did not waver. He reached out for the edge of the door and slammed it shut. In the flicker of a half second, he saw both father and daughter flinch. But there was no flurry of fists on the other side of the door. The knob did not twist and rattle. There were soft footsteps in the hall and then Cain heard the squeak of springs.

The rocking horse. She's riding the rocking horse.

Soon after, Angel Currie began to cry. Cain stood near the door and listened with near self-loathing as she sobbed, like any little girl who has had her heart broken. And like any father torn apart at even the petty grief of a child, Theodore Currie tried to comfort her with reassuring words and soft coos.

Eight

Darlene Hill could not look into the coffin. She stood next to it with both hands on the lid and she trembled. She looked up at her husband, who stood with slumped shoulders next to her. She glanced with crazed eyes at the somber funeral director hovering on the other side of the casket. Surely, they could not expect her to do this.

"I can't," she said.

They stood in the viewing room at Whipple's Funeral home. It was dark. A far off clock punched the silence with regular clicks and clunks. The room smelled of flowers, though there were none to be seen.

Ramone Hill stepped closer to put an arm around his wife. He was enormous and sweating through a blue dress shirt. When he hugged her, Darlene seemed to disappear in the meat of his armpit.

"Take your time," said Carlton Whipple, a tall, thin man in a dark suit. He looked like an undertaker. Whipple had returned to Mulberry from California ten years ago after a failed bid to break into acting. As the joke around Mulberry went, had Carlton Whipple not given up his dreams to become a funeral director, he would have played one in the movies.

Darlene Hill squirmed under her husband's massive arm. Her hair was dark and wild and her face was pale and gaunt. Her lower lip was in constant motion as she trembled and muttered.

"I can't. I'm sorry Ray. I just can't."

She pulled away from him and hurried from the room. Ramone heard her sob as she went. A door slammed closed in another room. Ramone and the funeral director shared a look.

"Maybe it's best," said Carlton Whipple.

"Yeah. Maybe."

Whipple pulled open the upper lid of the coffin like a showman. The corpse of Dennis Hill lay propped on bright blue pillows inside. Ramone glanced at his son and tears immediately rolled from his eyes. The boy was wearing a white shirt under a blue blazer. He looked like a proper little lad. But the patchwork at the side of his face was obvious. There were glaring discolorations and puckers on the skin where attempts had been made to mask the sewn up wounds.

"I don't think so," Ramone said in a voice that was choked with tears. "You did fine work, but...I don't think so. I don't want people to see my boy like this."

Whipple nodded and closed the lid. The body would be flown to New Haven in the morning. Cosmetics was his only role in this nightmare.

Ramone rubbed his eyes and stepped away from the coffin. He paused, staring through the webs of his fingers.

"Can you open it up again, Mr. Whipple?"

Whipple nodded once more and complied. Ramone leaned down into the coffin, gently probed the collar of his son's shirt, stood straight again.

"The necklace. Where is his necklace?"

"Necklace, sir?"

"The cross necklace," Ramone said in a tone that was sharper than he'd intended. "A gift from his grandmother just before she died. He never took it off. Never."

Whipple knew nothing of the necklace. He went into a back office and checked the paperwork from the hospital and found no mention of it.

"Perhaps it was lost in the...in the water."

"Yeah," Ramone said. "Maybe."

He began to weep in earnest.

Nine

For the first time since he'd arrived, Cain was asleep minutes after he lay his head on the pillow. He was still spending nights in the living room on the first floor, but he was thinking about changing that soon. There was a mattress on the second floor and tomorrow, there would be a bed in the turret room.

Clouds had rolled in late in the day and rain soon followed. Cain spent three hours wrestling furniture and boxes from the turret room to the second floor. Once that exhausting chore was over, he started all over again, lugging everything downstairs to the first floor and then through the front door to the yard.

By the time he was through, it was pouring outside and he was spent. Everything from the pink room was packed inside the trailer, which he had backed up close to the house.

There was more work to do tomorrow. Much more. But carrying things up to the turret room and setting up would be much less like labor. It would feel more like preparing for a guest.

Now deeply asleep, Cain did not stir when two figures walked side-by-side down the staircase. He did not hear or sense them as they stood over him. He did not wake when a corner of the sleeping bag was pulled from his shoulder. And when small, cold lips pressed against his shoulder blade and warm air breathed across his skin, Cain's sleeping brain incorporated it into a dream.

"No! You must not bite! Not now, Angel. Get away from him."

There was a low growl and a hiss. But the small face drew away from the sleeping man's bare back.

Cain smacked his lips in sleep. He twisted in the sleeping bag and tried to shrug it back up over his shoulder. The two figures stood over him, watching. Rain tapped on the windows outside.

"Why is he here, daddy?"

"I don't know, Angel."

"Why are you here?"

"Because you are."

Silence except for the rhythmic chatter of rain on glass.

"I want to go to my room."

"I'm sorry, darling."

A blast of wind rattled panes and made the house shutter. Outside, a tree limb cracked.

"You shouldn't have brought me here."

"I know that. I missed you. I was wrong."

It was dark and there were no human eyes to see the vicious smile of the dead little girl as she lifted her head and stared up at her father.

"I'm going to chew you up, daddy. One of these days, I'm going to chew you up and swallow you."

"Angel..."

In the dark, while Cain slept in peace, Theodore Currie backed across the living room. He retreated up the stairs to the second floor while his daughter, snarling and gnashing her teeth, followed him into the darkness.

Ten

"What do you mean leaving? You can't leave. We're in the middle of an operation here."

Rathbun was in a rage. More accurately, he was in a panic. But he tried his best to make it look like a rage. He banged his fist on the desk. He hurled a glass across the room. Reyes and Loomis, nonplussed, continued to throw clothes into gym bags.

"Those are our orders. We're needed somewhere else."

"Somewhere else! So soon before the solstice and you're abandoning the whole operation?"

Loomis snickered. He zipped a gym bag and threw it like a basketball to Reyes, who caught it and added the bag to a stack.

"What operation? You don't believe this horseshit any more than we do, Rathbun."

"I don't believe it, but I damn well know enough to stay here until it's over. I'll be calling Brazel on this. Mark my words."

"Brazel," said Loomis, "is the one hauling us outta here."

Rathbun was stunned. He had not been notified about any of this. It was an outrage. He should be the one getting out of this God forsaken place, not these two jarheads.

"What about me?" His voice betrayed the creeping sense of alarm.

Loomis shrugged. "Brazel said you'd be staying put. You oughta take it up with him."

"You better believe I will. This is unacceptable."

What was unacceptable was the thought of staying alone in this goddamn Quonset hut for a week or more. Rathbun was no pansy. But the woods were creepy at night and he already felt outnumbered by the clan-like population of Mulberry. Furthermore, how the hell could he exert himself if necessary when he had no one to back him up?

He sat back behind his desk and took deep breaths. He had a mind to pick up his cell phone right now and call NASA-Langley. Brazel would be mad as hell if he called from other than a land line, but fuck him.

Rathbun looked at the phone on his desk but did not touch it.

"When are you leaving?"

"Tomorrow morning. Driving down to Bangor and off we go."

"Where are you going?"

"Tsk tsk, Rathbun. You know better."

"You're a real shithead, Reyes."

Eleven

Even after the diagnosis, even after the long, horrible conversations with a roomful of physicians, Cain had believed everything would turn out fine. People survived cancer all the time. The news was replete with stories about celebrities who overcame. It seemed, sometimes, that everybody was stricken with the dread disease at one point or another. It was a growing plague brought about by the abuses of man and his untamed gluttony. Cancer dripped from the clouds factories oozed into the air. It snaked through the crevices and ducts of buildings that bulged with wires, coils and tentacles of the newest technology. It came in neatly wrapped packages of tasty carcinogens with creamy centers. People ate the disease and then threw the package into the trash, to be burned and sent skyward, to rain down more toxins on an already choking planet.

Men, women and children every day gobbled up the disease and carried it around in their pockets. Everything was a tumor waiting to be born.

People talked about cancer as though it were unavoidable. They had sisters, uncles and grandparents who were afflicted. They quit smoking, started popping vitamins and hoped for the best. But every day, the news wailed on about new sources of toxicity that would breed cancer like insect eggs. Cancer of the breasts, lungs, throat, skin, bones, brain, stomach, liver, testicles...Cancer here, cancer there. Cancer, cancer everywhere.

But people survived. They came home weak and bald after chemotherapy and that's how you learned they had been afflicted. There were horror stories about the procedure, but there they were. A day or two in the hospital and they were back at home to begin recovery, with expensive medications and a new appreciation for life.

Some relapsed, others kicked the tumor's ass and never had to fight it again.

For Kimberly, there would be no long struggle with radiation and chemotherapy. There would be no battle at all.

She went for a jog one autumn afternoon while Cain wrote a gripping climax to a novel he planned to squirrel away for a dry spell. Nearly three hours passed before he realized she had not come home.

He drove along her usual running route around the lake, not yet worried. Kimberly never interrupted him while he was writing. She may have gone for drinks with friends. She may have stopped at the market for steaks to grill or the bookstore for something to read. It could be anything, but Cain had gone looking anyway.

He found her sitting on a bench near the water. Her head was in her hands and she was sobbing into her gloves. Cain squealed to a stop, left the car in the road and ran to her. He was sure she had been attacked, possibly raped. Maybe she had been mugged and was hurt.

She looked up at him with red, wet eyes and pulled him to her.

"Jonathan, it's awful. I've been trying to get home for an hour and I can't remember how to get there."

For Cain, it was a terrifying moment. His first thought was of Alzheimer's, a disease that had whittled the life and memories from his favorite uncle when the man was in his 40's. Alzheimer's was a word Cain did not even like to utter.

The first doctor they spoke with, an intense, dark-eyed man who looked to be no more than 30, was reassuring at first. All sorts of things can cause temporary memory loss, he told them. A bump on the head that seemed harmless at the time. It could be a hormonal imbalance. It might be the onslaught of a migraine, a problem with medication or even simple stress. All tiny little disorders that could be easily remedied. The doctor told them not to worry much as he scheduled the tests.

Two days later, Cain saw the pictures from the CAT scan. The tumor inside Kimberly's brain looked like one of those small, candy Easter eggs that come in all sorts of colors. The sight of it was more frightening to Cain than any horror he had invented in his novels or in his dreams. This was a murderous, egg-shaped fiend that lived inside his wife's head. And because of its location within the brain, removing it would not be easy.

"You have to understand that it can be done. But the work is very delicate. It will require specialists..."

That night, he and Kimberly wept like children in their bed. Cain kept trying to reassure her, but his words sounded fake and hollow, even to himself, and he would start sobbing again. She would get better, he was still convinced. But the pain of recovery would be excruciating and long. It tore him apart to think of the agonies she would endure. It infuriated him that something so vile could invade his tender, beautiful wife like some tiny, evil burglar that snuck in while they slept.

Kimberly did not have to suffer the agonies of surgery and the long road to repair. Things got worse very quickly, more quickly than the oncologists had anticipated.

The night after they had cried together, Kimberly lost control of her bladder while they watched television in the living room. The following day, she did not recognize her husband or the house around her. She recovered from that lapse quickly, but then she fell to the floor in the fetal position and began to convulse.

It was the last moment Kimberly Ann Cain spent inside the home she had picked out with her newly wealthy husband nine years ago. She was swiftly admitted to St. Martin's Hospital where her condition rapidly deteriorated. Cain was always by her side, in a chair where he was close enough to hold her hand. He was there when she slept, and when the nurses came to bathe and change her. Sometimes she was lucid and they would talk. She would wake from a long sleep and say something startlingly vivid and clear.

"My God, Jonathan. You know what I just thought of? I thought of the time we went to Nebraska and that dog bit you in the ass. My

God, that was funny. We were out by the corn, taking pictures, when that little..." Kimberly had broken off into laughter that shook the bed. "...that little, scrawny mutt went at you like you'd insulted his mother or something. And you tried to kick it away but it ran around behind you and bit you...bit you...Oh, my God!"

Cain, sitting next to her, was laughing along with his wife who was now in tears and reduced to wracking hysteria that stole her ability to speak. He remembered the dog bite well, but she told it with such vivid recollection, he almost felt the fangs clamped onto his buttocks.

"Oh, and he bit you and wouldn't let go and that...that little, mangy thing was hanging off your pants and growling. And you were running in circles and...and whooping and trying to slap it and the dog just whirled around in circles behind you like you were...you were...like a circus act, and...Oh, God!"

When the nurse stepped in, she found a man thrashing in a chair and his wife rocking back and forth and slapping her hands against the mattress. The nurse was alarmed and started to call for help down the hall. Cain assured her they were all right and she left them with a curious look.

Kimberly was sniffing and rubbing her eyes with the bed sheet.

"Christ, Jonathan. That was so damn funny."

"Yeah. Easy for you to say." His whole body hurt.

"And I got a picture of it. The dog is a little blurry, but that makes it even funnier. Holy crap! What ever happened to that picture?"

Cain had been trying to catch his breath. He felt like he'd been punched in the stomach.

"I dunno. In the basement probably."

"Go find it. Next time you go home, go look for that sucker. I'd love to see it. I swear, I'll pop a blood vessel, but so what?"

Cain had found the picture, too, packed in a box that was jammed with old photographs. And it was goddamn hysterical.

But when he returned to the hospital, Kimberly did not remember the ass-munching dog or the husband who had suffered at its jaw. Kimberly was shrieking vulgarities at nurses who tried to remove the clothes she'd soiled.

And worse, and worse, and worse. For two days, Kimberly got worse, with no soft memories for reprieve in the meantime. By then, surgeons wanted to cut immediately. Kimberly was completely blind and worse, she had a few remaining moments of lucidity and she screamed at the loss of her vision.

If Cain went to hell after his time on this planet, no cruelty there could be worse than those final days of watching his wife deteriorate. Kimberly suffered the emotional terror of realizing what destruction was overtaking her. Cain suffered knowing that she suffered so acutely.

He cried and prayed. He cried and shouted hateful things to a god he did not believe in. He wanted to fight the doctors who came to jab needles into his wife. He wanted to toss visitors through the window. Kimberly's mother was a drunk who lived in Buffalo. The woman never came to the hospital. Cain told his wife that she had. Then he called the bitch from a hospital phone and told her off in a screaming tirade of profanity that left him weak.

In the end, Kimberly died without drama. It happened in the hours before dawn, while Cain slept in a chair, his head slumped on the pillow next to hers. He had a memory of his wife gently squeezing his hand before the shriek of machinery sent nurses running. He believed in that squeeze. He believed his wife was his wife again for a flickering moment before she passed. And for a second, in the dark next to her, he thought he heard a faint goodbye.

See you on the other side, Jonathan. I love you.

That is what he believed.

Twelve

It was disorienting how quickly the pink room metamorphosed into the blue room. Pink walls were sanded, primed and painted over. Pink curtains were replaced with blue ones. The runner on the floor was blue, as were the pillows on the bed. The ocean blue fan from Thailand was hung on a wall as were the Homer and the Van Gogh. The frilly, girlish mood of the room had given way to the regal, restful shades of cobalt blue.

And the recreation was damn near startling. Sure, the windows were situated differently here than they were at home, as was the closet door. They were small matters, though. What counted was the replication of their bedroom down to the tiniest detail.

The blue and white quilt Kimberly had made herself was draped across the queen bed so that it hung evenly on all sides. Two pillows on each side of the bed (feather pillows on his side, foam on hers) with shams that matched the curtains.

The papasan with its blue cushion was tucked in a corner near the window where Kimberly could sit and read while waiting for her husband to get his ass out of bed. The vanity was where the bureau had been and the top was cluttered with perfume bottles, brushes, combs and scrunchies.

The nightstand was on Kimberly's side of the bed, farthest from the door, and a drawer was left slightly open. Spilling from that drawer was a notebook, more scrunchies, a bottle of massage oil, a box of tissues. On top of the nightstand, a digital clock, a blue candle in a jar with a matchbook wedged beneath it, a heap of books, a few pens and a pencil. There was a bottle of Poland Spring water there because Kimberly always awoke thirsty in the night.

The tall, slender bureau was near the door, flowers in a blue vase atop it. The trunk was at the foot of the bed, battered and mysterious. A blue blanket was draped over it in case she got cold in the night.

Gowns and dresses, pants and blouses that emerged from the trunk were now hanging neatly in the closet. An army of shoes of all varieties lined the closet floor, where Angel Currie's smaller, jauntier shoes had sat. There were discarded purses in there too, each with scraps of paper and trinkets that hinted at the last time they were used.

This was an adult's room, the room of a grownup couple with charmed lives. The decor spoke of their collective tastes. The only childish remnant here was a goofy, blue frog that sat against a pillow with arms outstretched. It was a gift from Kimberly to Cain after he wrote a novella about a town cursed by a rain of frogs. Only, Kimberly was the one that slept with the frog and hugged it tight when her husband was up writing into the wee hours. Because of this affection, the frog had the battered, loved look of a stuffed toy lugged around by a child until age and maturity severed the relationship.

The blue room was beautiful. Bamboo blinds had been hoisted to let in the sun. Cain sat on the foot of the bed, tired from the exertion of the last few days, but rejuvenated.

The day before, while he'd been finishing up with the paint, he'd felt a prickling at the back of his neck. He turned to see Angel, lowered down on her haunches in the doorway. She was naked and dirty and sucking her thumb. It appeared she had been crying. The springs of her hair were almost gone, flattening and uncoiling with grime. But when Cain had leveled the paintbrush at her, she growled and got to her feet. Her naked flesh was alarmingly gray and bloodless. She hissed and spittle flew from her lips.

"You'll pay for this, prick. You ruined my room and you will pay."

Then she spun and dashed down the hall, the thump and thump of her footsteps fading off into nothing. Theodore Currie never came to watch the redesigning of the pink room.

It was painful sitting here, in the familiar surroundings of his old life. He imagined Kimberly leaning into the closet and mumbling about having no decent clothes. He imagined her at the vanity, putting just touches of makeup around her eyes. He imagined her flopping down onto her back upon the bed, with a tired moan and then a giggle. He imagined looking at her naked back as she was turned away from him in bed, silently scribbling poetry in her notebook

Painful, very painful. But less so, now. Cain stood and walked to the window, looking out into the northern sky, which was still bright blue and hours before stars would twinkle. Whatever magic Theodore Currie had invoked in this place, Cain was relying on it now. The magic of strings, the magic of the sky, the magic of unseen energy from the earth below the Second Empire home. Whatever it was, one element or the delicate collaboration of all, Cain really didn't need to know. If Kimberly had been snatched into a dimension so cosmically close and yet impossibly far, this is where he would find her.

"Come back, darling. Come back home."

He wanted her now. This very moment, now. He wanted to turn and see her standing in the doorway, with smiling eyes and arms stretched out to him. He wanted to smell her soft perfume and feel her breath on his neck. He wanted her long hair to tickle his skin as he buried his face in it. He wanted to feel her hands slide up his back in their embrace.

Cain understood why Currie had not waited a year to beseech his daughter to come back to him, understood it perfectly now. There was no waiting through this kind of pain. Ask a wave to wait before crashing to the sand. Ask a lightening bolt to pause before cracking from a cloud. There is no waiting. The laws of the universe were at work here — the very laws of physics that control all things in heaven and earth. Theodore Currie had reached into the stars and with science and will, tore free the lost beloved who had been snatched from him. Cain wanted his shot. The pink room had been turned blue. And with it, wrong would be turned right.

Thirteen

He awoke back on the first floor, lying flat in the sleeping bag and absolutely certain he had heard a noise. It wasn't fear that thumped through his heart this time; it was anticipation.

Cain could not explain why he chose to return to the bottom floor. It seemed natural to sleep in his own bed, in a room that looked and smelled like his own. Yet, some nagging, preternatural voice told him it was wrong. It wasn't the right way.

He sat up in the dark and listened. The wind was kicking up outside and tree branches battered each other like bones. There was a far away wailing of a night animal and something metallic clanging closer by.

Inside the house it was quiet and still. Yet, Cain felt something new — some intangible change that was neither seen nor heard. He'd had that feeling before and not so long ago. He shimmied out of the sleeping bag and hastily pulled on a pair of shorts. He thought about grabbing the baseball bat, dismissed the idea, picked up the flashlight.

He climbed the staircase quickly and then took more care winding his way up to the turret room. Blood pounded in his ears like the vacant, breezy sound from a seashell. He ignored it and tiptoed down the hall toward the closed door.

Be there. Please be there.

He twisted the knob and pressed open the door. It swung inward and thumped against the bureau. The vase atop it trembled against the wood and then was silent. Cain could smell the flowers. He switched on the light.

Nothing. The blue room was sleepy, unchanged and empty.

He looked around a moment, switched off the light and started to back out. He paused, thought for a moment, switched the light back on and stepped into the room. The closet door was fully closed. There was no reason to believe anyone was inside there. Cain stepped toward it anyway, his heart racing now, hands slicked with sweat. A cold uncertainty wormed into his thoughts.

What does it mean if she is in there? Why should it matter?

He shook the thought away. He took a breath and reached for the knob. He pulled the closet door open with hope and trepidation. He peered into the dark square, with hanging skirts and waiting shoes.

Nothing.

Fourteen

As far as Bucky Letroy knew, he was the only agent working in New York City who still did most of his wheeling and dealing on a rotary phone. It was a big black thing that sat on a corner of his desk, half buried in stray papers, magazines and calendars. The phone had an honest to God ring that startled rather than annoyed a person. It had weight, too. You could kill a person with a phone like this.

Sometimes, he paced around the room with the base dangling from his fingers, the phone pressed to an ear. When things got really heated, he'd stray too far and the phone cord would reach its limit. Bucky would come to a jolting stop like a dog on its leash, and the cord would snap from the wall, ending the conversation. It was usually for the best.

Bucky also liked twirling the cord in his fingers as he sat at his desk and that was what he was doing today. It was bright in the large, cluttered office because there were no blinds on the windows. It smelled like street exhaust because the windows were open. Bucky had his shoes off. He always took his shoes off when a conversation leaned toward long. Sometimes, he forgot about them and went marching into the hall in his stockings.

"You're okay, Gene. Try to trim 30,000 words and we'll go from there. You've just got to...I know 30,000 is a lot of copy. Didn't it feel like a lot when you wrote it? Jesus Christ, we agreed you'd...No, no. Jesus, don't scrap it. For chrissakes. You've got a month to...Gene. Gene! Will you listen to me?"

Goddamn candy ass writer. Gene Stackhouse was a mildly talented author of five teen novels filled with the usual teen angst. Tame stuff, but he'd found an audience. Suddenly, a year ago, he'd decided he wanted to write science fiction thrillers and the result was chaos. Bucky had to hold his hand through the first half of the novel and during the second, Stackhouse disappeared into his work at blinding warp speed. Now the strange tale of an aging poet caught in a wormhole with his cat had swelled to 160,000 words, and Stackhouse was in a panic.

Bucky, who was convinced the writer was a burgeoning pedophile, wanted a 125,000 word novel, and less if he could get it.

"Look," he said, rubbing his feet together under the desk and twirling the phone cord in his fingers, "start cutting. It won't be that painful, I promise. Once you get going, 30,000 words will disappear like...No, Gene. I'm not driving down there. You don't need...Gene, no. For chrissakes, get a goddamn grip."

Stackhouse started screeching. Bucky got up to pace and the phone cord came snapping out of the wall.

As usual, it was for the best.

He plugged the cord back into the wall but kept the phone off the hook. He walked to a corner of the office where a fish tank sat on a scarred bookshelf. There was one fish in the tank and it swam back and forth menacingly, like a pint-sized shark. The tank had once been filled with bright, colorful specimens but they had died one-by-one over three deadly days of apparent plague. Nothing killed the gourami. It had been left for days without food, subjected to intense heat in the summer, deadly cold in the winter. Bucky had a deep admiration for the gourami. He began dropping flakes of food onto the surface of greenish water.

He was restless. When deals fell into place, and the writers he represented made their deadlines, the calmness and silence of his world was unnerving. A troublesome Stackhouse here or there was not enough to fill his days and right now, his days needed filling.

Sometimes, he made the grave mistake of examining his life, and the uncertainty of it pained him. Maybe this freewheeling, bachelor lifestyle was losing its appeal. Maybe he was running the bars out of loneliness these days more than hedonism.

Bucky had no real friends, beyond the clients that tended to think of him alternately as a pain in the ass and a savior. He had no real family, either. His younger sister married some genius in software design a few years ago and now she was off in California learning to be a snob and working on her own drinking problem. His older brother was on a God kick down in Memphis. Jesus Christ. Tommy smoked more pot and dropped more ecstasy than any rock star and now he was praising God for every fucking thing. Weird ass family, the whole lot of them.

Restless, yes. And troubled. The drunken wrecks, the suicides and the outright loonies he met in this land of literature made him wonder about his own grip on things. He was drinking too much. He was clinically depressed and he knew it. His dad had been clinically depressed, and it really showed when he got naked and jumped off the Brooklyn Bridge that fine summer so long ago.

It would be wonderful to have a buddy to call on at times like these. Maybe duck into a dark bar, get loose and talk about the problem. But Bucky didn't have buddies like that. The people he drank with, ate lunch with, talked about women with, were sharks in the same cove. It was all about what he could do for them, what they could do for him, or who would screw whom the quickest.

Goddamn depressing, is what it was. New York was depressing. New York was all business while the rest of the world was on vacation. Well, screw it. Bucky Letroy had been known to take a vacation from time to time. Maybe it was time to slither away from the city for a while.

He clapped his hands together twice to acknowledge the decision and walked back to the desk. He picked up the phone and started to dial. He paused. Smiled. Put the phone back on the cradle.

Fifteen

The morning of June 17th came with chilling cold. It felt cold enough to snow. Completely perplexed by the drastic change in weather, Cain stood in his T-shirt and shorts for a solid minute wondering if he'd slept right through summer. There was dew on the long grass. There was frost on the steps and you could still see shoe prints leading up to the porch.

Cain blinked several times. He rubbed his face and shook his head. Coffee was brewing inside. It was just a few hours after sunrise. He was not an early riser. Sleep was tough to shake off any time of the day, but on early mornings like this, it seemed to follow him around like a cloud until noon.

Why are there shoe prints on the steps?

Shivering, he bent for a closer look. The fading impressions of a man's shoes looked ghostly in the frost. There was one print on each step and then several across the porch. The prints circled back from the door and disappeared at the bottom of the steps.

Someone had crept up to the door, and not so long ago. It was a strangely chilling feeling. He glanced toward the edge of the woods where the gravel driveway disappeared into the trees. Birds were clamoring there but there was nothing to be seen.

He stepped back inside where the smell of coffee floated into the living room. By the time he returned to the porch with a mug in hand, the frost was off the morning and the footprints were gone.

The problem was, he was too damn eager. His imagination nagged him like a small child tugging at his sleeve. Let's go now! Why wait! Let's go, let's go, let's go!

Cain sat at the windowsill, pen in hand but writing nothing. He had filled five notebook pages and by his count, that was good enough for morning work. Now he sat looking out and wondering what it would be like.

She'll be sitting Indian style on the bed, wearing gray boxer shorts and that burgundy half-shirt. The dorky frog will be tucked faithfully under one arm. Her hair will be up in a pony tail and she'll be gazing around the room with growing glee. Her eyes will be wide and happy and her mouth will be half open in wonder and joy. She recognizes the room around her and remembers: the vase by the door, the painted fan from Thailand, the deep blue drapes. She will recognize the room as her own and she has missed it so, so much. She will wonder what is keeping the husband that goes with it and then she will see him walk through the door. With a squeal, she'll bounce from the bed. Bare feet will barely touch the floor as she glides to him, arms open, face glowing with happiness. She'll slam into him, still in the air, and wrap those arms around his neck. He'll savor every bit of her pressed against him. He'll lift her up and smell her. Oh, the smell of her...

The thing to do was to wait a bit longer. But the thought of it. The idea that Kimberly might await just a few dozen steps above him was a powerful one. It was anticipation at its zenith.

He closed the notebook, tossed the pen on top of it, and left it on the windowsill. He stood from the wooden chair, forced himself to stretch and walked to the staircase. La la la. Just going upstairs. No reason to hurry at all.

Halfway up, he started to trot. By the time he was on the second floor, he was rounding the corner toward the next stairwell as though his ass were on fire and there was a bucket of water just ahead. He bounded up the winding stairs and reached the upper floor. He stood staring at the closed door. Such a mysterious door. Such a powerful door that opened on a truth that was supposed to be hidden from man. But Cain had found it through another man's genius and through his own unwillingness to turn love over to the monumental unfairness of this world or any other. This door and what lay beyond it was his.

She'll be sitting Indian style on the bed...

He twisted the knob. He pushed the door open.

Angel Currie squatted on the bed, corduroys around her ankles. Cain heard the coarse sound of liquid pouring onto fabric beneath her. A dark circle spread across the quilt beneath the dingy girl as piss soaked into the bed.

He stepped into the room, teeth jammed together, hands squeezed into fists.

"You bitch. You little, fucking bitch!"

Angel's lips curled into a sneer and she laughed the mocking laugh of a cruel schoolgirl taunting a weaker classmate. Cain rushed to her, lifted her off the bed by one cold, bony arm and still she laughed. Urine continued to stream from her, spraying the side of the bed and splashing across the floor. Angel cackled as he pulled her away.

"Get away from her! Get your hands off her!"

An angry, jagged voice from behind him. Cain wheeled. Theodore Currie was standing in the doorway, disheveled and pale. A row of red, fresh wounds wound up the arm he held in front of him, pointing at Cain.

"Let her go, you bastard."

Cain started to say something. Then hot pain bit into the hand that squeezed the arm of Angel Currie. He yelped and turned toward her. Angel's face was fastened to his arm, teeth gnawing at the skin just below his thumb. He pressed his hand against her face and tried to force her away. Her face felt hot and damp, like the belly of a bat. She resisted him, continued to bite. The pain was exquisite.

Cain was aware of a hand on his shoulder and he jumped, yanking his hand away from the torment of Angel's mouth. Incisors tore through the skin along his thumb before pulling free. Now Cain spun again to find Theodore closer behind him, reaching and grabbing.

In fright and loathing, he screamed and shoved Currie back toward the door.

"The hell off me!"

Theodore went easily, stumbling back and colliding with the bureau next to the door. The bureau slammed against the wall. The vase toppled, bounced and fell crashing to the floor. The explosion was loud and flowers flew. Cain watched them skid across the floor in a spray of water. Then Angel was clawing at his back and he screamed again. He wheeled once more, grabbed her arm, flung her toward her father. She slid almost gracefully into his arms.

Cain stood panting, hands up in the posture of a boxer.

"Get away from me!" he screamed at them. "Both of you!"

Theodore had righted himself and he clutched his daughter against his waist with both arms. Angel still beamed like a child with a table full of presents. She playfully nipped her father's forearm and he jerked away.

Theodore's dull, milky eyes never left Cain's. "This is our place. You stole it from us."

Cain was breathing hard. "No," he said. "You shouldn't be here anymore. I need this room now."

"But you can't have it."

"I will have it. Just two more days, Currie. For chrissakes, stay out of my way."

Theodore was backing toward the door now, pulling his daughter with him. The girl continued to smile and titter and bite at her father's arm. Corduroys hung around her hips, dark with urine.

"You have no idea what you've done," Theodore said, backing into the hall now. "You will become insane with the consequences of what you have done."

Cain watched them carefully. He stepped toward the door, ready to slam it closed behind them. "Just stay out of my way. Okay? Just...please. Go away."

He closed the door. He stood against it, breathing hard. He waited for their departing footsteps, but heard none. He waited another minute and then opened the door. The white, tear-stained teddy bear lay on the hallway floor, its head gone.

Part III
Solstice

One

Few people in Maine cared much about the scientific properties of the summer solstice. As the date approached, there was not much discussion in bars or bait stores about the solstice shifts through the Gregorian calendar due to the insertion of leap years. Fists did not fly over lively discussions about whether or not the planet is heated most efficiently when the northern hemisphere receives direct sunlight.

For most, it would be another day in June and an opportunity to give thanks for surviving another wretched winter. The arrival of summer meant the arrival of tourists and that was both boon and bane. Boon because tourist dollars kept the state fiscally healthy. Bane because tourists were absolute pains in the ass.

By the middle of June, Maine might see temperatures soar to 80 degrees, but few people would voluntarily jump into a lake or stream to celebrate. Maine water never got truly warm. By the first day of summer, it was still frigid enough to hurt.

Mulberry and the regions around it did not know that mid-June 2005 was to be a cosmic anniversary. They did not know that sudden and pronounced strangeness routinely visited their patch of the planet, although few who lived there escaped it entirely.

Primitive men who lived on fault lines only knew that the ground sometimes rumbled beneath them. They knew nothing about tectonic plates or extensional ridges, so the occasional quakes were a matter of course to be dealt with and not dwelt upon much.

In Mulberry, an unlikely convergence of geographical and cosmic forces were at work again, and the strangeness began in the early afternoon June 18.

Kenneth McAbe, a renowned architect who had retired here five years ago, set down the book he was reading and stood in the quiet study. His back cracked as he stretched. He began to peel his clothes off slowly, like a man in a trance. The sweater vest, the crisp yellow shirt, the gray slacks; all of it landed in a heap beside the chair.

Dolores had gone to pick up her sister in St. Agatha. Soon the two squawking sisters would be back at the McAbe household talking nonstop. Dolores was 69, Edna was 74 and both of them were fond of yard sales, knitting and Jesus. Kenneth decided that today, he would give them something entirely new to squawk about.

He made himself comfortable on the kitchen table, near the door through which his wife and her sister would enter. He was naked except for black socks over white, bony ankles. He waited in the silent house, trying to imagine how they would react. The thought excited him and he began to get an erection, the first in many years.

Shirley Kinney, who owned a row of camps on Long Lake, sent her two sons out to play and then went into their bedroom to collect their pets. She snatched two hamsters from one cage and put them in a box. She was bitten several times before winning a battle with a gerbil in a cage of its own. Into the box it went. Shirley walked to the kitchen, tossed each of the rodents into the microwave, and watched them twitch and jump until, one by one, they exploded.

Randy Todd, a welder who lived closer to Olive Hill, went from room to room in his rambling farmhouse, searching for his mother. She had been dead 12 years, but Randy was sure he heard her calling to him from nearby. She needed her medicine. The pain was becoming bad again. Randy, who sat with his mother for six months as she died of stomach cancer, knew that the screaming would commence soon if he didn't find her. And he was right. After an hour, she began to shriek in agony and Randy began busting down walls, shouting: "Momma? Momma?" as he searched.

Paul Dutil fell off the wagon and got drunk for the first time in eight years. When the gin was gone, he smashed the bottle and then began to carve smiley faces into his skin with a shard of broken glass.

Fred Descoteaux sat alone at the cluttered kitchen table, his head down, and wept onto his arms. He wept for an hour and sometimes pounded the table with his fist. Descoteaux sobbed aloud for the son who died in a highway crash on I-95 near Newport. The agony. The rage. Only Descoteaux never had a son. He had no children at all.

Strangeness that no one would talk about later. Tempers were short. Happy people became depressed. Faithful wives cheated on husbands and law abiding men committed horrible, inexplicable crimes against their neighbors.

Nobody was out in a pontoon boat June 18 talking about the rare alignment of the planets and the effect it had on the delicate balance of gravity. No one at Jacob's Smoke Shop stood among the magazine racks talking about hidden dimensions and things that seep in and out of them. Not one word was said about ley lines.

But Carlton Whipple had to flee the funeral home because the dead had begun to whisper from the mortuary. They were talking about him, he was sure of it. They were conspiring.

Martha Braintree was planting azaleas on her husband's burial plot when she heard him speak from below the ground.

"Dammit, Martha," Louis Braintree snapped. "I never liked flowers while I was alive. Why in hell would I want them sitting on me now? Stupid old woman."

Martha fled the cemetery and heard other corpses laughing at her from their graves.

On the other edge of town, Ben Rathbun was going out of his mind. His companions had made good on their plans to leave and he was alone. There was no one to talk to. He sure as hell wasn't going to mingle with the locals. The locals were out to get him.

Early that morning, just before dawn, he had done something remarkable. He had completely disregarded orders by driving to the Currie house. Even now, he didn't entirely understand why he'd done it. He felt like he was becoming somebody else, driven to new levels of independence by the hardships that had been thrust upon him.

He had parked halfway up the long, gravel driveway and walked the last 500 feet to the clearing. For many minutes, he only crouched there at the edge of the woods, staring at this house of misery and mystery. It was intoxicating to look at it, a sensation children must feel when they creep up to a spook house on a dare.

Heart pounding, years of rigid discipline screaming in his head that this was wrong and that he must turn back now, he had walked the extra 60 feet to the front door. It was exhilarating. It was liberating. He quietly climbed the front steps and moved toward the door.

Rathbun — this new Rathbun — had no doubt: were that prick novelist to open the door at that moment, he would have shot the writer in the heart.

But that didn't happen. Rathbun had crept away as quietly and as unnoticed as he'd come. From a strategic standpoint, the trip had accomplished nothing. From a personal one, Rathbun felt as though he'd grown six inches. The new Rathbun was bigger and bolder.

But that was then. Now, he sat alone in the Quonset hut and listened to a dog growling from somewhere close by. Three times he had crept outside, gun drawn, ready to blast a hole in the mangy mutt that had found its way here. Three times he had found nothing. He had gone back inside for good and started drinking.

Rathbun felt strange. Emotions he had become adept at suppressing were suddenly roiling in him like a gastric episode of the psyche. He thought about his father, the nuclear physicist, and finding new reasons to hate the bastard. If he were anywhere near Arlington, Rathbun might go dig the son-of-a-bitch up and shit on his dead face.

He thought about his mother, too, that worthless whore. Where was the bitch while young Ben Rathbun was withering in his father's shadow? Drinking like a starlet and screwing every man in the neighborhood, that's where. And a few of Rathbun's classmates, too, he was sure of it.

The dog growled. Closer this time. The beast was right outside now, by the sound of it. Friggin' mutt. Getting braver all the time.

Rathbun got out of his chair, slightly unsteady from the vodka. He crept toward the garage door, pulling the .45 from its holster as he went. Here, doggy doggy. That's a good boy. Let's see how brave you are with a slug between your eyes, Cujo.

He fingered the box on the wall next to the door, pressed a button and got into an offensive position, gun raised. The door jerked upward and Rathbun tried to peer under it. Here, doggy doggy. Here, dog...

The dog lumbered from the side of the hut as the garage door continued to rise. It was a ghastly thing to look at. A hole had been punched into its left side and purple organs bulged out, roasting in the sun. The dog growled, displaying long canines under its curled lip. Its eyes oozed a creamy, yellowish substance and mucous dripped from the nostrils.

"Jesus..."

It was a black Labrador with a red bandana around its neck. It began to shuffle into the garage, pulling itself forward with the front legs, the hind legs crippled and dragging across the concrete. The dog growled and bared its teeth, uninhibited by the disability.

"You...fucking dog. You were dead in the ditch."

Rathbun, backing further into the hut, realized he was talking to a dog and a dead one at that. He took aim and fired. The blast was deafening inside the steel building. The bullet grazed the top of the dog's head and tore away fur, leaving a grayish streak of brain like a Mohawk.

Still, the dog crept closer. Rathbun could smell it now, and it smelled like death. Terrified at the implication, he took aim again and fired ten shots in rapid succession. The dog spun on the concrete floor. It bounced this way and that. One of its legs was blasted in half and the animal fell face first to the floor. A rich mixture of fluids spread around its body in a widening pool. Sickened, deaf from the gun blasts, Rathbun screamed and ran past the mangled dog and out the door. He sprinted across the gravel driveway to the trees on the other side. He bent and vomited vodka and bile into the grass. He vomited for ten minutes and then crept warily back to the hut. He stepped inside and braced himself for the horrible sight of the mangled, dead beast.

But like the joke about the dyslexic atheist, there was no dog.

Two

It was just before 2 a.m., June 19, when Kimberly came back. There was no blinding flash of light. There was no electrical buzz. Kimberly returned to her husband by calling out from the dark.

"Jonathan?"

Asleep outside the turret room door, Cain twitched in his sleep. He stopped breathing. His body tensed.

"Jonathan? Are you here?"

Dreams to the dreamer feel marvelously real. Few have not had the experience of waking from a sound sleep, convinced that the world of the dream was the reality. But a voice in a dream has only to travel across microscopic portions of the brain. The voice does not carry. There is no real world clarity and sharpness to the acoustics.

"Jonathan? Where are you?"

It took the sleeping mind of Jonathan Cain half a minute to make that distinction. The echo of the soft sound. A certain lilt of the voice as wonder turned to panic. The invasion of physical sound on the fuzzy silence of his sleep.

Kimberly.

His eyes snapped open. He sat up so quickly, he would feel pain in his lower back hours later. He threw his arms out so forcefully, the sleeping bag zipper tore open with a long protest of metal and fabric.

"Jonathan?"

Cain tore his way out of the sleeping bag, stumbled in the dark hallway, lunged for the door. His shoulder struck a wall and he groped frantically to orient himself. His fingers brushed across the doorknob and then lost it. He whipped his hand back and forth until knuckles struck the glass knob. He twisted it and threw himself into the room, cool air rushing out.

And she was there, aglow in the light of a candle that flickered from the nightstand. Kimberly sat up on the bed like a woman who has risen from a dream. A red, silk gown flowed around her body, brilliant with waves of reflected candlelight. Dark hair fell around her shoulders, gleaming. Her eyes were full of low fear and confusion, but the look softened when her husband came into the room. The small mouth quivered toward a smile, bewildered and reluctant at first, relieved and satisfied at last.

She was beautiful. Cain rushed to the bed and fell upon it. Kimberly bounced beside him and he took her in his arms, wrapping one about her waist, another around her neck. For Cain, the moment was a rush of tidal emotions that could easily rip him apart. It was like nothing he had anticipated, even in the most torrid of his daydreams. The mind of man was not designed to experience the rapture of reclaiming a love who has been lost to the grave. What Cain felt was an alien emotion that stimulated an unused portion of the brain. Every sense was heightened. He could hear her breathing over the crackling of the candle flame. He could smell her faint, sweet aroma. He studied each individual hair as he buried his face in it. His fingers dwelt on each curve, each rise or hollow of her body as his hands slid over her. He tasted salt on her cool skin as he kissed her neck, her cheek, her lips. He felt her hand slide up to the side of his face, feeling him, verifying his existence. He heard her sigh in his ear. He drew back to look at her, could bear it no longer, resumed kissing and feeling her.

"Jonathan..."

Her voice was a melody. It tickled him. It was like a narcotic moving languidly through his body. He did not want to say a word. He wanted to sit here feeling her, listening to her, breathing her in.

"Jonathan..."

She pulled away slightly. Cain, feeling as an unborn child must in the height of comfort in the warm womb, gave in reluctantly to the inches between them. He smiled at her, unable to speak. Kimberly smiled too, though the expression of disorientation lingered.

"How did I get here? Where have I been?"

He took her face in his hands. "You're here. That's what matters. For now, can't that be all that matters?"

She kissed his thumb, but the look of growing wonder did not depart. "But this isn't our room. Jon, where are we?"

Bliss fragmented by earthly matters. He was happy his wife was comprehensive enough to wonder. He was relieved that she was intact and sane after the long journey, though he never really doubted.

He stroked her bare shoulders.

"You've been away, Kim. For a long time. I'll explain it all to you, but not right now, okay?"

In the soft light, Kimberly nodded and smiled. She looked around the room, appraising. She stared into the dancing candle flame.

"There should be 65 more candles. Only I can't remember why."

He hugged her and lowered her to the bed, like a tackle in slow motion. Her head fell back upon the pillows and a sea of hair spread out around her. One thin, red strap fell over her shoulder and the silky gown dropped appreciably. She looked down at it and smiled. Cain folded in around her and they became impossibly entwined.

He lay awake listening to her breathe into morning. Faint, gray light was gathering outside and still he remained awake, stroking her shoulders and smelling her hair.

She lay with her back against him under the covers, which he had washed at a laundromat, adding baking soda to wash away the vile traces of Angel Currie's piss. Their hips were joined like puzzle pieces and Cain would not have moved if the house was on fire.

The sun was up in the sky before he drifted to sleep, body buzzing with happiness and exhaustion. He fell into a light doze that was pocked with short, bizarre dreams and then he slept. The candle burned out and the sun rose higher, slanting into the room and warming it. There was no discernable sign that the earth was tilting steadily toward the sun or that the longest day of the year was imminent. There was no hint at all of the solstice. Except, of course, for the woman lying next to Cain on the queen size bed. The beautiful, mesmerizing woman who had been loaded into a coffin and buried under soil nearly a year ago.

She was gone when he awoke. Cain jerked out of sleep shortly after noon and for several moments, battled with the idea that Kimberly's return had been a dream. He had snapped, at last. Anguish and imagination had come together and whisked him off into the land of delusion. And were it so, Cain would have welcomed it.

But the pillows still smelled of her. Strands of long, dark hair were coiled in the sheets. Kimberly was with him again.

He dressed quickly and trotted downstairs. She was not in any of the rooms on the second floor. Cain moved through them one by one, calling to her softly.

She was not on the first floor, either. She was not on the porch and she was nowhere to be found outside. Troubled now, he searched the house all over again and called her name a little louder. He stood panting in the kitchen, frantic and out of ideas. Inspiration struck. He ran to the cellar door and pulled it open.

A sour smell wafted up and he ran down into it. He moved quickly through the cellar, calling her name. He walked a circle around the chimney as if they were playing hide and seek. She was not here. She was nowhere.

Rushing back to the staircase, Cain spotted more bones poking from beneath them. He heard the high buzz of flies from back there and became aware completely of the fresh stench of decay.

Another snack for the Curries?

A grisly thought but there was no time to pursue it. He ran upstairs and slammed the door behind him. He trotted to the living room and up the staircase. And up and up.

He returned to the turret room. The closet door was slightly ajar. Had it been that way when he awoke? He couldn't remember. He stepped to it. Reached for the knob. Opened it.

Clothes and shoes and nothing more.

He closed the door and looked about the room. The candle jar was blackened from a long burn, the matchbook near it. Feeling foolish, he got down on his knees and looked under the bed. Not even a dust bunny to greet him.

From behind him, she spoke: "Did you lose something, Jonathan?"

Cain spun, still on all fours, and she was standing in the doorway, still wearing the red gown, her hair wild with sleep. She leaned against the doorframe, watching him. Cain stood and walked to her, pulling her close and kissing her.

"Where were you?"

She looked up at him. "I don't know. It's the strangest thing. I don't know where I've been. And I feel..."

He grabbed her shoulders. "What? What do you feel?"

"I feel like not all of me is here. I know that sounds crazy."

He kissed her on the bridge of her nose. Suddenly, the day was rich with possibilities. Would he bring her into town and show her the wilderness splendor of northern Maine? Would they stay inside and talk for hours? Or would they flee this place forever and chart the dubious future of forever avoiding the horrified curiosity of people who could never know she was back?

"Who are the others, Jonathan?"

Cain drew back, startled. She looked at him with such tepid curiosity, he wondered if he had misheard her.

"Who..."

"The man and the little girl. I've seen them wandering. And a little boy all by himself. They don't seem to notice me. Who are they?"

He turned away from her and walked to the bed. There was something he wanted to give her, but now was not the time. She had questions and why should he be surprised by that?

He avoided the subject as long as he could. He straightened the pillows on the bed. He walked to the window and opened it wide. He stared out into the woods that were so powerfully green, it looked like a painting.

"The man and girl are people who used to live here," he said. "It's hard to explain who they are beyond that. Can I just tell you..."

Cain had turned to face her, but she was gone. The doorway was empty. He rushed into the hall where he was greeted by silence. More troubled than before, he dashed downstairs and began the search once more.

Three

Rathbun was outraged. He was somewhat drunk too, but the outrage needed no fuel.

"What do you mean, he's not available? Jesus Christ, he's in charge of this operation!"

"I'm sorry, Mr. Rathbun. All I know is what I've been told."

"And what," Rathbun seethed, "have you been told."

"That you are to remain where you are and observe. If nothing is to be learned, you may receive orders to clear out. Until that word is forthcoming, you are to stay put. That's word-for-word, Mr. Rathbun."

He was standing at a phone booth in St. Agatha, outside a store where kayaks could be rented all day or by the hour. Next to the store was a wide stream that connected two lakes. A man and woman, each in their own kayak, struggled ten feet from shore trying to master the complexities of rowing with a two-sided oar. Rathbun hoped they'd fall in and drown.

"Billy, this is fucking ridiculous and you know it."

Rathbun typically liked to irritate William Goddard, a punctilious gay man and Brazel's personal assistant, by calling him Billy. Today, though, he was hoping to appeal to the young man's generosity. He needed a contact number. Anything. He was alone here and somewhat frightened. He was frightened by what was happening to his mind, and frightened that he was falling further and further outside the inner circle. Jesus, if they'd only let him bust his way into the Currie house, he might find something that made sense. He would have that knowledge before anybody and might restore his long gone reputation as a credible scientist.

"I'm sorry," Billy said. "I don't even know where he's gone. Something stirring with the anti-gravity people at Princeton, is all I know."

"Great. Jesus, that's just great."

There was a pause and Rathbun feared Billy might have hung up. But then he spoke, low like a conspirator, although Billy knew as well as anybody that all conversations at Langley were recorded.

"I can tell you this. The whole Currie thing sort of lost its drama the moment Franklin learned Olivia had died. The intensity was gone. It fizzled, Mr. Rathbun."

He stood clutching the phone very tight, no longer wondering if the kayak couple would spill into the stream and float away. Billy Goddard would say no more, but he had said enough.

It was Olivia they'd wanted all along. Son-of-a-bitch. It wasn't about science at all. If they were interested in Theodore Currie's work, it was only a peripheral curiosity. No, Brazel was interested in Olivia and hoped the strange house in Mulberry might draw her out. Because Olivia's husband had known more of the government's dirty little secrets than anyone alive. And his widow might know enough about it to bring down senators. Or maybe a president. Or a president in the making.

"Goddamn," Rathbun said to the phone booth. "Goddamn it all."

Four

Two nights before the solstice, Cain made love to his wife for the first time since she had fallen to cancer. It was sweet and slow. It was intense and sustained. In his throes, he had lowered his neck to her throat and picked up the tiny apple in his mouth. He played it across the tongue as he thrust into her. She gasped and squeezed him tighter. She moaned and then took the apple into her own mouth when he lowered his face to offer it. He had presented the apple necklace to her earlier, when he found her here once more in the turret room. She remembered nothing about its significance. For now, the tiny apple was just a trinket, shared during a sexual embrace.

He barely heard the creak of hinges as the bedroom door swung open. A flicker of movement caught the edge of his peripheral and his eyes were drawn to the doorway.

Theodore and Angel Currie stood watching them. Angel stood in front of her father, clutching her headless teddy bear in one hand and sucking the thumb of her other.

"Go away," Cain whispered.

Kimberly thrashed beneath him. "Oh, Jonathan."

He turned to her and the ecstasy of the moment was restored. The silent pair continued to watch from the doorway, but Cain became unaware of them.

She flickers in and out, that is all. A temporary condition. In time, she will be with me completely. It is all just the progression of her return. She will be with me forever soon and no longer lost.

He told himself this over and over and ultimately, he believed it. It was morning and she was gone again. He sat at the top of the turret stairs, flicking playing cards down the winding stairwell. Bonus points for gliding one around the corner and to the floor below. Later, he would go down and collect all the cards. He would return here for one game of solitaire or another. Cain knew a hundred games of solitaire and he would play them all while he waited. He would wait forever for Kimberly to become a permanent resident in the world where she belonged. They would leave this house and find a place to hide together. A sunny island where nobody knew them and no one would ask questions. All those lost, little memories would come back to her and he would tell her all that had happened. There might be shock. There might be disbelief. In time, she would grasp what he had gone through to get her back. She would come to understand this and their love would only deepen.

There was a brief shuffling from below, like a mouse moving in a wall. Cain leaned forward but could not see around the bend in the staircase. Hopeful, he stood and bounded down the stairs, stepping over playing cards as he went.

"Kim? Kimberly?"

Silence. There was nobody at the bottom of the stairs. But three of the cards had made it down to the second floor, a heaping helping of bonus points added to the final score. Cain bent to pick them up. He paused, frowning. One of them had been ripped in half. It was the queen of hearts.

Five

Bucky Letroy had a half dozen compact discs he used only on long road trips. The discs were full of music he had burned himself on a home computer. There was classic rock 'n roll from Springsteen, the Beatles, the Doors, the Who, the Dead. There was old stuff, new stuff and more than a little from the 70's. It was all mashed together, with no regard to genre or era.

He never played these discs if there was someone else in the car with him. No way. Uh uh. It just wouldn't do to have some colleague or bar buddy find that Bucky Letroy, a hard-drinking grizzly of a man, was fond of some truly embarrassing shit.

It was his fervent hope that, should he die someday in a horrible crash, the discs would burn up with him.

He had four or five tunes from the Carpenters burned onto the discs. There was some Fifth Dimension in there, a stray Bee Gees song or two, a whole bunch of Cyndi Lauper. When driving, Bucky let the CD player spin his burned music in random order. He might get down to a head slamming AC/DC song followed by a selection from the Partridge Family a few miles down the road.

Many a highway traveler had been spooked at the sight of the big, bearded man with hard, wild eyes, driving 85 mph in the passing lane and singing Ann Murray at full volume.

As he crossed the long bridge over the Piscataqua River from New Hampshire into Maine, a truly sappy song from Journey gave way to something raucous from the Stone Temple Pilots.

Tapping the wheel, he pulled to the side of the highway, late morning traffic buzzing past him. He had examined a Maine map and determined it would take another eight hours from here to drive to Mulberry. Half of that time would be spent on I-95 before he spilled onto Route 1. Bucky guessed Route 1 in northern Maine was probably the kind of stretch where you could get away with driving with a bottle between your legs. Christ, from what he had heard about northern Maine, he could probably stick his ass out the window and fart at moose and state troopers, too.

Six more hours. It would be easiest to stake out a motel room and resume the trip tomorrow, but Bucky decided to go for it. He was excited about being out in the woods. As a boy, his father took him fishing up in New Hampshire and Bucky remembered it as sort of surreal. There were long roads that wound between the mountains and sometimes an hour would pass before they saw any buildings. He'd never been as far north as Maine, but he imagined it as even more remote. In Bucky's mind, he was going to a place like the Congo, without the giant insects and military uprisings.

He hadn't called Cain to tell him about the trip because Cain would have tried to talk him out of it. Besides, Bucky liked to sneak up on people and then subdue them with enthusiasm. He'd run Cain ragged for a day or two. Bucky planned to rent a fishing boat, gawk at some moose, maybe prowl the hick bars for some hotties. The trip had a twofold purpose. It would snap Cain out of his funk (Bucky was still convinced the writer was brooding instead of writing) and it would provide the agent with a refreshing break from too much introspection.

He slapped the shifter back into drive and squealed back onto the highway ahead of an approaching rig. From the stereo speakers, STP had faded out and now Bonnie Tyler was singing about her heartache. Bucky nudged the volume up and sang along with her.

Six

Cain absolutely had to go out. The milk supply had run dry. There was no beer left and the only thing to eat in the house was tuna with no bread. Kimberly had not eaten or expressed the need to and that troubled him. What troubled him more was that she vanished for long stretches and he had no idea where she went. There was no dramatic vapor trail to mark her passing. There was no pop to announce a journey between this dimension and another one. His wife, purloined from the grip of the netherworld, simply went away.

He drove to the IGA where throngs were attacking the beer cooler and the deli like it was a day before disaster. Tourists (Cain could pick out the tourists by now. They were the ones who bought all the goofy souvenirs) were loading up on everything that could conceivably be used to make the camping experience more authentic. They filled carts with bug spray, canvas tarps, rope, strange looking utensils designed specifically for campfires, flashlights, coolers, hatchets and boxes of matches. They bought fishing hooks and bobbers. Chips and chocolates for the kids, booze and smokes for the after-hour gathering around the campfire.

Cain wove through the crowds, picking up only the things he could not do without. He said hello to people who recognized him. He stopped to talk about that poor boy who fell out of the boat.

Cain was preoccupied. Earlier, Kim had appeared at the front door, looking out on the tall grass that gave way to trees. She still wore the red nightgown and it was wrinkled and worn. Her hair was starting to tangle and it no longer gleamed. She did not react with affection when he stepped up behind her and wrapped his arms around her waist.

“Why did you bring me here?” she asked him. “Why do you keep me in a strange place? It’s cold in here. I don’t think I like it much.”

Her voice had a hard edge he remembered from aftermaths of arguments that were never resolved. There were few of those, but Kimberly's irritation always manifested itself in the dry, clipped sentences uttered in an otherwise silent spell that haunted their house like a ghost.

"We don't have to stay here forever," he told her. "Only long enough for you to recover from your trip."

She'd turned on him with hard eyes and a mouth twisted into a scowl.

"Trip? Is that what this has been? Jesus Christ. It's like you yanked me out of a long sleep when I wasn't ready to wake up. That's pretty selfish, Jonathan."

Cain reacted as if he'd been kneed in the groin. Kimberly apologized for the remark, stroked his cheek and went upstairs to look through her closet. She never returned.

Now he was hurrying to load groceries into his car when he was approached by Reggie Lyons. Lyons wore a fishing vest and hat and looked somewhat like a tourist himself.

"How you been, writer man?"

"Doing good, Reggie. Just starving up there because I keep running out of food."

Lyons laughed. "You should get out more, if you don't mind my saying so. Go out and get drunk at the Hearthside. Let me take you out fishing, catch some monster bass."

Cain laughed back. He hadn't caught a fish bigger than a guppy since he was a kid and admitted as much. Lyons launched into a lengthy fish tale about a New Jersey businessman who had gotten so excited about pulling a trout from Cross Lake, he'd suffered a heart attack in Lyons' boat. That segued into a story about a man who'd fallen through the ice one winter and who survived after many minutes beneath the frigid water.

"When the guy came to a week later, he swore pretty mermaids had taken care of him while he was under the ice. Beautiful fish ladies kissed him and sang to him. He still swears it, in fact. Of course, the guy was a bit of a loon before he went under."

Lyons asked about the G-men living in the Quonset hut. Cain lied and said he had not seen them. Then he remembered that he had forgotten to buy bread and the two men walked back into the IGA. Lyons trailed Cain and told him more stories. He stopped a half dozen times to introduce the celebrity resident to men and women who seemed both impressed and suspicious.

Cain was getting antsy. He imagined Kimberly back at home, wandering and calling his name. Becoming afraid.

The lines were longer than before and Cain stood for 15 minutes with his bread, Lyons hailing people over to introduce him. Finally, he paid for his purchase, promised Lyons he'd go drinking with him, and beat a hasty retreat to the parking lot.

Now home, he thought. And wasn't it funny how he had come to think of the Currie house that way? Home and maybe a long talk with Kimberly. It was time she knew the truth. With knowledge, maybe they could combat the sudden disappearances, the memory lapses and the strange temper flares.

Cain would accept his wife in any form in which she came. Ultimately, he wanted her the way she was before vileness had invaded her brain and killed her. He wanted his wife back. For good this time.

The black Mercedes was parked near the front of the house. Tinted windows threw dazzling stars of light under the late day sun. Crickets jumped around the car as if worshipping it.

For ten seconds, Cain sat in the Explorer, doing nothing. The vision of the strange car was like a mirage. Surely there was no unexpected visitor here. That could mean calamity. That could mean...

He jumped out of the truck thinking about Rathbun and his two spooks. But the Mercedes wasn't a government car. The Mercedes looked vaguely familiar.

He left the groceries in the car and rushed into the house. In the sparse living room, Bucky Letroy was leaning against the windowsill, flipping through the notebook. He was a giant of a man, with rumpled clothes and a beard that could have used a trim two weeks ago. He looked up and smiled when Cain walked in. He set the notebook down, crossed his arms.

"Glad to see me?"

"What the hell are you doing here?"

Bucky was unfazed. He chuckled. "Hey. Nice to see you, too."

Cain collected himself and ushered his agent outside. He grabbed the groceries from the Explorer and set them on the porch. He reached into the bag and pulled out two bottles of beer. He handed one to Bucky and gave no sign of going back inside.

"Really, Buck. What the fuck?"

Bucky twisted off the bottle cap and downed half the beer in one swallow. He sighed contentedly as though he had not polished off a six pack on the drive up. He wiped a bare, meaty arm across his lips.

"Really, Jon. Other than the beer, you're a terrible host."

Cain leaned against the Mercedes. "Why are you here?"

The sun was hovering over the tops of trees behind them. The woods were quiet. Every sip of beer, every step in the gravel driveway seemed loud.

"I wanted to take a trip. Get outta New York for a while," Bucky said. "Stackhouse is having a conniption over his mid-life crisis novel and bugging the shit out of me. Everyone else is off cashing their checks and so I had some time to kill."

Cain gazed at him. "Why here? Why didn't you call?"

Bucky waved his arms in the air and sat down on the stairs. He grunted and panted as he sat, cradling the beer bottle like something fragile.

"It's not a big deal, Jonathan. I won't cramp your style. I wanted to spend some time in the woods and maybe get a tour of the legendary Currie house."

"It's a short tour," Cain said perhaps too quickly. "There's not much to see."

Bucky squinted up at him, one eye closed against the sun.

"Yeah, well. I already took a tour and there's plenty to see. In fact, I think we oughta talk about a few things."

Cain thought: shit.

Seven

Bucky resumed his place at the window while Cain paced through the living room. Sunlight was fading outside and the sky was a darkening blue. Night birds had begun their twilight cacophony and warmth fell from the air. The diminishing light inside the Currie house cast a spectral glow, the feeble illumination making everything seem dim and haunted. There was a quality of unreality about it. A cool breeze floated through open windows, fragrant with smells of the woods.

"You've gotta leave, Buck. It's not what you think, but you've gotta leave."

Bucky was on his fourth beer of the visit. He was calm and studious. He watched Cain the way an interrogator watches the unwinding of a criminal suspect in a small, square room. Cain didn't like it. He continued to pace. He snuck glances at the staircase and Bucky caught it every time. He followed Cain's glances briefly and then resumed his clinical gaze.

"It's not what I'm thinking? Why are you so defensive, Jon?"

"I'm not defensive, goddamn it. You snuck up on me and pretty much invaded my privacy. Now, we're close, Buck. But this is bordering on..."

Bucky held a hand up to stop him, beer dangling between two fingers. He shook his head slowly.

"I'm not here to dick with your privacy or to snoop. Why should I care what you do up here, as long as you get me 400 pages of fresh copy? But I've been worried about you. I think you're pushing yourself too hard. I think you're getting some...some weird ideas."

Cain stopped in the middle of the living room. He stared at his agent, striving for anger, mustering only wariness and unease. He felt like a man caught wearing women's clothes or a teen discovered whacking off in a locker room.

"Weird ideas. What weird ideas are we talking about?"

Bucky studied him, leaning against the sill and filling the window. He tapped the beer bottle with a sausage sized finger. He sighed.

"I've seen the room at the top of the stairs, Jonathan. Looks a lot like your old bedroom back at home."

Cain flung his arms in the air, incredulous. Beer splashed from his bottle and onto the floor. He turned his face to the ceiling as if running out of patience with the line of reasoning.

"God help me," he said. "I decided to get rid of all the fluffy, pink toys and make the bedroom more comfortable. And familiar. Really, Buck. You're letting your imagination get the best of you."

Unflappable. Always unflappable was Bucky Letroy. He pointed the neck of the beer bottle at the floor near Cain's feet.

"You get the room all dressed up cozy and then spend your nights in a sleeping bag?"

Cain turned his eyes to the floor as if seeing the sleeping bag and pillow for the first time. He seldom rolled it up or moved it out of the way. It was really the only splash of familiarity down here. Now, it looked like a down-filled tube of evidence stretched across the floor.

"You're full of shit, Bucky. Seriously. You're my fucking agent, for chrissakes. You know what I'm like. I get spooked up there on the top floor once in a while, okay? Is that really a goddamn testament to my state of mind?"

"Not by itself, no. But the bedroom isn't the strangest thing I came across. There's also the matter of a little girl's overalls on the staircase. And some beat up pants and a shirt in a room on the second floor. A little girl's clothes here, a man's clothes there. Hmmm. In the Currie house. I wonder who they belong to."

Cain's mouth opened and then snapped shut. An icy hand stroked his spine as though he'd been goosed. His mind was working through the implications of what Bucky had said. His mind was reeling with it.

Bucky was not finished.

"There is a very nice nightgown hanging from the knob in the second floor bathroom, too. Pretty and red. The kind a grown woman would wear just before settling into a hot bath. There's also a teddy bear kicking around and the thing has no head. I also found a..."

But Cain had started for the stairs. Bucky jumped in behind him and reached for his shoulder. Cain wheeled and shoved the hand away. His face had gone white. His eyes were wild. He turned and ran up the stairs.

Eight

On the night of June 20th, there was not one person in Mulberry stewing over the complexities of string theory. The concept was not on their minds as the planet moved through space to deliver its promise of summer.

A total of six people in the tiny town had read about the strange theory and two were actively interested in it. But those people were barbecuing or catching fireflies with their children the night before the solstice. And anyway, nothing they had read or heard made any impact on their already complicated lives. What was there to ponder?

One of the two men mildly interested in string theory was a veterinarian named Claude St. Croix, who kept his monthly subscription to Discover magazine faithfully up to date. Claude was vaguely interested in the concept, but he was more absorbed by stories about the myriad creatures that live in Madagascar.

On the night of June 20th, Claude was suffering with visiting in-laws who insisted on playing cards deep into the night, and who asked him almost hourly why he never became a *real* doctor. Tonight, Claude was tolerating the visit with great difficulty. Twice he had excused himself from the card table to step into another room and stare out at the lake. He felt strange. He felt he was being challenged somehow and he didn't like it. His daddy used to challenge him, too, by taking away a cherished toy for every grade point under a hundred Claude brought home from school. Claude always wanted to take away something daddy loved every time the old bastard beat his mother.

Tonight, on the third trip away from the card table, he was increasingly agitated. The in-laws seemed to be torturing him with a steady stream of questions designed to make him appear inferior before his wife. Only, those questions were cleverly disguised as idle chatter about the weather, about the Bush administration, about the situation in the Mideast.

"What's the matter with you tonight?" his wife asked him as he excused himself from the table. "Don't you feel well?"

Claude said he felt just fine and then sneaked into the first floor bedroom, which the in-laws had invaded for this two week trip. He found his mother-in-law's purse and scrounged in there until he found the heart medication and the asthma inhaler. She was an insufferable old woman with steel gray hair and eyes to match. She would grab your arm every time she addressed you and not let go until you were completely unnerved.

Evelyn also smelled like cinnamon and Claude had grown to hate the smell. It was faint and sly and somehow part of the woman's psychological arsenal. Claude was beginning to understand that he hated the old broad.

He grinned as he cupped her medicine and stole out of the room like a mischievous child. He quietly stepped out the back door, walked to the lake, and hurled the medicine bottle like a right fielder firing to the plate. He waited for the gentle plip it made when it hit the water and smiled.

The inhaler sailed even farther out over the lake before descending and landing in the water with a slightly louder splash. Ripples of light on the water became frenzied where the items had submerged. It was as though the lake was as excited about this uncharacteristic sin as he was.

Claude giggled into his hands, imagining Evelyn Mulready's frantic, wheezing gasps when she went searching for the inhaler later in the evening. He buried a chortle on the back of his arm as he fantasized about the soaring blood pressure as she emptied her purse in search of the pills. Then he went back inside and his pinochle game improved immensely.

Claude knew, but didn't care, that string theory had evolved into M-theory, which posits that all those tiny, vibrating strings connect to make one giant membrane. He knew, but didn't care, that this development meant that all things in the vastness of the cosmos were intricately intertwined, and that all things are influenced by all others.

Still, Claude had never carried this concept to a higher level. He was 48 years old and would live another 25 years. Yet in all his days, the veterinarian with the troublesome in-laws would not once wonder if tiny changes in the gravitational dynamics of the universe could have an impact on the wee little orb on which he lived. He would never interrupt a card game to say something so abstract and profound as: "You know? It occurs to me that if the universe is a membrane, then all the planets, all the rocks and dust in the solar system must tug at each other once in a while like unruly children. And that's got to cause changes in the magnetic fields right here on earth, particularly around ley lines. It must wreak absolute havoc with higher dimensions now and then, wouldn't you say? Pass the corn chips, please."

Claude would spend his days more fascinated with the creatures of the world and more concerned with the depletion of untold species due to man's abuses of the environment. After time, he wouldn't remember throwing an old woman's medication into the lake. And if he did remember, he would not recall that it was just hours before the summer solstice or that he had been feeling very strange.

At the Hearthside, two fistfights broke out and one of them was over a lobster bib. Reggie Lyons broke up both fights and accidentally broke a man's pinky finger in the process. Later in the night, he picked up a wealthy widow with a bad set of false teeth but a body that would make a younger woman envious. He took her home, nailed her in his bed and later found himself wide awake and battling an inexplicable desire to kill the woman and dress her in his dead wife's clothes.

Bobby Erenfried, meanwhile, was horrified to discover, all at once, that he was gay. He was 41 years old and had always loved women. But here he was, sitting at home alone and fantasizing about a teacher he had not seen since junior high. So acute were these fantasies that he imagined the tall, lean teacher with the lovely blond locks was standing outside and calling for Erenfried to come out into the night. Bobby would have been concerned about this, but he knew damn well that Mr. Brown had died of the rare necrotizing fasciitis many years ago.

A woman named Samantha LaBlond headed south to Bangor because she wanted to see how many brutish men she could screw for money in one night. A 34-year-old single mother, she dressed in the only slinky gown she owned, sprayed on perfume, and drove toward the big city. She was guessing she could bag a dozen men tonight and take home six hundred bucks or so. She would screw them silly in dingy motels or the back of cars. She would take it any way they wanted to give it.

Samantha was almost feverish with the idea right until she shot through the other side of St. Agatha on Route 11. All at once, the idea disgusted her. Had she really left Kelli and Ray Ray at home without a babysitter? Was she really thinking of betraying her dead husband for the first time in two years?

Samantha was horrified. She looked at her reflection in the rearview mirror and saw a city slut staring back. She squealed in revulsion and clapped a hand to her mouth. The dark eyeliner. The bright red lipstick. The way her neckline plunged into her cleavage. She looked like a diseased whore.

The blast from the tractor trailer horn exploded into the night. It startled her and she turned away from the rearview just in time to see the big, round lights bearing down on her. They looked like giant eyes reproaching her. Samantha screamed and tried to steer around the truck, but it wasn't even close. Before the collision that would kill her instantly, Samantha thought: "Oh, you dirty little tramp. You dirty, dirty little..."

And then she was dead.

Nine

Cain was beside himself. There was no sign of Kimberly on the second floor. There was nothing but gathering gloom in the turret room. And clothes were scattered throughout the house just as Bucky had told him. Panic burned in his belly. Something had happened here. It was as though the inhabitants of the house had been plucked right out of their clothes, like peas popped out of their pods.

"Jesus," he said, falling onto the bed with the silky gown clutched in his hands. "Jesus Christ."

Bucky was in the doorway a moment later, red and winded. He'd been chasing Cain around the house and doing a poor job of keeping up. Now he was bent over in the doorway with his hands on his knees. He took deep breaths and wiped sweat from his brow. Then he straightened and took a step into the room, pointing at Cain.

"You," he said. "You've got to get a grip. Do you see what's happening to you? Do you see how deep into it you are?"

Cain lifted his head. He looked up at the winded man with cold eyes.

"No, Bucky. Why don't you tell me. Impress me with your knowledge of the life of Jonathan Cain. Please. I'm dying to hear it."

Bucky stood where he was, looking around the room. He walked to the closet and opened it. He winced and shut the door. He ran a finger over the blue fan on the wall and it made a rippling sound. He turned to Cain with a soft look.

"I've seen it before, you know. About 20 years ago. Guy named Ramsey. Lost his whole family in a plane crash and went slowly and completely nuts. You remember Ramsey? He wrote the series about the carnival workers."

Cain said nothing. There were too many emotions swirling for him to muster a rational thought. He was exhausted. He was afraid. He was confused, frustrated and aching with self-doubt.

"Ramsey dropped out of sight for a while," Bucky went on. "Wouldn't talk to anyone, wouldn't go out. I wasn't representing him, but I knew the guy who was. Everyone was afraid he'd off himself up in his high-rise apartment. Then one day, he showed up unexpectedly with a 550 page cooker. His best work ever, I swear to God. A final installment in the carnival series. Brilliant stuff. It was fat, but not a wasted word. Swear to God.

"Anyway, Ramsey looked like a school teacher, all neat and studious. Kind of a nerd, I guess. Only, when he started coming around again, that had changed. He looked younger. More stylish. The glasses were gone, he'd gotten a good haircut, and he was dressed sort of casual, like a guy who'd fit in at the trendy clubs. A total transformation. He didn't look like a man who'd just lost his wife and two kids in a plane that crashed into a mountain.

"Everyone who knew him was happy as hell. He'd come around. We figured he'd worked through his shit and that writing was part of that process. He was over the bad stuff, you know?

"Then Gabe, the guy's agent, dropped in on him one day. Knocked on his door and the door opened right up on its own. He could hear Ramsey in there yelling at someone, not argument yelling, but a kind of authoritative voice you use with kids. Then he heard what sounded like a woman joining the argument. A family squabble, you know? I'm sure you see where this is headed."

Cain said nothing. He fondled the red gown and waited to hear footsteps. Or a voice calling his name. He would tear right by this loquacious agent of his and join his bride wherever the hell she popped up this time.

"Anyway, this Ramsey guy was in the bedroom, wearing a dress and high heels. He had makeup on and earrings...the whole works. Guess he made a fucking ugly woman. But the fact is, he was carrying on a multi-part conversation. He was himself. He was his wife. He was the kids who wouldn't behave. And the creepy part —

as if that ain't creepy enough — is that the whole place looked like the family still interacted there. Toys were scattered all over the place. One bathroom was a mess with kid stuff, the other with all the shit women keep around. There were four settings at the dinner table. I guess that's what the argument was about, the kids were late getting ready for dinner. And Mr. and Mrs. Ramsey were giving them what for in the bedroom. It scared the hell out of Gabe. He said this guy made Norman Bates look only mildly troubled."

Cain rolled the gown into a ball, was troubled by the gesture, straightened it out again on his lap.

"So, you think I'm up here parading around in Kimberly's clothes, is that it?"

"No. No, Jonathan, I don't. But I think the circumstances of this...this place are just too damn significant for you right now. Currie was up here trying to raise the dead through his voodoo science. You're up here missing Kimberly. It's not a big leap, man. You're a believer. You have that imagination."

"My bailiwick."

Bucky nodded. "Yeah. And you wonder. You wonder what happened to Currie up here. You wonder if there was anything to his notions of strings and dimensions. You take out his clothes and imagine him there in that study downstairs. You sit and think about how he weeps for his daughter while scribbling out the formulas in a notebook. You find the girl's clothes and you carry them around for a while. Trying to get a feel for the two of them, I don't know. You start mumbling to yourself. Your imagination runs wild and you start acting out scenes between the two of them. Maybe you try on Currie's clothes to see if they'll..."

Cain jumped off the bed. His feet landed hard on the floor and it rattled the walls. Bucky flinched but didn't move. Cain was livid and pacing next to the bed.

"Holy shit. You really think I've gone over the edge, don't you? You think I'm taking on the personalities of these dead people and...what? Squeezing into Angel Currie's little overalls and sucking my thumb?"

"No. No, man. I think you wore Currie's clothes around just for kicks, maybe."

"For kicks! You think I put on a dead man's dirty pants and shirt for kicks? I'll tell you what, Buck. I barely get my own clothes on day after day. I don't have much use for someone else's."

Bucky was quiet a moment, deliberating. Cain sensed he had something to say and was working his way up to it. It was unlike the agent to suppress a thought, no matter how desultory the train of his logic.

"What, Bucky? You got something to say, say it."

Bucky sighed. "You remember that pen you used to carry around? The one marked Mammoth Pens? Only you managed to scratch an "I" in there so that it said 'Mammoth Penis?' You thought that was the funniest thing in the world. Like a fifth grader."

"I still think that's damn funny. What's your point?"

Bucky reached into the pocket of his jeans. He pulled out a pen and held it out to Cain.

"Look what I found in the pocket of that shirt you say you never wore. What do you think the odds are that Theodore Currie also had a mammoth penis?"

Cain took the pen. He looked at the funny words on the side. It was his. He didn't recall the last time he'd seen it, but it was his. He clicked the button at the top and the tip poked out on the other end.

"It's mine. I don't know how it got in Currie's shirt."

"And you don't know how Currie's shirt got on the floor. And you don't know why Kimberly's nighty was hanging on the knob. And you don't know why the little girl's overalls are laying around. And you have Kimberly's clothes hanging in the closet, Jonathan. Not your own, but hers."

Cain dropped back onto the bed. He held his arms in the air as if in surrender. The gown hung from one hand like a flag.

"Alright! Alright, Bucky. Okay. You win. I'm a friggin' lunatic acting out the scenes of a scientific tragedy up here in northern Maine. I get to dress up pretty. I get to be a bunch of different people. I always wanted to work in the thee-ATE-er, you know. I mean, fuck."

Bucky took a step toward the bed. He reached out and squeezed Cain's shoulder, like a baseball manager consoling a tired pitcher.

"I didn't come up here to browbeat you. I don't think you're a lunatic. But something strange is going on with you and staying up here by yourself isn't helping. You know?"

Cain laughed without humor. He rubbed his eyes and shook his head. He wondered if his wife was hiding nearby and maybe listening to the conversation. Kimberly knew Bucky and had been fond of him. But would she slink into the room to say hello? Or would she hide in a dark place and wait for him to be gone?

Cain got to his feet once more.

"I need you to leave, Buck. Not right away, because I know you won't go without a fight. I'm going to tell you a story and you can believe it or not. After that, I need you to take off, either way. I have things to do. Is it a deal?"

Bucky cocked his head and looked at him. He was suspicious but intrigued. "You'll tell me the truth? All of it?"

"All of it," Cain said, and pulled at the sleeve of his T-shirt. "I'll start by showing you a couple of my cool, new wounds."

Downstairs, with the supply of beer and a few bottles Bucky hauled from his car, it was story time. Cain sat in the wooden chair, Bucky on the third step of the staircase. The wind was picking up outside and it added a fine backdrop to the tale being told inside the Currie house. Occasionally, animals screamed from the woods and tree limbs cracked and groaned. Neither man heard.

Cain started with his visit to Olivia Currie's mansion in Marblehead. He described the old quadriplegic until Bucky steered him back to the point. Cain admitted he had learned more from Olivia than he had revealed before. He admitted he was intrigued for reasons that did not altogether pertain to a book about the scientist.

"The mother believed him. And that was spooky. She's a smart old woman, and not a superstitious bone in her body. She's the one that gave me the name of Theodore's colleague."

"The one you spent a week with."

"Right."

He told the agent about his first night in the house. He told him about thrashing around on the second floor like a frightened ten-year-old and his run in with the monster telescope and the flapping blanket creature. He recreated the scene of his first visit to the pink room. Cain told the story like a writer. Bucky was rapt, but impatient, and Cain sensed it. He went for fresh beers. They drank in silence for thirty seconds, each mulling the story in his own way. Then Bucky clapped his hands together and indicated intermission was over.

Cain sighed. "So, one night, I'm sleeping down here, and something wakes me up. I don't know what it is right away, but then I hear music. Fur Elise. From upstairs."

It took nearly two hours to tell the entire story. Alternately, Cain was lost in the telling of the tale and then reawakened to the idea that he had not seen his wife in nearly 12 hours. At one point, he excused himself to pop his head into the turret room. He checked the rooms on the second floor for good measure. Not a creature was stirring. Cain returned to the stairway and continued the story like some form of penance.

Bucky did not interrupt often. When Cain described the numerous appearances of the little girl, and finally of Theodore Currie, the agent listened attentively in silence. He only asked Cain to back up when he described certain points. The apple necklace, for instance.

"Where's the necklace now, Jonathan?"

"I'm getting to that. Jesus, will you let me tell the story?"

Cain drifted away while recounting the night Kimberly had appeared in the turret room. It was as though he were telling a romantic tale to a grandchild, years after the event. It was the night Grammy and Grampa met for the second time, kids, a little less than a year after Grammy died.

He tried to describe the feeling of seeing her again and found he could not do it adequately. His eyes glistened with tears and he didn't realize it. Cain spent a long time recounting his first moments with Kimberly and Bucky did not interrupt. He explained his fears the first time his wife disappeared and his utter joy at seeing her again soon after.

"She just vanishes and reappears. Like that. No sound, no clues as to where she's gone. It's horrible, Buck."

Bucky said nothing.

When the story was over, there was an appropriate silence. Cain returned to the turret room and again found it empty. Apprehension growing, he returned to the first floor to find Bucky putting on his sneakers. Cain felt a surge of relief. The agent was keeping his part of the bargain. He had heard the story and now he was making tracks, for better or for worse.

But then the big man said, "Come on. Let's take a ride."

Cain was gathering up beer bottles and carrying them to the kitchen. He stopped, confused.

"Where the hell are we going? It's midnight and we've both had ten beers."

"You had eight, I had twelve. Come on. Get your shoes on."

Cain delivered the bottles to the kitchen and dropped them in the sink. He returned to the living room with growing alarm.

"Seriously, Buck. What the hell are you thinking?"

Bucky shrugged on his coat. He pointed to Cain's bicep.

"See that ugly little wound you got there?"

Cain looked, confused. The wound was starting to heal, but it still looked raw. It was circular, like the bite of a very small shark.

"Yeah, I see it. Felt it, too. What's your point?"

"And the other one on your wrist?"

That wound was fresher. It was red and the skin was still raised around it. Still, Cain didn't think there was any sign of infection. He was confounded by the agent's train of logic and his sundial pace of getting to the point.

Instead of explaining, Bucky did something bizarre. He lowered his head to his arm so that his face was pressed against his bicep. Then he pulled his arm away, bent his elbow, and moved the arm back toward his face so that now the wrist was pressed against his mouth.

"If I wanted to bite myself," Bucky said, "these are the two points on my body where it would be easiest. Try it, Jonathan. You'll see what I mean."

Cain was at first confused. Then he was furious. If he'd still had the bottles, he would have hurled them at his agent.

"You prick. Now you think I chomped myself because I'm so out of my mind, I need to invent a little girl to punish me?"

Bucky was calm. "Jonathan, bear with me. I'm trying to use syllogistic reasoning here. I can't just eat a story about string theory resurrection in one bite. You know? A few things just seem too easy."

"Easy? Bullshit. What's easy?"

"Well, like this secret agent guy you say has haunted you since you got here."

"Rathbun," Cain said. "Ben Rathbun."

"Rathbun. Right. A man with father issues and an inferiority complex. Probably has trouble with women and can't hold his liquor."

Cain blanched. He held up a finger to make a point, forgot what the point was.

"You're losing me, Buck."

Bucky walked across the room instead of answering. He plucked the notebook from the windowsill and waved it at Cain. Then he held it in both hands, flipped to a random page, and began to read.

"Ben Rathbun smote the kids who taunted and rejected him in school by out-achieving them. He obliterated them with his brilliance. It was the same, maladjusted scheme that propelled him through college. Only there, the social awkwardness he had suffered his entire life began to inflict him with more pernicious psychic injuries..."

Cain slapped his forehead. It was a perfect "doh!" moment. He felt betrayed by his own work. He felt caught naked with a whore while trying to convince a weeping spouse he was not unfaithful.

"Fiction. It's fiction, Bucky. I started jotting down a profile of the guy for kicks and went a little nuts with it. I'll change the name if I ever use it, of course. But Rathbun is not a figment of my imagination."

"A profile. And pretty much the way you described the guy to me. Nice and neat. Like bite marks where the mouth has easy access."

Cain stammered. He finally gave up trying to answer and grabbed his shoes from a corner of the room. He flew past Bucky, headed toward the door.

"Okay, shit for brains. Let's take a friggin' ride then."

Bucky was blown away by the consummate solitude of the woods. There were points on the drive where he could not see artificial light no matter where he looked. The trees pressed close on both sides so that it felt like they were not upon a civilized road at all. He felt overpowered by nature and he loved it. He was surrounded by woods and the creatures he could hear moving around in there. The sky looked like a giant screen with superimposed stars. So many stars. Bucky thought back and could not remember ever seeing so much of the galaxy. It was breathtaking. It made him feel small and his petty problems even smaller. He was exhilarated.

Ten minutes into the drive, he insisted Cain pull the Explorer to the side of the road and shut the headlights off. The darkness that fell in was consummate. Smothering darkness. And the sounds were incredible. Far off, they heard something howl long and mournful. It was a Hollywood howl, Bucky thought. He pictured a sleek coyote with back arched, nose pointed high into the night, screaming into the sky full of stars. It gave him chills. It delighted him. Bucky was sold on the Maine woods.

It took a little more than 15 minutes before they turned onto the barely-there tote road that led to the Quonset hut. They bounced along the dirt road with branches slapping against the Explorer. It was like a funhouse ride. Bucky didn't care that he spilled half his beer.

The corrugated hut was dark. There were no cars in the lot. The place felt as abandoned as it looked. Cain was already muttering as he got out of the truck, emboldened by alcohol and by his desire to prove his sanity.

There was no proof to be found. There were a few tire tracks in the gravel lot, but they could have been days or weeks old. Bucky was not impressed by them. He bent to try the garage-style door and almost fell backwards when it came up.

"Jesus! What are you doing?" Cain hissed from nearby.

The door rolled up on its tracks with a clamor, like an army tank rolling across rough terrain. The sound roared across the silence. Headlight beams from the truck sliced through the darkness and into the hut.

It was empty. Mostly empty, anyway. A square desk sat at the center of the room like a forgotten relic. There were lockers on one wall and a few empty liquor bottles against another. There was no computer or stacks of paper. There were no cots and blankets. The hut looked like a storage point that had not been used for a season or more.

"I'm not seeing any government types," Bucky said.

"Fuck you. This is goddamn bizarre."

Ten

No whistles blew and no church bells rang to mark the official arrival of summer in northern Maine. At 2:46 a.m., the town was asleep. Campfires left untended were reduced to heaps of orange embers that burned out like the dying eyes of jack-o-lanterns. Boats tethered to docks bobbed in the water as though they were dreaming, like dogs chasing butterflies in sleep.

The town was asleep, but it wasn't still. Loons called out over the lakes and coyotes screamed from the darkness. Domestic dogs howled from backyards and frogs groaned from wet places. In Mulberry, people were accustomed to the orchestra of the night. Most were sleeping deeply by the time it reached a crescendo. They had been in bed for hours. Night came early in a town where the best fishing was over by 8 a.m.

In the hours after midnight, the oddities of the solstice affected mostly dreams. Men, women and children slept poorly. They thrashed in their beds and some sobbed. A few climbed from their beds and walked like zombies to open doors or windows as if for guests. One man stepped inside a closet, locked the door, and curled up to sleep among a heap of unlaundered clothes.

The dark was the domain of woodland animals, and they were not immune to weird forces of nature they were hardwired by evolution to detect. For a half mile stretch running parallel to Route 11, not far from Olive Hill, night creatures dropped dead by the dozens. Birds suddenly dipped in their flights and crashed into trees. Raccoons fell from branches and lay convulsing on the ground. A quarter mile from the Currie house, a 200 pound buck sniffing lazily at a sumac bush brought its head up suddenly, turned as if to bolt, and then toppled. For 15 minutes, the deer thrashed in last year's pine needles, froth spewing from its snout until finally it lay still, the victim of a heart attack.

Birds and squirrels would be found dead along roads from Mulberry to the far side of St. Agatha. Other creatures crawled away to die and would be scavenged by other animals or found by hunters in the fall. A dog or two would be found dead at the end of leashes after a night of howling in back yards. Victims of fear, most of them. They died of fright at the sight of things that did not normally inhabit their world.

For Cain, dreaming was not a problem. Not right away, anyway. He lay awake in the dark, troubled.

What if Bucky is right? What if I've lost my mind and all of it is delusion, both the good and the bad? No dirty, biting horror named Angel. No sad, repentant father named Theodore. And of course, no beautiful, resurrected wife. Maybe it's not the returned dead who flicker in and out of the world here. Maybe the flickering is the fading light of my sanity, the vestiges of rational thought, flickering the way a dying flashlight will if you tap it with your palm a few times...

Because truly mad people don't realize when they've slipped over the line into lunacy. Cain believed all he had experienced in the Currie house, but of course, that's what madmen do. They breed the delusion, nurture it, and above all, they believe. They believe and no amount of outside logic can sway them. To madmen, sane people are crazy.

Cain did not believe he was crazy. He believed the dead walked in the Currie house and he was very much in love with one of them. But Bucky's inexorable train of logic had rattled him some. The bite marks, inflicted in areas of his body so easily accessible to his own mouth. The supremely inconvenient disappearance of Rathbun and his muscle-bound friends. The words he had written in his notebook, the pen found in Theodore Currie's pocket, the utter silence of the house since Bucky's arrival.

Cain lay awake, convinced he was sane, vaguely worried he was not. It wasn't much of an inner debate, really. By his estimations, he was 99.5 percent sure of his mental soundness. But that remaining .5 sure was a bitch.

The very idea that he was thinking about it was fraught with trouble, but also some measure of relief. If he was sane, then all he had to do now was find Kimberly again and find a way to keep her. If he was crazy, at least she was there somewhere in the spinning world of his dementia. Ultimately, the objective remained the same.

But I'm not crazy, he thought. *I believe in string theory and ley lines. I believe in the strength of the solstice and in the grace of gravity. I believe in multiple dimensions and in things enticed from them. My father's house has many rooms.*

The science was soothing. Cain was starting to feel the soft lightness of sleep. His head sank deeper into the pillow and his muscles relaxed. *I believe in string theory and ley lines. I believe in the strength of the solstice...*

As those reassuring thoughts moved through his head, his lips began to move slightly, like a child's reciting the Lord's Prayer. And like a prayer, it comforted him so he went through it again, and one more time after that. And finally, with the strange mantra upon his lips, Cain fell into the funnel of sleep and at last the disputation over his sanity was through.

Hard drinkers tended to fall sooner than most in Mulberry, lulled by the sleepy embrace of the woods. Among them was Bucky Letroy, who slept on a mattress in the back room on the second floor of the Currie house. The mattress smelled musty and the entire room had a stale aroma about it. Bucky grumbled as he pulled the sleeping bag over his shoulders. He lamented the absence of late television and then fell asleep in less than ten seconds.

There were no crazy half dreams in the midway point between sleep and consciousness. Alcohol that propped him up throughout the day tended to knock him down handily at night. Bucky first started to hiss through his nose and then the snoring began. It rumbled like a tractor, growing impossibly louder with each new exhalation. Then, when it seemed the violence of his snores would knock doors off their hinges, Bucky would gurgle, stop breathing and then snap awake. He would smack his lips together and roll over onto his stomach. There would be a period of silence, a thrashing in the blankets, and then the freight train would start to roll again.

Just before 2 a.m., Bucky sucked in a breath that sounded like a chainsaw ripping through hardwood. The back of his tongue dipped into his throat and clogged it. He tried to suck in more air and the sound it made was like a pig snorting. He tried a few more times to breathe and found he could not. He lay on his back, choking on his tongue, face turned to the ceiling. Finally, he blew out a gust of trapped breath and his airway was clear. He awoke clearing his throat as if he'd swallowed a handful of thumbtacks. He spun on the mattress and twisted the sleeping bag around a giant, white leg. Hopelessly snarled, he sat up and ripped the sleeping bag away, tossing it to the floor beside him. He tried to peer around in the darkness to see if he'd brought a bottle up here with him. Carefully, he probed around the edge of the mattress in search of some Jack or some Jim. Mostly naked, arms flailing in the dark, Bucky looked like a rhino rooting in the mud.

He stopped at once and became still. He cocked an ear toward the door. There was a sound out there in the darkness, a soft sound from far away. It was like singing from somewhere below. Bucky was intrigued but unmotivated. Had he found a bottle nearby, he might have dismissed the noise altogether and slugged down some liquid sleep instead.

He lumbered to his feet and found his jeans at the end of the mattress. Stumbling and grunting, he pulled on the pants and wove his arms through shirt sleeves. His steps were heavy on the floor as he went for the door. The walls shook around him.

Bucky stepped into the hall, arms out to probe the darkness. He stopped halfway to the stairs to listen. Singing. No. Humming, soft and low. A pretty tune. He worked his way to the stairs, an unpleasant image in his head.

I'll find Jonathan down there, dressed in his wife's pretty gown and humming as he strokes the headless teddy bear. He'll look at me with an effeminate flutter of eyelashes and speak in the high voice of a woman. Hello, Bucky Letroy. What's a nice boy like you doing in a place like this?

Jesus.

Bucky stopped at the top of the staircase and stared down into blackness. There was nothing to be seen from here. He started down, moving slowly, thinking about how he would deal with his favorite author in the grip of true madness.

At the bottom of the stairs, he felt around for a lamp. He pulled the chain but no light was forthcoming. Great.

"Jonathan?"

Silence.

"Buddy, are you there?"

Silence. And then humming from across the room, near the front door. Bucky stepped in that direction, eyes adjusting to the dark. He followed the singing and tried to place the tune. Something classical. Something catchy. It conjured images of fantasy castles in make-believe kingdoms.

"Hello? Somebody there?"

He walked to the foyer and felt cool air brush his chest through the unbuttoned shirt. He squinted into the darkness and saw that the door was open. The world was black beyond it, but he could see pale grass swaying in the breeze and stars twinkling overhead.

Humming from outside, absent and halting like someone contentedly knitting or working in the kitchen. A gentle sound, almost soothing.

"Jonathan?"

Bucky stepped into the doorway, pulling his shirt closer around him. The humming stopped. Wind swept through the pines like whispering. There was no more singing but the songs of the night. Crickets chattered. Tree limbs groaned.

"Hello?"

He stepped onto the porch and stared out over the yard, where the Mercedes and Explorer looked like crouching beasts in the night. He squinted, trying to gather all the light the world could muster.

There. Where the gravel gave way to long grass, something had moved, a pale spot on the darkness. He focused on that spot and walked down the steps. The darkness was smothering. It seemed to move in on him from all sides, like ocean water. The gravel was cool and rough under his bare feet and he stepped carefully, trying not to lose sight of the spot where he had seen that flicker of movement.

There. Again. A quick jab of white, like the tail of a deer as it turns to run. Only nothing scrambled through the tall grass toward the woods. Bucky inched his way over the driveway, moving closer to that spot. A breeze blew into his open shirt, chilling him. He shivered but kept moving.

"Hello? Stay where you are, little hummingbird."

Closer. Closer. He reached the grass and stepped into it, feeling dampness under his feet. He leaned forward and waded into it, tensed and expecting a flurry of motion as the visitor took off running. But nothing bolted. Nothing sprang at him, either. Sprawled in the long grass, the headless teddy bear lay with arms outstretched, as if wishing for eyes so it could stare at the stars. It was a grisly sight in the darkness. Bucky poked it with one bare toe. The fur felt moist and mushy and he quickly wished he hadn't touched it. No way he was picking the thing up.

He stared out over the grass toward the trees. Nothing moved there but the pines that swayed like hula dancers. Bucky felt a chill. He needed a drink and then sleep. He turned back toward the house.

The child stood a few feet before him. She almost glowed in a white nightdress and Bucky jumped. He caught a scream in his throat and fought to keep it there. He took an instinctive step back and then held his ground. The girl was staring up at him with sad wonder. Her hair was dirty and her face was pale. Her mouth quivered as if in fright. She took a step closer.

"Do you like my singing, mister? Don't you think it's pretty?"

Bucky stood still as the girl approached.

"Who are you? Why are you here, little girl?"

The girl smiled and it was awful; the kind of smile, Bucky thought, that graces the face of a vampire in a late night movie. It never touched her eyes.

"Don't I sing pretty, mister? Don't I sing like an *angel*?"

The wind swept across her and the white gown flapped. Bucky thought she might fly right over his head. He took another step back, his eyes locked on her, hypnotized, repulsed and confused.

"Like an angel. Yes, I sing just like an angel."

Bucky didn't see the tall man moving up the driveway toward him. He didn't see the small, round object the man held high above his head. He took another step backward and tripped over the headless teddy bear. He screamed, felt his feet tangle, and then crashed into the grass, flailing and choking as though he were drowning. The snow globe crashed down on the bone above one eye and a supernova of light filled his head. The little girl stood above him beaming as her father brought the snow globe down over and over toward Bucky's head and face. He shrieked and felt hard glass slam against his teeth, knocking three of them into his throat. He tried to roll away from the blows and there was piercing pain on his upper back. Small teeth sank into his skin and ripped away a jerky-sized strip of flesh. Bucky screamed some more and felt small hands on him. The little girl climbed along his back and now he could feel her breath on his neck, just below the ear. He could hear her humming. It was a soft little tune a person might hum while absorbed in work. Then lancing pain bit into his ear lobe and he felt it rip away. Another blow crashed down on the back of his head and the world washed away in another flash of that dazzling, blinding light.

Eleven

Early on the morning of the solstice, Rathbun woke from a distressing dream. In it, he was completely deaf from the gun blasts fired inside the Quonset hut. The dog was dead, only now it lay on the front steps of the Currie House. Theodore Currie was leaning over the animal, speaking aloud and explaining how he would use string theory and natural anomalies to bring it back. Rathbun stood very close, trying to hear the magic of Currie's words. But the only sound in his head was a high ringing that seemed to leak from his ears like blood. He tapped the sides of his head with his palms. He tried cupping one ear and leaning toward Currie and his sermon of science. Currie's lips were moving and he gestured with his hands, but Rathbun could make out nothing.

"What is he saying, idiot? This is your chance to take the work as your own. Do you hear nothing?"

It was Brazel, standing next to Rathbun dressed like General Patton. He held a riding crop in one hand and repeatedly slapped it against his palm.

"That's it, then. The calculations are gone forever. Give this man to the dogs."

Rathbun turned as if in slow motion. Behind him, a pack of snarling Rottweilers crouched, ready to spring. Each wore a red bandana around its neck.

Rathbun turned back to Currie, but the scientist was walking away with the dead dog in his arms. He was moving across the porch and into the dark house. Rathbun screamed for him to stop. He screamed that this was his last chance. He needed to know the secret. He needed to understand it or he would perish.

He awoke completely disoriented on the motel bed. A sweaty hand was wrapped around the grip of the gun beneath his pillow. He had flung the blankets away and now conditioned air chilled his sweat slicked skin. Rathbun rolled onto his back, resting the .45 on his chest. He glanced from side to side, taking inventory of the small room in the predawn light. He was surprised that Gen. George S. was not standing tall and rigid in a corner, riding crop in hand.

Rathbun felt like a man sliding down the amusement park ride called insanity with his eyes wide open. For two days, he had felt entirely fragmented. Trying to analyze the way he felt, he could come up with nothing better than that. There was Ben Rathbun the scientist, Ben Rathbun the soldier and now this new personification, something alien and unnatural. Rathbun the unstable. Rathbun the befuddled.

He had abandoned the hut soon after the experience with the dog. Had the corpse of the animal remained there in a heap of gore, he might have been all right. It was not the appearance of the beast he had killed that frightened him. It was the way it vanished like a hallucination.

The motel on Ringwold Road, near Frenchville, was quaint and friendly. Rathbun hated quaint and he despised friendly. It was called the Breath of Air Inn or the Open Air Motel. Something ridiculous like that. There were moose antlers on the wall and wood carved boats. Goddamn hicks. They were surrounded by God awful wilderness and yet they had to celebrate it indoors, too.

Brazel didn't know he had moved out of the hut and Rathbun didn't care. Brazel didn't return his calls. Brazel had clearly abandoned the operation, leaving his best man behind and in the dark.

In the development of this new emotional imbalance, Rathbun had made a decision. Left to his own devices, without backup or direction, he would continue this operation in his own way, with a direct approach. The big dogs might be more interested in Olivia Currie, but he was still focused. There was still the unfinished business of the Currie house to attend to. There were answers to be found, knowledge to be gleaned.

Okay, stolen. There was nothing noble about his intentions and he gave up trying to convince himself otherwise. He planned to get out of Bumfuck and real soon. But not before obtaining whatever the house had to offer. One way or another and for himself this time, not for the agency or anyone within it.

He sat on the edge of the bed, rubbing his thin legs and yawning. Maybe this was a good thing, this new Rathbun and his careless disregard of discipline. Maybe this is how shit would finally get done.

Twelve

The turret room was washed in a faint, gray glow when Cain awoke. Not yet dawn, but close. He blinked his eyes quickly, trying to adjust them. Shadows filled the room. And a scent. What was it? Something soft yet acrid, like a sweaty man carrying lilacs. Cain blinked again and turned his head toward the doorway.

Kimberly stood next to the bed looking down on him. Her arms were crossed over her bosom and she was scowling. Hair fell straight and matted over her shoulders. Her faced was lined and tired. Wrinkles curled like insect legs around her eyes and mouth.

"I don't know why you think you can keep doing this to me, Jonathan. I don't know why you have to be such a selfish bastard."

Cain sat up, reaching for her. She batted at his hands with one of her own. She grimaced and bared her teeth. She wheeled and marched toward the door. Cain tried to lunge after her, but fell short, falling halfway out of the bed.

"Kimberly, wait!"

She turned and shot him a look filled with hate. Cain thought she might spit at him. Then she was out the door and she slammed it behind her. The room shook. The sound echoed. Cain kicked off the blankets and went after her.

Hollering, unafraid to wake the dead, Cain moved from room to room in his underwear. He threw open doors and jogged from place to place. The time for patience and calculating had ended. His wife was unraveling before him. Cain knew little about the science that had brought her here. But he had hunches and he always believed in them. He had to get her out of this house. Here, she was becoming contaminated by whatever poison had reduced the others to gibbering ghouls wrapped in the remnants of their earlier lives.

"Kimberly? Honey, come out. I need to talk to you."

He shoved open the door to the back room on the second floor. The sleeping bag was coiled in a heap on the end of the mattress. It looked like something that had been discarded before dying. Cain frowned and moved on.

"Honey, please. We can talk about it. We can talk about anything you want."

He would tie her up if he had to. As unsavory as the idea was, Cain would throw her down and tie her with belts if it were the only way. He had no real grasp on her mental state. The woman who had snapped at him minutes earlier was not the wife he had sought for so long. It was not Kimberly of the 66 candles or Kimberly of the apple orchard. She was becoming deranged.

She is vacant and corrupt, like the final agonies of cancer.

The thought was unbearable. He would not see her go through that again. He would not go through it himself.

"Kimberly?"

He swiftly descended to the first floor. This frantic race through the house was becoming as rehearsed as a morning jog and it pissed him off. No wife in the kitchen, no wife in the hall. No wife in the bathroom, no wife at all.

Jesus. He was becoming a little deranged himself. He felt as though he were under intense physical pressure, like a diver who descends too deeply. His thoughts were huge but skittish, like bold print letters trying to crawl off a page.

A few stray beer bottles on the floor and on the windowsill reminded him of his agent. Where the hell was Bucky? He needed him gone, that was for sure. Kimberly might never reemerge with the strange presence in the house. Cain would be forceful on this point.

"Goddamn it, is anybody here?"

His voice resounded through the house. It sounded like fear masquerading as anger and impatience. Cain was becoming more and more frantic. The pressure on him seemed to build and with it a sense of urgency.

Out of here. Get her out of here and far away. What you're feeling is minute compared with the forces that bear down on the others...

"Kimberly, please come out."

He glanced toward the top of the stairs. Nothing moved. He stood still and listened. Nothing stirred. He kicked the floor with a bare foot and headed toward the front door. The eastern edge of the sky was fish-belly pink as dawn turned to early morning. The cacophony of daylight creatures was beginning, a soft conversation of chirps and whistles from deep within the wilderness. The air was almost completely still and it smelled of damp wood. Cain stepped through the door in time to see a skunk waddle down the steps and clumsily scramble away. Then his eyes were drawn to the heap below him, closer to the door.

Bucky was sprawled face up on the porch and he was a hideous sight. Part of his skull had caved in and grayish brain poked through the fragments. His face had been torn apart so that bone showed through pink ribbons of flesh. Blood and chunks of skin littered the flyaway beard. His shirt was open and it appeared as though something had gnawed off both of his nipples.

Biting a knuckle, backing inside the house, Cain glanced at the big man's hands. Several fingers had been chewed from each of them. Jagged stumps remained so that it looked as though the dead man were trying to communicate in some grisly form of sign language.

Maybe the skunk did that. Nasty critters, skunks.

He backed into the house and away from the door. He felt his stomach lurch and fought against the sensation. He tried to breathe evenly, eyes closed. Cold water. He needed cold water on his face. He turned back into the house, away from the atrocity on the porch.

The solstice. The pressure of the alignment. Bear up against it guy, or it will crush you like the ocean depths.

A boy stood in the living room. He was shirtless and barefoot, clad only in swimming trunks. His skin was very tan for June and his hair was golden blonde. The boy stood in the center of the room looking at the floor. He looked this way and then that. He spun around to face Cain and he looked vaguely familiar. His eyes were the color of denim and there were freckles across the bridge of his nose.

"My cross. I want my cross."

There was no anger in the words, but Cain found them chilling just the same. The voice was strangely adult and seemed to come from far away, as though a clever ventriloquist was playing a parlor trick.

"You took my cross and I want it back."

Cain stood, staring. He was still biting down on a knuckle and he forced himself to stop. He moved his hand away from his face.

"Who are you?"

The boy was scanning the room again, eyes sweeping low as if examining the floor boards. His head moved from side to side as he searched.

"My nana gave it to me. I want it. I need it. I want my cross and I want to go back."

Cain, feeling pressure at his temples, feeling desperate for his wife and sickened over his agent, stepped slowly toward the boy.

"Who are you? How did you get here."

The boy looked up at him. Now his eyes were slitted and his mouth turned down in a frown. The boy was maybe 12 years old but now he looked much older.

"Stop fucking with me, old man. You lifted my cross and I want it, you hear. I mean to get it one way or another."

Cain inched closer and saw that the boy's hands were clenched in fists. But he was backing away and that meant something. Cain didn't know what, but it was significant.

"When did I take your cross, kid? I don't know you."

The kid was backing toward the stairs, but his eyes were full of hate. Cain saw tears welling there. He felt both sympathy and loathing for the boy.

"Was it the boating accident? Are you the kid who died? You can't remember anything about that, can you? None of them do. You can't remember dying because it never really happened. You just went from one place to another and now you're here. You don't know why, do you? You just know that the trip was long. So, so long. It's eternity in between, isn't it? Tell me, kid. Tell me how long it is in there."

The boy was crying now. He had backed away until a bare heel struck the edge of the first stair. It startled him and he jumped. He looked down and then quickly back at Cain, eyes dripping tears but still hot with hate. The boy was trying to stand his ground.

Cain stopped, ten feet away. He felt vile. He felt like a mean child who tears the legs off a spider and then torments the helpless, twitching torso. For all the strangeness that had sucked him back into this world, the kid was just a scared little boy searching for the one thing that had lured him here. A shiny, gold cross he wore around his neck to protect him. A failed icon the boy still believed in. Cain remembered plucking it from his cold, pale skin. He remembered dropping it into his pocket, intending to hand it over later to a parent or a cop. A simple, religious heirloom that probably cost ten bucks at Wal-Mart. But it meant so much to this quivering boy, it was enough to lure him from beyond and back to a world in which he didn't belong. A world that would make him crazy.

The boy was standing at the foot of the stairs, blubbering. His hands were still clenched in fists but it was a hollow show of defiance. The boy was helpless and lost. They all were helpless and lost and Cain understood the unfairness of it. This house was an abomination of physics and cosmology, a cruel trap constructed of lumber, ley lines and cheap enticements. This was science, psychology and human greed mixed together by fluke alignments in far flung places. This was an abhorrent display of violence against the dead, committed by the selfish mind of man. This house was a monstrosity.

"I'm sorry, kid. I'm really sorry."

The house was the very culmination of sin. For all his talk of souls and the ethereal beauty in all of us, the ultimate drive of man was greed. For all his windy talk of God and salvation, man remained selfish and nothing more. The soul, as it turned out, was for the taking. The very moment it was discovered, a man devised a way to capture it. Man always devised a way to capture what he wanted, over time. Theodore Currie, the scientist, described it as energy slipping into another place. But it was only words. With his strings and his alignments and calculations, he had devised a way to lasso a soul and drag it back from the place in which it rested. Nothing less. And Cain had followed. Others would surely be close behind; like the desperate men on the edge of town who waited to pounce on the science and to steal it for their government. No soul would rest with the avaricious hand of man in control of powers he had long thought beyond his grip.

"The laundry basket. In the bathroom off the kitchen. You'll find a denim shirt in there. Your chain will be in the pocket."

He was disgusted, with himself and the rest of his species. Sorrow and longing had brought him here, but selfishness had done the rest of the work. He wanted his wife back. He wanted to hold her again. He wanted to hear her laugh. He missed her. He missed her so awfully, it was like his bones had turned to fire. But in retrieving her, what had he done? What rest would she find in a world she had been destined to leave and was now bound to forever? What bliss had he ripped her from in order to satiate his own unbounded needs? The natural order had been interrupted and that may have cost his guiltless wife her place in eternity.

The boy cast a suspicious glance at Cain and then he was gone. His feet drummed against the wood floor as he bounded toward the kitchen. Cain stood tiredly at the foot of the stairs and watched him go.

"I'm sorry," he called out. "All of you, I'm sorry. I'm really fucking sorry."

Thirteen

Reggie Lyons was not one to battle with insomnia. Reggie Lyons was one to give in completely.

The morning of the solstice, he awoke grumpy and dazed. He had not slept well. He dreamed of his wife and the daughter she had miscarried 25 years ago. The daughter was wrapped in a pink blanket, grotesque and purple. The lump in the blanket was misshapen and oozing, but Cathy clutched her lovingly and cooed like a proud mother. Reggie was horrified. In the dream, he tried to take the blanket away from his wife, but found he had no arms.

He awoke slapping the mattress as though it were on fire. When the dream swirled away and he got a handle on his thoughts, he realized he still had arms. He remained grateful for a good three minutes before gratitude gave way to annoyance.

He'd been sleeping 20 minutes at a time and waking invariably disturbed and frustrated. Finally, at about 4 a.m., he got up. He brewed a pot of coffee and switched on the television. He fried four eggs, over well, and ate them with grape jelly between two slices of toast. He flipped through the paper while finishing his coffee. He rinsed the dishes and left them in the sink. He took a shower, dressed and went out.

As constable, he really wasn't required to do anything when all was quiet. Still, Reggie liked to make his rounds whenever he could. He drove out to Rooster Lane to check on a long row of camps that had not yet opened for the season. The lake was so still, it looked like a mirror. The air was cool with no sun to warm it. He got out and walked from cabin to cabin, checking for broken windows or smashed in doors. He examined locks and looked for signs of trespass. There were none. All was well on Rooster Lane.

He drove off and two miles north, turned up Nomar Court where Ellen Reed lived in a big, old farmhouse at the end of the dirt road.

Ironically, the driveway was paved, and Reggie had never grasped the logic of that.

Reed was 92 years old and mean as a snake to just about everyone. She was cordial to the point of flirty with Reggie though, and he was fond of her. Ellen was mother to the late, great Rover Reed and Reggie frequently felt pangs of guilt that he had walked away from that long-ago wreck and Rover had not.

He drove up the paved driveway, stepped out of the Jeep, and crept to her stairs with a newspaper and a sack of blueberry muffins from his cupboard. Ellen Reed was as old as dirt, but there was nothing wrong with her hearing. If she detected Reggie skulking out here, she'd bust ass with her walker getting outside and then he'd never get away.

Silently, like a burglar in retreat, he sneaked back to his Jeep and drove away.

He drove back to Route 11 to check on his store. There were no cars in the lot and no broken bottles on the pavement. He swung by the Hearthside and saw that there were no drunks passed out in the lot. It was serene just about everywhere. On the first day of summer, most of Mulberry slept in after a troublesome evening of ghosts and dreams.

Reggie was breezing past Olive Hill, on his way to the edge of town near Frenchville, when he spotted the dark sedan ahead of him.

The sun had crept up in the brightening sky and it sat fat and lazy over the trees. Morning clouds were rolling away and the day was warming.

Reggie set his coffee cup in a holder and leaned forward in his seat, trying to get a fix on the car a few hundred feet ahead of him. In the pastoral scenery around Olive Hill, the big sedan looked menacing and ugly.

The car had slowed to a crawl and now Reggie slowed, too. He supposed it could be the gay couple out looking for moose again. He had told them that early morning was the best time. But he still wasn't buying it. It could not be a coincidence that he'd spotted the dark sedan once more near the Currie house.

Reggie stepped on the gas at the same time the car ahead of him cut to the right and disappeared into the trees where the long driveway began.

"Son of a bitch."

He stepped down harder on the gas and almost overshot the driveway when he came to it. He braked and cut the wheel sharply, skidding onto the gravel and almost flipping into the trees. He stomped the gas and the Jeep spun forward again, climbing the hill with branches slapping at the windshield.

The hurry was needless. Around a bend, the sedan had stopped in the middle of the driveway. Reggie braked quickly to keep from slamming into the back of it.

He could not see the driver through the rear window. The narrow lane was smothered by trees on both sides and it was dark. He squinted at the car and decided the driver had killed the engine. This was more and more suspicious all the time.

Reggie stepped from the Jeep and onto gravel. He walked slowly toward the car, keeping his eyes on the driver's side window. There was no movement in there. Surely they heard him coming. Surely there were not two gay men in there enjoying a muscular embrace.

He stopped short of the window (becoming constable had required some training and he remembered the protocol for traffic stops) and wrapped on it with his knuckles. Nothing happened for several seconds. Then the window began to lower with an electronic buzz and Reggie was staring at the side of a man's head.

"Hi there," he said. "I'm Reggie Lyons, town constable. You got business up here?"

The man turned his face toward the officer and Reggie recognized him. It was the spooky fellow who claimed to be part of a geological survey. Lived out in the old tin hut paid for with government money a few miles from here. Didn't come into town much.

The man looked at him and smiled. He looked tired. The eyes were red and puffy and the short hair looked as though it was fresh off a pillow. The man had a thin face and a long nose and looked exactly like someone who might be on a geological survey.

"Officer. Hello. No, I don't have business up here, per se. I'm going to be leaving Mulberry soon and I thought I'd see a little bit of it before I go."

Reggie stepped up and leaned in a little to get a better look. There were no passengers inside the car. There was no coffee in a holder or any maps on the seat.

"You want to see Mulberry, this is the wrong end of town to do it in. Private land up in here, mostly."

The man nodded. "Yes, yes. I see that now."

"I'll help you back on out of here and point you in a better direction, if you'd like."

The man shook his head. "No, I think I'd like to just sit here for a bit, if you don't mind. Listen to the birds. Enjoy the silence."

Reggie was growing impatient. He was coming to the opinion that the man was whacked out on something or just outright loony. He had that look about him, for starters. The eyes were kind of vacant and glassed over. He did not seem to be aware of much around him.

Reggie leaned in closer and rested a big hand on the window frame. "I'm afraid I can't let you do that. You're on private property, as I mentioned. And if you don't mind, I'd kinda like to see some identification before you back your car out of here."

"Sure," the man said, and he sounded sleepy and withdrawn, like a man in a comfortable trance. "Sure. Of course."

Reggie watched as the man fumbled behind him for a wallet. Wouldn't it be something if he had to take in a fed? The Staties would get a kick out of that. They seldom got more than a bar brawler or wife beater out of Mulberry.

The man thrust out his hand. Reggie extended his own to fetch the information. But it wasn't a license or government card the man was offering. It was a silver gun that looked like it had been freshly polished. Reggie was staring into the wide O of the barrel and he knew that he had fucked up.

Police protocol my ass. Moron. You took your eyes off his hands and now look at you. Stupid, hick cop. You'll just have to survive this like you survived everything else, with cunning and finesse and outright toughness. You'll come through this fine and shit, how the boys at the store are gonna laugh...

There was a flash and then a tendril of smoke rolled out of the barrel. The bullet slammed into Reggie's forehead and gouged a hole there the size of a nickel. Blood trickled down over his nose. For a moment he seemed to hang in the air as if on the strings of a puppeteer. Then he fell over with a thud and his body rolled toward the edge of the driveway. It hung there momentarily, a final testament to the tenacity of Reggie Lyons. Then the weight of his belly gave in to gravity and he rolled over a patch of long grass and into a ditch. He came to rest in a narrow stream, face down as if peacefully peering into the water.

In the Crown Victoria, Rathbun watched the big man roll into the ditch and then listened as he made a small splash down below. Mulberry's finest was out of sight and out of mind.

"Fuckin' yokel," Rathbun said.

He slipped the gun back into the holster and stepped out of the car. He peered over the embankment, grinning. Then he turned and began walking up the sloping, twisting driveway to the Currie house.

Fourteen

Strangeness. All over strangeness. Nothing overtly connected to the solstice. Nothing to be discussed with wives or fathers, sisters or brothers. Just the fleeting peculiarities that came upon Mulberry at intervals and then passed like a fever.

Kevin Proctor woke early to cut firewood and then take his girlfriend's dog for a walk. He took a new route this morning. He walked up the short road to Route 11, dragged the beagle half a mile, and then turned onto another short road that sliced toward the lake.

He came to a tall, stately house with a view of the water. He knocked on the door until a woman answered, eyes slitted with sleep, a terrycloth bathrobe pulled around her.

"Kevin?" It was his girlfriend's mother. She was normally a pretty blond with luscious, heaving breasts.

"Ms. Timberlake. Hello. I think there might be something wrong with Kelli's dog."

Ms. Timberlake glanced down at Kevin's feet and began to scream. The beagle named Geek had been cut in half, as if with a chainsaw. All that remained was a lolling head on a short stump of blood-smeared fur. An abbreviated dog with shredded organs hanging from its truncated body.

Sarah Breemer got up before her children and began to boil water in a giant pot. She hummed while waiting for it to bubble and stared out the window. It was going to be a nice day. A good day to take the kids down to the beach, though it was still too cold to swim. Maybe better to take them on a picnic.

On the stove, the water was boiling. Bubbles exploded against the metal pot with a satisfying sound. Humming, Sarah watched the water boil and thought: double, double, toil and trouble. How does the rest of that go?

She rolled up the sleeves of her robe, placed both hands into the pot and slowly lowered them into the boiling water until palms rested on the bottom of the pan. The skin immediately began to blister. Sarah held her hands down while letting her head roll back on her neck. The pain was immeasurable. She opened her mouth and sighed as if in ecstasy.

Luke Macwhinnie woke his twin boys with lashes from a belt. He slapped Roy in one twin bed, Davey in the other. Both boys woke up screaming and the beatings continued for fifteen minutes. When he was through, Luke ordered the 8-year-olds into the shower and sat laughing on the toilet as they jumped and cried from the spray of water on fresh wounds.

Alberta Norris, a former school nurse, put laxatives in a batch of brownies and then left them covered and cooling on a neighbor's front steps.

Willie Coppenstance, a retired pilot, called his brother in Phoenix and announced sadly that their mother had died, though she was alive and healthy and living in Boston.

James Peterson went into the backyard, dug up the remains of a half dozen dead pets, and then left them on the foot of his 6-year-old son's bed. He giggled as he stole out of the room. He roared with laughter in the safety of the hall, imagining little Tony waking up to the stinking, skeletal corpses of Mighty Mike, the hamster, Tom Tom, the coon cat, Rocky, the Collie...

Existing in Mulberry was sometimes strange and painful when the tilt of the planet turned spring to summer. The thrum of energy from beneath the soil was ten times as strong on any given solstice. Today, with the planets gliding dutifully close in their orbits and the moon cycling toward full, it was off the charts.

Two dozen people in the region would suffer nosebleeds. The same number would lose fillings and a few would suffer cataclysmic headaches. For the most part, it was just a collective malaise that would burn itself out like a sparkler on the Fourth of July. No big deal.

Fifteen

Bucky Letroy did not go easily into the trunk of the Mercedes. Long, doughy arms flopped against the car frame. Giant legs dragged in the dirt like anchors. The flesh under his arms was loose and damp and covered with bites. Chewed flesh felt slick like slugs under Cain's fingers. Bucky's head lolled from side to side as if turning away from this grisly operation.

But it was exhausting work more than it was disgusting. After thirty minutes, Cain had half of Bucky's body shoved face first into the trunk. He heaved a shoulder against the big man's hip and more of the corpse slid inside. Panting, Cain hoisted the legs and maneuvered them into the trunk. He had to force the bare feet into a space where a spare tire had been removed.

The remains of the agent barely fit inside the spacious trunk. Bucky's massive bulk caused the lower end of the Mercedes to sink considerably. It was an ugly sight. Cain felt sadness more than anything else as he watched the maw of the car swallowing Bucky whole.

"I'm sorry, Buck. You were a great agent and a great friend."

He brought the trunk lid down and slammed it shut. Panting, soaked with sweat, Cain leaned against the car. The sun was rising higher and the day was growing warm. It would be hot before long. Hot and dry.

He took inventory of the myriad items he had hauled from the trunk before depositing the remains of his agent. More than a dozen booze bottles. A like number of paperback books, all of them battered and filthy. A couple skin magazines. Two rolls of toilet paper. A pizza box with an intact, moldy pie inside. A machete, a long tube for siphoning slime from the bottom of a fish tank, a greasy George Foreman grill, a cowboy hat, a lacy pink bra, a basketball, a ping pong paddle. Bucky's trunk, like his life, had been filled with a colorful array of incongruous playthings. Cain found it sad and charming in an offhand way.

Breathing normally now, he bent and picked up the siphoning tube. He collected an armful of liquor bottles and set them beside the car. He leaned into the Mercedes and searched for a lever that would open the gas lid. He found it next to the driver's seat and pulled it. Behind him, the lid sprang open.

One by one, Cain filled the bottles with gasoline sucked from the tank of Bucky's car. He managed not to swallow any, but he was getting lightheaded anyway. The high reek of gas was overpowering. That on top of this strange, expanding pressure inside his head and Cain was feeling pretty odd indeed. The world seemed to glow with a radiance that was both alien and remotely comforting.

For the first time, he showered in the opulent bathroom on the second floor. He washed in water as hot as he could stand it. He scrubbed from head to toe and then started all over again. He shaved in the shower and then stood for 15 minutes just soaking. He pressed his face against the tile under the shower spray and closed his eyes. He let his mind play a reel of memories for him, starting on the night he came home to find 66 candles burning in his small, squalid apartment and Kimberly waiting radiant and trembling with her news. He recalled in exacting detail the trip to New York to sign his first contract. He remembered each little town across the country on his first book signing tour. Kimberly joined him at every store and easily outmatched his ability to entertain the bored bookstore denizens. She made them laugh with amusing stories about her creative, bumbling husband and then whispered in his ear when he ran out of things to sign inside book jackets.

He tried to recall the feeling of unreality when the first big checks started rolling in. They made plans for exotic vacations and then cancelled them nervously, fearing the tenuous nature of wealth. That went on for two years. It was Kimberly who finally took his chin in her hands and explained to him that he was extremely talented and immensely worthy of this success.

"You deserve all the good things that happen to you, Jonathan."

"Except you, maybe. I don't know if anyone deserves that much."

So much good fortune that followed. So many blissful nights and beautifully prosaic days. Together, always together. And yet it was not long enough. Not nearly long enough. Cain would happily go back to that squalid apartment and create novels no one would read just to have that life again. He'd gleefully go back to unloading trucks with bleeding, raw fingers just to sleep uncomplicated sleep next to her each night. Wealth wasn't worth this. Nothing was worth this. A tumor smaller than a marble was enough to burn it all up.

He dug fresh khakis from the suitcase and pulled on a white shirt. His hair was slicked back like he used to keep it and he was wearing brand new shoes. He looked good. He was starting to feel good. The pressure at his temples had subsided some and now he felt only a numb humming throughout mind and body. He was relaxed. He was ready. This wouldn't be so bad, really. Maybe just a little unpleasant at first.

He straightened his collar. He rolled shirtsleeves up just below the elbows. He started up the stairs at a leisurely pace.

The study was empty. The telescope stood uselessly near the door, lens aimed at the ceiling. The desk was an abandoned landscape covered with books and papers no one would read. If there were decipherable directions to the human soul in there, no eyes would fall upon them.

"Stay out of my way," he said to the room, before closing the door. "Stay out of my way and I'll stay out of yours."

One down.

The bathroom was still steamy from his shower. No dead men or dead children gibbered from the bathtub. No apparitions lunged or leered.

"I don't want to see you. I don't want to hear you. Please."

The space that would have made a great reading room was inhabited only by a coil of rope and a ladder that never served its final purpose. Cain stared around the room and felt the silence like a physical thing.

"Good luck with that, Mr. Currie. I have a feeling you know a noose will do nothing for you now."

The sleeping bag was still in a heap at the bottom of the mattress in the space that was meant to be a master bedroom. The last stand of one Bucky Letroy. The sleeping bag appeared as though it had been shrugged off. Cain supposed he would never know what had happened to the jolly old agent. Maybe that was for the best.

"Be still, Angel. I'm sorry that you're here, but it's not my fault. Be still and let me go about my business now."

No one sneaked up behind him in the hall. No undead figures waited around corners. Nothing thumped far off and the haunting tune of Fur Elise was not to be heard. All was quiet in the Currie house.

He paused at the bottom of the winding stairs that ascended into magic. He stared up and whispered an easy prayer into the gloom.

"Be there, darling. Be there with your quilt and poetry and the papasan you used to sleep in when you swore you weren't tired. Be there so I can carry you from this place and please don't make me force you."

Cain climbed toward the top of the turret.

Sixteen

Franklin Brazel stared in disgust at the cell phone. Then he snapped it closed and slammed it down on the desk.

"Nobody can reach Rathbun. The idiot."

"He was pretty upset when he called."

"Rathbun is always upset. The asshole."

Across the desk was William Goddard, a small, neat man who sat with legs crossed at the knees. He was eternally calm and polite and he had weathered many of Brazel's emotional storms. A Yale schooled psychiatrist, he had once provided blueprints for the emotional and physical torture used to extract information from the sturdiest of enemies at Guantanamo. Goddard had never seen the work that resulted from his assessments. He thought torture was crass. These days, his skills were reserved almost exclusively to guide Brazel through the frequent pitfalls of human nature.

"Perhaps you should send somebody up to Maine to snoop around," he said now, knowing precisely how Brazel would respond. The trick was to get the man to say it for himself.

Brazel shook his head. "No. Nobody is going to Maine. We're not going anywhere near the place."

"That may be best."

"You better believe it. Right now, we need to find out if Olivia Currie left behind anything she may have learned from her husband. We don't need things complicated by trespass violations from the court."

Goddard unfolded his legs and crossed them in the other direction. "But you do want to get inside the house, do you not?"

Brazel waved the comment away as if it were a trifle. "Of course, of course. We will get our day. I have no doubt. But I can't let that be the focus of my concern right now. I don't have to tell you that the old woman could be more dangerous now than she was alive."

"If she did keep that kind of information, you mean."

"That's what I mean. Where have you been, Goddard?"

Brazel leaned back in his chair. The clipboard was on his lap. He held a pencil in one hand and tapped the eraser against his teeth. The office was spacious, dark and quiet. The sound was like a woodpecker giving an oak tree a taste and finding it good.

"I suppose it's possible Rathbun got spooked and simply ran off," Brazel said.

"He's not the bravest of men," Goddard agreed. "If you don't mind my saying so."

"That he's not, Goddard. That he's not. Take away his goons and he's a bit of a coward."

"He may be on his way back to San Diego as we speak. He may have never gone near the Currie house."

"You're right. I'll bet that's exactly what happened. I'll fry his ass one way or another. That moron has been with us too long."

"He really is a liability," Goddard said. "If you don't mind my saying so."

Brazel sat back and thought about it, staring at the ceiling. He nibbled the eraser, found it distasteful, began tapping it on the clipboard.

"I'll tell you what. It's unlikely the twit is doing anything on his own. He's a coward, we both agree. But just in case, as of today, we don't know Benjamin Rathbun."

"Benjamin who?"

"Precisely. See to it, Goddard. All traces of him eliminated. Not a report or a memo that can be traced back here. Obliterate him."

Goddard unfolded his legs again and stood next to his chair. He clasped his hands together and waited for final thoughts before departing. He knew what they would be.

“I tell you,” Brazel said. “The Currie family has been nothing but trouble. The whole goddamn lot of them. Nothing but trouble, each one of them.”

Goddard waited. Brazel tossed the pencil onto his desk and got to his feet.

“We don’t know Benjamin Rathbun. Not a trace of him. He could really screw this up. The asshole.”

“He really is,” Goddard said. “If you don’t mind my saying so.”

Seventeen

Cain paused with one hand on the doorknob, the other pressed against the cool wood. He whispered another silent prayer: to Kimberly, to himself, to the twisted science that had brought them together again. He needed so badly for her to be here. He needed so desperately for her to be herself again, confused for now, but compliant.

"Please," he whispered. "Please." He pushed the door open.

Kimberly was waiting for him on the other side. She sat on the bed smiling shyly, like a schoolgirl awaiting the arrival of her first date. Her hair was tied up at the back of her head and diamonds twinkled at her earlobes. She wore a black, strapless evening gown and the red apple lay against her throat, a splash of color where pearls would have been advised.

She was radiant. She was majestic. Her cheeks were pink and her eyes gleamed. Her chin quivered and she held out her arms to him, a solitary tear rolling down one cheek.

"Oh, Jonathan."

He ran to her and dived into her embrace. He was swept by a fragrance of lilacs and by swooning relief. He wrapped himself around her and they fell onto the bed, arms everywhere at once, faces pressed together, each of them crying now. He rolled to one side and pulled her on top of him. They kissed a long kiss and then he rolled the other way, pinning her beneath him.

For Cain, this was nothing less than time travel. This was a time before the Currie house, before the debilitating pain of missing her, before the cancer and sickness. This was the continuation of their lives as it was supposed to be, with a delirium of contentment and no darkness on the horizon.

"God, Jonathan. You feel wonderful. I feel I've been away forever."

His hands were on her arms, her hips, her breasts. He kissed her under the ears and felt her melt under his touch. She breathed in his ear and writhed beneath him. Cain felt himself falling into the mesmerizing fathoms of euphoria and had to physically pull himself from its black hole grip. He raised his body from the bed and propped himself on his arms, leaning over her like a bridge.

"You're beautiful," he said.

She smiled. And it was a pure Kimberly smile, unadulterated by any of the terrors of the past year. She hooked her hands around his neck and laced her fingers together. Cain lifted himself higher and she came up with him. He touched the end of his nose to hers.

"Come on," he said. "Let's blow this taco stand."

The smile fell from her face slowly, like it was being tugged away by strings. She unhooked her hands and fell back to the bed. Her eyes bored into his, studying him.

"Why, Jonathan? Why should we leave here?"

He kissed her quickly.

"This isn't our home, Kimberly. We don't belong here."

Without moving, she seemed to withdraw from him. A sad uncertainty stretched across her face and her eyes were tearing again.

"But it's safe here," she said. "I didn't understand that before, but I do now. We're safe here. Won't you think about staying? For me?"

"No." He put a finger to her lips. "We can't stay here. But we'll find another place, darling. Someplace big and beautiful and we'll..."

But she was struggling beneath him, thrashing to sit up. He moved back to give her space, watching her. Her face was pinched with aggravation. Another emotion had appeared as swiftly as the earlier one had vanished.

"Kimberly..."

She pulled away hastily, angrily. Her hand went to her throat. Fingers wrapped around the apple necklace in a fist.

"Bastard!" she said. "You goddamn son-of-a-bitch." And ripped the chain from her neck. Cain heard it snap as it broke and he reached for her hand too late to stop her. She held the hand back, like a child trying to keep another away from a favorite toy.

"You thought you could lure me back and keep me with this, Jonathan? This cheap little trinket from some shithole town you dragged me to? You're a fucking fool, Jonathan. An asshole, bastard fool."

He reached for her, hoping to pull her closer and soothe this wrath. He reached for her shoulder and her hand blazed forward, hooked into a claw, nails sweeping toward his eyes. Cain saw only a flash of pink. With a swipe, the hand came down and nails tore through his cheeks, ripping bloody tracks through the flesh. He recoiled and brought a hand to his face, blood trickling between the webs of his fingers. He looked up into the raging turmoil of her face. She sneered and threw the necklace. He reached for her again and her eyes cut away from him. She stared over his shoulder and a sleek, sinister smile crossed her features.

Cain turned on the bed to face the door behind him. They were standing in the doorway like a small army. Angel stood by the side of the boy, who wore the gold cross across his naked chest. Angel was smiling, her face bright and pink, as healthy as Cain had seen her. The boy was staring with his jaw open, numb and bored.

Behind them stood Theodore Currie. He held a puckered lump of naked flesh that squirmed in his arms like an oversized maggot. Cain saw wisps of white hair flying from around the head of that lump and recognized the hard gaze of Olivia Currie.

Kimberly was moving in close behind him. Calmly, she spoke and he could feel her breath on his neck.

"You have to stay with us, Jonathan. We need you here."

He turned to her. The eyes were dark and vacant. Had they been that way before? Had she changed or was he just now seeing?

"No," he said. "I can't. Come away with me, darling. We don't need them."

She snarled and a low, grinding growl rolled from her chest. She shoved past him, climbed from the bed and stepped toward the others. She fell in next to Angel, taking her hand.

Cain twisted on the bed to face them. Collectively, they looked like ghouls haunting a world to which they had come unwittingly. There was something soulless about the eyes. There was a gibbering insanity in the way they stared. And Kimberly was not set apart from them. She gazed on him like a creature that no longer recognized him as the man who loved her. There was no trace of the affection he had seen there moments ago.

He got to his feet and glared at them. His eyes moved from one to another, challenging them. Theodore stared implacably, without malevolence or empathy. His limbless mother, laying across his arms, only goggled. Angel grinned and the boy gaped. They disgusted Cain. Completely disgusted him.

When his eyes fell upon Kimberly, he tried to implore her in the secret, silent way all couples possess after years of marriage. Nothing but loathing was returned.

"I am leaving this house," he said, and his voice was flat but strong. "I am taking my wife with me and I want you all to stay away."

The black gaze of dead things, no more alive than the eyes of souvenir animal heads hanging on a wall. Kimberly spoke and the voice sounded far away.

"You can't leave, Jonathan. We need you here."

"We can't let you leave us. We have no place to go."

"I've come to see my boy. You will not take this away from me."

"You have to stay with us."

"Yes, stay with us forever."

They were advancing now and Cain took a step back without thinking. The backs of his legs pressed up against the bed. They came at him slowly, feet shuffling as though they had forgotten how to walk. He braced himself, arms outstretched, and waited. He tried to look at them as fiends — as vile things no more human than plastic, funhouse monsters that lunge from the dark at the carnival. But his eyes were drawn to Kimberly. Even as she moved in on him with the pack, lips drawn back to reveal teeth like a savage, he loved her. He opened his mouth to tell her and then they fell upon him.

"We're a family now. There is no going back."

"It is eternity in between. You have to stay."

Hands pulled him to the floor; hands that clawed and ripped at him. He felt mouths against his skin and teeth piercing him. He pushed and shoved, but it was a feeble effort. There was no will in it. He reached a hand out to his wife, but he could not find her. A hot swarm of bodies bubbled around him, a faceless mass of tugging hands and meaningless words.

"You will stay with us forever."

"We need you."

"We must have you."

"Forever."

More heartbroken than afraid, Cain gave in to them. Love wanted to keep him but pain lashed away the emotion. Bitterness made an advance and was swiftly swept away by stinging agony. There was no room for the lesser emotions in this moment of ascending horror. Love and rage were worthless and inert. The moment was governed by the physical pain of fingers and teeth that tore at him. Pain and suffocation whisked him from the psychic torment of all that he had loved and lost. It was loud and sweaty pain and it moved in on him like locusts.

Eighteen

Thunder. It was always thunder in this place. That sudden, intense explosion that filled the world and then rolled away. Startling. Unnerving. The sound wanted to bounce him out of the foggy gray place in which he resided. He wouldn't have it. He would ignore the sound. He would ignore the whispers around him.

"Leave him."

"Someone is coming."

"We have to go."

"I want to eat him, daddy. I want to eat him up."

Silence. Sweet, eternal silence.

Cain opened his eyes. The silence was the most troubling of it all. He waited until his vision cleared and tried to orient himself. His cheek rested upon the cool floor. There was a sensation of wetness beneath him. He blinked and saw that blood pooled on the hard wood. He had a calm sense that the blood was his.

So what?

He stared some more. There was something shiny soaking in the blood; a splash of gold against the crimson. Cain blinked again and lifted his head. The audacity of the movement sent a spike of pain through his skull. His vision blurred. He waited it out and focused again.

The necklace. It floated in the blood, the tiny, red apple almost invisible. He lifted himself onto his elbows and waited for the pain to come and go again. It did and he pulled himself on his arms over to the necklace, sliding smoothly through his own blood. He plucked the gold chain out of the mess and held it up. Blood dripped from the apple and tiny droplets splashed on the floor. Cain watched it, transfixed, and felt another wave of pain in his head.

Marry me, Kimberly...

The sound again. A soft thump from below. It was a sneaky sound, not bold like thunder at all. He was foolish to have thought that before, but the house did funny things with sound.

He climbed to his feet and found that it took less effort than expected. The pain was brief and manageable. He stepped toward the door and then quickly propped himself against the wall to rest. For the first time, he felt the sting of wounds on his back, his legs, his stomach. He did not go searching for the wounds. That pain was manageable, too. He looked around him, instead.

The room, once pink, then blue, was now a disordered space of many colors and it was splashed with blood. Blankets were torn off the bed. The night stand had been overturned and white pages of paper were strewn and specked with red. The bureau had fallen also, and clothes of many hues were scattered like exotic flowers across the floor.

He looked at the closet door. It was open just a sliver. Why, he wouldn't even have to turn the knob to take a look in there. There would be a whoosh of air as the door swung open. Clothes hangers would do their little dance and talk their secret talk.

Cain closed his eyes and pressed his face onto the back of a bloody hand from which the bloody necklace dangled. He missed her. He missed her so completely, it was worse than any blow to the head or any deep, jagged wound on his body. Missing her was always the worst of it. Nothing else compared.

He did not look back at the closet. He did not take a final look at the turret room at all. He stepped into the hall and closed it behind him. He walked to the stairs and left bloody footprints all the way down.

Nineteen

Rathbun was just starting up the stairs as Cain was starting down. Both men stopped at the same time. Each stared at the other and said nothing for several moments. Then Rathbun held the gun in front of him and smiled. He took another step up toward Cain.

"Well, well. There you are. Quite a mess in the front yard, writer man. And now that I see you up close, you don't look so hot yourself."

"I could say the same for you," Cain said. "You look like you haven't slept in weeks, Rathbun. What's the matter? Solstice getting to you?"

Rathbun's smile faltered briefly and then it was back. He started up the stairs again and Cain started down Each man moved slowly, as if counting the steps.

"I've come to get what's mine, Cain. I hope you don't plan on keeping it from me."

Another step up, another step down.

"You're welcome to it," Cain said. "There are no secrets here I'm not willing to share."

"Good, good."

They met in the middle and stood on the same two stairs, faces just inches apart. Cain felt the barrel of the .45 against his ribcage but didn't much care.

"It's all yours, Rathbun. All of it. I won't be giving the tour because I've had it with the Currie house. I hope you understand."

Rathbun positively beamed. His breath was hot and rancid.

"Who needs you? I plan to make quick work of it, myself. Scraps of paper, notebooks, scrawlings on the wall...shit that looked useless to you, Cain, is going to make me one highly sought man in the scientific community."

Cain nodded and forged a little smile.

"And I wish you the best of luck with that. It's all gibberish to me, my friend. Every bit of it. There's nothing for me here. I thought there might be, but I was wrong. I should have listened to you from the start."

Rathbun withdrew the gun from Cain's ribs, but only a little. He beamed some more. He looked toward the top of the stairs.

"Hey, better you learn now than not at all, am I right? Go on your way now, Cain. Let the experts take over and go write your little make-believe books."

Cain nodded again, more enthusiastically.

"Don't mind if I do," he said. He started down the stairs, but stopped. He turned back to Rathbun, who was still grinning like a man who is only a very short way from achieving his loftiest ambitions.

Cain held out a hand. Blood was drying on his knuckles and between his fingers. Rathbun looked at it without comprehension.

"Take it," Cain said. "It may look like only a trinket right now. But you'll want it when you get all the way to the top of the turret. They like shiny things."

Rathbun looked a moment longer and then snatched the necklace from Cain's hand. He looked at it, snorted, and stuffed it into the pocket of his pants.

"So long, Rathbun."

Cain walked down the stairs. His legs felt heavy. The wounds were stinging now, pain that was gigantic. His head throbbed and a piercing sound whistled inexorably in his head. He walked to the bottom of the stairs, wishing there was a railing to hold on to.

From above him: "Hey, Cain. Just one more thing."

Cain turned in time to see the flash from the gun. Something slammed into the right side of his body and it spun him. He heard himself let out a gush of air and then there was burning in his gut. He looked up the stairs where Rathbun was still taking aim.

"I never intended on letting you live, my friend. Another lesson to learn the hard way."

Another flash, another booming explosion. It felt as though someone had punched him in the shoulder and he fell backwards and down. He seemed to fall forever with the echo of the gun blast in his ears.

I'll bet that's gonna hurt like a bastard when I hit the floor.

It didn't. Not much, anyway.

Twenty

It wasn't thunder this time, for sure. This time, it was screaming. And that sound was unmistakable if you had essentially made a career out of screams.

Cain's eyes fluttered open and he lay listening to the sounds of horror from above. Rathbun was screeching like an animal in agony and pounding on the walls. There was terror in that sound, but Cain thought it was mostly pain. It chilled him. He knew the man upstairs had found himself faced with things he could not comprehend and that those things had a tendency to bite.

There was a ten second span of silence and Cain believed it was over. Then there were three quick gun blasts and then the screaming commenced.

"Oh God, help meeeeeeeeee..."

Then the voice became garbled and the house grew considerably more quiet. Cain began to imagine the unutterable scene in the turret room and found that he could stop. His imagination had been dulled over recent days, and for that he was profoundly thankful.

He had to get up. He tried moving his arms and legs and found it was an almost impossible task. The pain was gone, but now there was weakness. It was weakness that reminded him of the suicidal booze binges that left him unable to rise from his bed for days.

The house was bright with incongruously optimistic sun pouring in. He guessed it had been less than a half hour since Rathbun had turned the gun on him. For the second time today, he could feel blood beneath him and there was more of it this time. God knew how much he had lost. Cain considered it a miracle he had regained consciousness.

That's what the house is all about, of course. Dubious miracles you want to send back like undesirable items from a mail catalog.

He rolled onto his stomach. He tried to raise himself with his arms and found that they had turned to springs. It was like trying to muster one last push-up after a Nazi trainer had forced you into dozens. But he only needed the one. He only needed to get to his feet one more time. Because this madness had to end.

It wasn't that they came back corrupt and deranged, though that surely was enough. He would never know what happened to the soul on the journey back from its resting place. He did not care to know. But he understood that it was something like eternity in between, and that even the cleanest soul would turn vile over that unimaginable span. What was sent out of the world a saint came back a demon. But the true evil was the man who arranged the journey.

It had to stop because sooner or later, the next scientist or grieving husband would try to improve on the work. And countless souls would be snatched from their peace by men who presumed themselves lofty enough to do the work of God.

Cain wanted forgiveness. He wanted to atone. Hell was a place created by man and he had contributed. Whatever he could do for penance, it was not enough.

He got to his feet and stumbled toward the door. His hands and feet were cold and he was shivering all over. When he walked, forward momentum tried to send him sprawling and he had to avoid that. He did not have another push-up in him.

Outside, it was painfully bright. He turned his head away from the sun as if banished from it. He lurched toward the Mercedes and leaned to pick up the bottles he had left on the ground. A wave of dizziness overcame him and he caught himself on the side of the car before he could stumble. The world seemed to turn gray in front of him, though sunlight still stabbed his eyes. He took deep breaths. He shook his head. He reached for the bottles and, one-by-one, tucked them under an arm.

Cain looked across the driveway at the barbecue and it seemed like miles. The sight of it also brought back a twofold memory: the memory of his aborted meal of steak right here in the shadow of the Currie house. And the memory of those long ago barbecues with Kimberly at Prince Edward Island or Canobie Lake.

His selfishness had brought about such failure. Now, those sweet memories had been contaminated as well.

He lurched over to the barbecue, spilling gasoline onto fresh wounds and graying out again with the pain. He thought about Kimberly sitting tanned and pretty in the lounge chair while he mowed the lawn, and the sting of gas on a gunshot wound lost its bite.

The long lighter he had used to light the coals was sitting on top of the barbecue. He grabbed it and found that his hands barely had enough strength to grip it. It was as though his fingers were frozen. It was completely astounding he had managed to hang on to the bottles.

Over-burdened now, he shuffled toward the house looking, he imagined, like an exceedingly drunk man serving drinks and lighting smokes at one very strange party.

Welcome to the Currie House, one and all! It's a place where lost loves come home and they can't wait to see you! A light for your pipe, sir? Fill your glass, madam? Yes, here you'll see the dear departed once again, so stop that weeping. And my, how you've missed them! And my, how they're so glad to see you! They'll just eat you up, they're so glad to see you again! Welcome! Welcome to the Currie House, one and all!

He began splashing gasoline onto the house next to the porch, in front of the Mercedes and next to the trailer that held all the happy contents of the pink room. Let the flames start here, he decided. Let the car explode and the trailer perish in the wall of flames.

He felt a quick pang of sadness and guilt thinking about Bucky Letroy in the trunk of the shiny car. It passed quickly and he tossed the empty bottle away, moving back toward the porch with his armful. He strained to lift his feet up high enough to negotiate the stairs, but he remained upright. The miracles were just never ending today.

He pushed the front door open and splashed gas inside. Tiring, he hurled the bottle into the house and it bounced across the floor into the living room, spraying more fuel on the way.

The reek of gas was making him feel nauseous now and his legs were wobbling beneath him. He leaned over a porch rail, took aim, and used the last of his arm strength to hurl one of the remaining bottles at a window. There was a sharp crack and the window shattered, the bottle disappearing inside and clattering across the floor.

He emptied the last bottle onto the porch. Gasoline pooled out over the wood and streamed down the sides. He tossed the bottle aside and made for the steps, feeling very lightheaded indeed. The world seemed to be moving up and down and all around, like the crystalline view through a kaleidoscope. He needed to get off the porch or he would perish in flames.

His feet found the top step, but overshot the second. Cain stumbled forward, tried to catch his balance, failed. His knees hit the ground first and then he crashed onto his chest. He felt air rush from his lungs on impact. He waited for it to return and feared it wouldn't. He took a large gulp of air that tasted of gasoline. He squeezed his right hand into a loose fist and found that the lighter was no longer there.

Find it fast. Find it and light it, even if it means you go up in flames with everything else.

He rolled to his right, toward the steps, and the lighter was an inch from his face. He snatched it up quickly and struggled to position it in his hand. He slid one finger over the ignition button and gave it a light squeeze, testing the resistance. It would take the last of his strength, but he would do it.

Cain lifted his head and looked up at the house. From the ground, it seemed to stretch all the way into the heavens. In a real way, he supposed it did.

He twisted his head so that he was looking at the turret. Sun gleamed off the highest window but there was nothing to see there. No Kimberly staring out with sadness and one more parting word. There had been no goodbye, real or imagined. From where he lay, as distant from her as he'd ever been, that final scene on the hospital bed had been a blessing. He'd tainted that as well.

"I'm sorry," he said, lowering his face into the dirt. "So goddamn sorry."

He stretched his arm as far as it would go, until it hovered over a pool of gas that had gathered in a small pond at the bottom of the stairs. His hand shook. His entire arm was trembling. But his finger was on the trigger and it only needed one squeeze. Let flames destroy this sin he had helped to create. Let it end here after such a dastardly beginning. He began to squeeze.

And then a shadow fell over him. A shoe pressed down with force upon his wrist. Cain's fingers opened involuntarily and the lighter dropped harmlessly into the pool of gas.

Cain moaned. The shoe remained on his wrist, strong and persistent. Grayness rolling in from all sides now, he twisted his head up as far as it could go. He stared up into a face that seemed miles above him, the face of the man who had thwarted his only chance at atonement. Cain moaned, dropped his head back onto the dirt and said: "Shit."

Epilogue

The Second Empire house on Olive Hill stood through the summer undaunted by the various dramas it had witnessed. It had existed through too few harsh winters and blazing summers to show signs of weathering. Red and white paint remained bright and vivid. There were no signs of rust on metal railings that topped the turret roof. Floor boards did not sag and doors still closed neatly within their frames. For all practical purposes, it was a solid home in a prime spot in Mulberry, Maine. It stood proud on the hilltop as summer reached its peak and then the dog days of August had come and gone. The house, like all inanimate things, was unburdened by the human vulnerability of impatience.

For a time following the afternoon of the solstice, there was non-stop activity both inside and outside the walls. For weeks, a steady march of men and women, some in suits, others in lab coats, had examined every crevice. No room was left uninspected. No crumb or scrap of paper was deemed too insignificant to be plucked with tweezers and dropped into plastic bags. Every item was subjected to a cursory examination, labeled dutifully, and hauled away in boxes or bags. A square of stiff paper was pinned to the belly of the headless teddy bear and marked 4C. Its head, located after a time in another room, was labeled 4D and both disappeared into a cardboard box which was then loaded into a long police van parked in the yard.

The Mercedes was examined for a full day before it was towed away to the State Police barracks in Presque Isle. The body of Bucky Letroy remained stiff and stinky in the trunk where it would be poked and measured several more times before it was removed inside a State Police garage.

Technicians emptied the small trailer that contained items from what was once referred to wryly as the pink room. Supervising investigators instructed them to photograph each item and then load it back into the trailer. There was not much by way of evidence there, until a tech wearing latex gloves picked up a small snow globe and found it sticky in his hands.

"Hey, sarge. Got some blood over here."

The technician was examining the child's toy when a soft, metallic tinkle arose from it and the notes of Fur Elise began to float incongruously over the crime scene. The technician jumped, unaware that the globe played music. He then held it at arm's length while waiting for the sergeant to come over for a look.

Reggie Lyons' body was found in a small stream next to the long driveway. When word of his death spread throughout Mulberry and St. Agatha, mourning began immediately. Town managers in both towns ordered flags flown at half staff and an elaborate funeral was planned. The hubbub surrounding the town constable's death fueled further gossip about the Currie house and its short, dubious history. One tribe of locals drinking at the Hearthside even talked of a midnight mission to burn the cursed house down. The idea reached a peak long before last call and then it died when a group of women on their way to Canada stopped into the lounge for a drink.

The body of Jonathan Cain was found next to the steps leading to the front door. There was a lighter next to his hand and he lay in a muddy pool of gas and blood. It did not take a master criminologist to discern what the writer had been planning, but his body lay there eight hours after discovery anyway, as technicians photographed the body and detectives took measurements.

Word of Cain's death sent reporters scrambling from all directions. They came from as far away as Los Angeles and from as nearby as the Bangor Daily News. The morbid circumstances about the demise of a best-selling author had journalists wetting themselves with glee and there was round-the-clock television coverage about the killings. There was little to be filmed by news crews, however, since the FBI had joined the probe and declared the entire area beginning at the end of the driveway a crime scene. Reporters clogged a section of Route 11, turning their cameras on any vehicle that drove onto or away from the driveway and shouting insipid questions at the drivers.

Press conferences held in the roadway were confusing frenzies of voracious journalists and reticent cops. Little was to be learned at the news gatherings but millions around the country crowded around television sets to watch frothing reporters have direct questions answered with vague police jargon.

The revelation that Bucky Letroy had been Jonathan Cain's literary agent was like gasoline spit on a campfire. Interest in the story flared anew and more journalists came to northern Maine. This time, they came from as far away as Britain, where Cain's novels had sold extraordinarily well.

CNN had three reporters in Maine and network producers had even developed an ominous musical theme to announce that more news on "Murder and Mystery in Northern Maine" was forthcoming.

Sales of all Jonathan Cain novels spiked dramatically. Websites were popping up all over the Internet as readers shared personal information about the writer and speculation about his grisly end. There was much talk about the cancer death of Kimberly Cain and about the history of Theodore Currie. Connections were being made. None were as fanciful as the truth.

Blood that could not be connected to anyone found inside the Currie house was discovered in the bedroom at the top of the turret. A heap of bones and decaying animal corpses were found in the basement. The first was strange, the second perhaps stranger.

No more victims were found, however, and the source of the blood and bones remained an enigma. The name Benjamin Rathbun was never uttered and there was no search throughout the house for his remains. His body would be found by a hunter months later in the woods, but the discovery would shed no new light on the "Murder and Mystery in Northern Maine." It would take weeks for investigators to identify the skeletal remains and then his name meant very little. He was traced back to San Diego and to the various colleges where he had studied. There was some indication he had worked with the government for a time, but no details of that work were ever uncovered. Benjamin Rathbun became a footnote in the reams of paperwork connected to the investigation. Few people remembered his name, even weeks after the body was found. He had become just a small development in a massive case with more questions than answers. There was no mention of NASA Langley and no one from that outfit came forward with information.

"Benjamin who?" a man named Franklin Brazel said when he heard the news on CNN. His assistant snorted from a chair across the room.

Maine State Police, the Aroostook County Sheriff's Office, the FBI, the Northern Maine Violent Crime Task Force and a host of other agencies with instantly forgettable acronyms held a press conference in the Mulberry Elementary School gymnasium on the last day of June. There was much back clapping among the agencies and very little new information shared with bored journalists and hundreds of curious residents. One by one, police spokespersons thanked the other agencies for cooperating in the investigation. There were solid leads and new developments all the time, they said. The case would be solved in time, thanks to the team efforts of the MSP, the ACSO, the FBI, the NMVCTF...

The feds were taking over the investigation into the shooting deaths of Jonathan Cain and Reggie Lyons, as well as the beating death of Bucky Letroy. The killings would be solved, the spokesperson said, through information and cooperation among the investigating agencies.

By the end of July, no one had been caught or named as a suspect in the killings. In updated news accounts, the FBI began to blame Maine State Police for errors made in the early part of the investigation. State Police refuted those claims through a spokesman and suggested that any mistakes were probably made by the federal agents who insisted on taking over the collection of evidence. State cops did not point blame at county cops. County cops did not point blame at the various tasks forces that had sent agents from Bangor and Lewiston. These people had to work with each other almost daily. There was no good to come from mudslinging in one's backyard.

A team of lawyers handling the estate for the deceased Olivia Currie did not put up much fuss while the investigation was continuing. It was not until early August that the Currie house was released as evidence and sagging crime scene tape came down. No more cars and vans went in and out of the driveway, which had been beaten down considerably over the past two months. Police had gathered up all that was to be gathered. The house was cleared for new owners.

Still, the house remained empty until the following spring. A board had been nailed over one broken window and the doors were locked. The house stood through violent rain storms and a four-day spell of 90 degree temperatures that was officially declared a heat wave. Then there were bitter cold nights at the end of September and winter had unofficially begun. October was the coldest in a half-century. There was snow by Halloween. By Christmas, there was already two feet on the ground and there was no end in sight.

The Currie house stood with snowdrifts burying the front steps and the porch around the sides of the house. By the middle of January, snow was up to the first-floor windows and a person would need to shovel for an hour to get to the front door. Nobody tried. The house survived another season and no harm was done.

On May 30, a full-sized U-Haul made the long, bumpy drive up the snaking driveway. The engine growled and rumbled all the way up and the tin trailer rattled excessively. There was much negotiating to be done to back the rig up to the front doors, but by the time the sun had begun to set, the U-Haul was ready to be unloaded.

By now, the snow was gone and the world was greening up. Flowers grew wild in the field around the house and the woods were full of chattering wildlife. It was warm, too, in the 70's most days. The nights were still cool and would remain so for another half month at least.

The new occupant spent the first night in the room at the top of the turret. The following day, the room was emptied completely and its items were loaded into another van that would be driven away by day's end. A team of seven movers were paid handsomely for their efforts. There were incentives for getting the move done quickly so there was no reason to milk the job. The workers moved old items out and new items in. Then they lined up to collect their cash and hastily made their exit. One of them had come away with an expensive telescope. Another snagged a computer, while a third had all the bedroom furnishings from the turret room.

During the first week of June, the Second Empire home was transformed. A team of carpenters and plumbers were brought in to complete the most basic finish work. Plaster cornices and crown moldings were installed over windows. The fireplace was completed in marble with an arched opening and a brilliant mantle. The kitchen was finished with a sink and new appliances. An antique Persian rug was spread out across the living room floor and heritage chairs and sofas were arranged just so around a gondola chaise and Andante tables.

Long taper candles were placed everywhere. The library was completed with bookcases, a mahogany desk and high-backed chairs.

Dark, elegant curtains were hung in all rooms and the dining room was completed with a luxurious table set, hutches and servers. Rich paintings were hung throughout the house, some reproductions, others originals, bought at European auctions with the Currie house in mind.

A modest bedroom was assembled on the second floor, with a four-poster bed with canopy and rich, purple curtains hung above carpeting of the same color. The study near the stairway was kept simple, with an armoire and a desk in front of the windows. There was a reading room with plush carpeting, ferns in three corners and a chandelier hanging overhead.

A special emphasis was placed on lighting. There were chandeliers in three rooms, and crystal vase lamps spread out strategically throughout the house. Light fixtures were added above the flying staircase and a row of wall lamps illuminated the journey up the turret stairs.

At last, the interior of the Second Empire home was as striking as the exterior. It had cost more than $100,000 to decorate and there would be more. The house was a work in progress. There was much to be done here and comfort was essential.

The turret room was the jewel of the house. It was completed by June 18 and all of the workers were hastily sent away. One of them, a painter from Arabia, had been paid $75,000 for his work. The others left the house with more modest, yet still obscene payments for their work.

The house was empty and quiet again. The hammering and chatter had ceased.

On the night of June 20, the new owner lit three dozen candles and stood silently in the doorway of the turret room to admire it in the glow of flames.

Paintings of various sizes adorned the walls, and all of them featured the Virgin Mary or scenes from the Nativity. The Adoration of the Shepherds covered the entire wall next to the closet, the Virgin Mother holding her child up for display as the visitors adored him and prayed. The Procession of the Magi was nearby as was the Annunciation. In each of them, the Mother of Christ appeared humble and proud.

There was a large bust of the Virgin Mother in an area where once sat a bureau with a child's dollhouse atop it. There were statues of all sizes on shelves around the room. Each of them glowed yellow in the light of burning candles.

Mother Mary was ubiquitous here, but never so imposing as in the painting that covered the entire wall over where once had sat a bed. The Arabian artist had spent three days completing "The Virgin and Child" and the final work was worth every penny paid.

Painted in egg-based tempera, the work portrayed the Virgin Mother gazing down on the infantile, yet exceedingly wise face of her child. The soft, golden hues of the artwork presented a comforting and reassuring scene: the Mother Mary's upraised hands over the head of her child, who beams with wisdom and optimism out at the world he would try to save. The serenity of the painting set the tone for the room, and the eyes wanted to linger there.

Yet close to the far wall, centered precisely to the window facing out on the northern sky, the tabular shaped altar beckoned the eyes at last. The wooden altar had been flown in from Mount Athos at great cost and now it sat evenly before the window. Upon it, a row of votive candles burned brightly to illuminate the bounty that lie there. Spread out in a rich heap of enticement were mounds of gold flattened into discs and brought over from Tanzania. Clumps of frankincense and mountains of myrrh imported from Somalia were now stacked high next to the gold. Some of the frankincense and myrrh had been mixed with seeds, roots and spices and fashioned into sticks. Those sticks now burned in holders at several points in the room and the fragrance was sweet and heavenly.

All the splendor of the room was meant as a show of love and devotion, but also as symbols of familiarity. The boon on the altar was more of an inducement, ancient gifts once carried for thousands of miles on the night of all nights in history. And tonight would be such a night. As time ticked on and the planet moved to its summer position, the solstice was imminent. The time of all times had come.

Gary Buchanan stepped into the turret room and paused before the marble font that stood just inside the doorway. He dipped his fingers into holy water shipped from Tiberius. He touched those fingers to his forehead, to his chest, to his shoulders. He closed his eyes and whispered a prayer. He stepped to the altar, arms upraised. He turned his eyes toward the heavens and spoke, in a heavy tone that was both imploration and command.

“Jesus,” he said. “Come forth."

About the author

Mark LaFlamme was born in Waterville, Maine. Since 1994, he has been covering the crime beat for the Sun Journal in Lewiston, Maine where he lives with his wife, Corey. LaFlamme can be contacted through his website at www.marklaflamme.com